The Emerald Threads

A Crown Jewels Regency Mystery
Book 4

Lynn Morrison

Anne Radcliffe

Marketing Chair Press

Cover design by Melody Simmons

Published by

The Marketing Chair Press, Oxford, England

LynnMorrisonWriter.com

ISBN (paperback): 978-1-917361-02-6

Contents

1

Lady Grace Percy stood facing the small mirror in her modest room, her hand resting upon her stomach as she tried to calm her nerves. Her mind shouted the same question at her that it had for weeks. *With child! How could this have happened?*

Of course, she knew *how* it had happened. She and Roland, though, had been trying to be careful. After the tumult of the season, the demands of the crown, and the dangers they had faced, neither was eager to settle sedately into some calm corner of England to begin producing heirs for the ducal line.

And yet that, despite their efforts, was what the future was about to hold.

Grace's knees wobbled slightly. Behind her, her lady's maid, Elsie, steadied her with a hand on her shoulder. "Easy, my lady. Is the corset... too tight?"

"It is fine," Grace said distantly, twisting the ring upon her finger. Her corset wasn't yet feeling too restrictive—although perhaps that was because Elsie, who knew more right now than her dear husband did, was deliberately leaving it a touch loose. Her wedding ring, however...

"You still haven't told Lord Percy?" Elsie asked, carefully keeping her voice neutral.

A baby should be a happy discussion, shouldn't it? For him, this would be a surprise. A shock. A line drawn through all Roland's carefully laid plans to take her to the continent in the spring as they continued enjoying their marriage and freedom from the responsibilities that would fall on his head once he inherited the title.

She checked her hands for puffiness, evading Elsie's gaze in the mirror as she lied. "I do not see how we can be certain yet. Are you certain I would not feel movement by now if I were?"

As she settled into her chair, Grace had one brief half-regret of not accepting her mother's offer to employ a more experienced lady's maid, one who might be better informed about the ways a pregnancy could progress. Yet, as Elsie ran the brush through Grace's chestnut locks, the steady rhythm soothing Grace's raw nerves, Grace knew she would not send her away. They would muddle through and hope for the best.

"It would be far too soon for movement if you are with child, my lady. Are you still feeling no sickness in the morning?"

"None at all." She hadn't even had a twinge of queasiness, even though Grace's older sister had vomited for months when she had been in a family way. "Perhaps the lack of sickness means it will not take. Perhaps I am imagining the whole thing. I would feel foolish if I upset him for nothing."

"You have missed your courses twice," Elsie said pragmatically, her voice very low. "And you are getting fatigued in the afternoons."

And there was a certain roundness to her cheeks that had not been there before. And a tenderness in her breasts. Grace had been unable to lie to herself about what the small changes in her body were heralding, even if she could still not utter the truth aloud. She could still not bring herself to tell her own husband while he was so happily looking forward to plans Grace already knew they would not be able to enjoy.

She couldn't tell him while there was still a part of her that felt this child wasn't real. A part of her that hoped it wasn't.

She was a coward.

Let him enjoy the planning for now, her pragmatic inner thoughts repeated serenely. *There are months and months to go, plenty of time to tell him later. A better time, when it will not be such an unwelcome surprise.*

So Grace sent her maid to let Roland know she was ready. For travelling, at any rate.

The smile Roland gave her when he entered her room was like sunlight breaking through rain clouds, and it melted the icy chill of worry forming in the pit of her stomach. "Are you ready to depart? We should make it there sometime in the early hours of the afternoon."

"I am ready," she said shortly as she stood and turned back towards the mirror, nervously checking again over the style of her hair. Grace had directed Elsie to do her hair sensibly, given that there would be several hours of bumpy roads to cover. It wouldn't do to arrive with half her hair sprung free of pins and clips.

They were on the last leg of their fall journey. In a few hours they would arrive at Alnwick Castle, the seat of power for the duchy and the home of Duke Gideon Percy, the fearsome Breaker of Northumberland. His was a moniker the bad-tempered old duke had earned fairly.

Grace shifted her gaze back toward her husband and found him studying her, concern twisting his handsome features and clouding his dark gaze. He stilled her hands and lifted the left to his mouth to press a gentle kiss across her knuckles. "Are you worried about facing my grandfather?"

"A little," she admitted. Even on her wedding day, he had

been unable to offer her a smile. She was unworthy of the role of future duchess, in his mind, and only timely intervention from the Prince Regent himself had kept the Breaker from trying to stop their wedding this summer. "Have you no qualms?"

He squeezed her hand conspiratorially. "I will not pretend that our stay at Alnwick Castle will be pleasurable, but we need only be there until the roads thaw. We will do our duty to the duke, and then we will make our escape to the continent."

A twinge of guilt twisted her stomach, and Grace pulled her hand free. She passed her husband his winter coat, playing valet to help him shrug it on. It was easier to keep the truth of her fears a secret if she did not have to meet his eyes. In a quiet voice, she asked, "But... what if something forces us to stay?"

"Nothing can force us, my wife. My grandfather has no hold over us any longer. He may have rushed us to the altar, but no one can rush us to the birthing bed, no matter how much he harangues about securing the ducal line. Everyone knows that these matters take their time." He whispered wickedly in her ear as he stood behind her.

Grace sucked in an unsteady breath, her heart pounding. What if he noticed a change in her body, right then and there? But he turned to grab his hat from the hook near the door.

"I'm off to see if the carriage is ready. Promise me you will put all concerns about the duke aside. Imagine the adventures we will have in the next year. I cannot wait to take you to Porto."

Grace forced a stilted smile onto her face and nodded confirmation. "It does sound very lovely. All right, let us get on our way."

No matter how pleasant Portugal was, she would not get to see it—at least not soon. By the early months of the new year, Grace would have to enter her confinement. Then Alnwick Castle would become their home, their prison, until after the baby had arrived.

Assuming she was indeed with child at all. Assuming that she managed to carry to term.

Grace pressed her fingers to her temples, shouting at her spiralling thoughts to be silent. She didn't move again until Elsie came back to get her, dressed in a simple travelling dress of dark blue wool, with long sleeves and a high neck. It was a plainer version of Grace's own heavy woollen outfit, but Elsie wore it as proudly as a ballgown.

"I could ride along with you, my lady," Elsie reminded her. "Then, if you need anything... if there is aught amiss, I would be near—"

Grace held up a hand to stop her there. "You will be much happier riding with Briggs, as we both know."

Elsie's face coloured prettily, and Grace stifled a small smile, the dour turn of her thoughts finally easing. She had only meant to imply that her lady's maid would be more comfortable not being cloistered in such a small space with her lady and her husband still mooning after each other like newlyweds, but perhaps there was another reason why Elsie looked forward to riding with Roland's new valet. Roland and Grace enjoyed one of the rarest of gifts—a true love match from within the ton. Grace wouldn't dare stand in the way of the chance of romance to bloom elsewhere.

———————

A short while later, Grace snuggled against Roland's broad form, soaking in what heat he could offer. He wrapped an arm around her shoulders, pulling her tight, while she adjusted the thick blankets covering their lower halves. They had mastered the art of keeping warm in the last several weeks, while the autumn days lost their battle against an early winter, bringing icy winds and heavy rain. It was a large part of their delayed arrival.

The wooden wheels bumped through the churned mud of

the roads, threatening to get stuck and sending ominous creaks through the carriage. Roland's elbow cracked against the door, causing him to groan. "There is not a part of me that is not bruised. We should have stayed in the south."

"Leaving Nathaniel to face your grandfather on his own after we had promised we would winter there?" Grace shook her head. "I would not wish such a fate on anyone, least of all your half brother."

"Needs must. Else I would not wish the backwater of Alnwick on *anyone*, least of all my darling wife," Roland countered. But his face got that far-away look that suggested his mind was already roving ahead.

"You have said little of Alnwick. Beyond your brother, is there anyone else you look forward to seeing? Perhaps some companion from your youth or a friendly servant?"

"In Alnwick? No. After I petitioned the duke to secure our positions in the military, we made one trip a year and otherwise kept our distance. I would go pay my respects to my grandfather, and Thorne would visit his mother." Roland pushed aside the curtain covering the window. Outside, the rugged hills of Northumberland rolled to the horizon, dotted here and there with grazing sheep. In the spring, the ground would roll like an emerald carpet. Now, the cold, short days had bleached the lands to a pale brown. Against the faded backdrop, a shimmering line glimmered in the distance. "That is the River Aln. We are getting close."

Less than an hour later, the road widened and the distance between homes shrank. Grace drank in what little she could see of the village—a line of shops, a village green, the steeple of the church.

On the other side, stark stone walls filled the view. The seat of Northumberland's name was no jest—Alnwick Castle was the second largest in England after the royal stead in Windsor.

No flowers or greenery blunted the weathered curtain walls that had provided protection in centuries past. They passed through the shadowed gatehouse entry without issue and emerged onto the grounds.

The first duke, Roland's great-grandfather, had undertaken a significant restoration project. Roland had told her of the expanded gardens, but had failed to mention the arched windows and crenellations. She drank in the pointed arches, pinnacles, and tracery on windows and doors. The style was described as fairy gothic, but only now did she understand why.

Her attention swivelled to the mass of uniformed servants filing out of the main entrance, forming a line along either side of the drive. Her stomach roiled again as she realised the lack of a duchess meant she would take on all the responsibilities of hostess and lady of a large household immediately. Never before had Grace cursed herself for ignoring her mother's attempts to educate her.

Roland laughed and pointed his hand at a pair of well-dressed youngsters with perfectly combed matching heads of mousy brown hair. The woman behind them had rested her hands on their shoulders, not so much to present them as to hold them in place.

Grace noticed the scuffs marring the boy's shoes and dirt staining the girl's knees and knew they were indeed the orphans she and Roland had rescued back in the spring. The twins held still only long enough for Roland and Grace to descend from the carriage. As soon as Roland helped Grace to the ground, the pair shrugged off the woman's hold and launched themselves toward them.

"Milady! Milord! It's us. The sprouts!" they shouted, though they needed no introduction.

Roland brushed his arm against Grace's in a silent bid for her to wait. He put his hands on his hips and eyed the children with mock suspicion. "The sprouts? That is not possible. Last I saw them, they ran as free as a banshee, their hair bedraggled and most certainly, a good few inches shorter than this fine pair of children."

Grace played along, tapping her chin while studying them. "Are you certain, lord husband? There is something vaguely familiar about them."

"It's really us, Lady Grace!" the girl pleaded.

"That's Lady Percy," the woman said, coming up behind them. "Ye ken well enough that ye're not to speak tae the adults unless they ask ye first. It's no' your place to be interruptin' them, aye? Wait till they bid ye speak, an' then ye may answer. Begging yer pardon, milady," she added, curtseying to Grace.

Roland stepped in before the children could land themselves in more trouble. "If you are the sprouts, then these packages in the carriage must be for you. Would you like to check?"

The children rushed past the pair, stopping only long enough to give Grace a glancing hug, and then climbed into the carriage to look for their gifts. Roland offered Grace his arm and escorted her forward to meet the servants still standing at attention. He directed them toward the oldest, a man wearing a stark black coat and an equally dour expression.

Despite the man's age, he executed a flawless bow, revealing the bald spot in the middle of his fringe of snow white hair. "Welcome back to Alnwick Castle, Lord Percy."

"Thank you, Withers. May I present to you my wife, Lady Percy. Grace, this is Withers, Alnwick's butler."

Grace executed a regal nod. "Lord Percy has spoken highly of you. I hope our late arrival has not caused too much turmoil for the household."

"We are prepared for every eventuality," the butler assured her in a gravelled tone, though Grace did not miss the glance he flicked toward the children cooing over their gifts. "Allow me to introduce you to the rest of the household."

Withers ran through a litany of names as the servants either bowed or curtseyed in turn. The housekeeper and cook were to be expected, but the senior and junior footmen, upper and lower floor maids, boot boy, stablemaster, and scullery maids spoke to the size and wealth of the duke's household. It would take Grace days to remember them all, but she made certain to commit the name of the housekeeper, a Mrs Yardley, to memory.

Withers ended on the woman overseeing the sprouts. "Our newest addition is Miss Fenton. She has come from the village to serve as governess for the children."

"Alnwick Village?" Roland asked, his face scrunched in confusion. Her thick accent suggested a very different hometown.

"Lately," Withers clarified with a sniff. "Her family relocated to the area after trouble in the Highlands. Sir Nathaniel made the decision to hire her."

"Speaking of my brother, is he so thin-skinned that he cannot risk a moment in the cold to come to welcome us?" Roland asked.

The butler's nostrils flared, but he otherwise hid his disapproval of Roland's decision to make public his connection to the son born on the wrong side of the blanket. "Sir Nathaniel is out, my lord. I will make him aware of your arrival when he returns."

Grace's smile slipped as disappointment washed over her. They had sent word ahead by rider, so he should have been expecting them. Unless—

"Did the rider fail to notify you of when to expect us?" Roland asked, clearly thinking the same thing.

"We received word," Withers replied. "His Grace was informed."

But His Grace's bastard grandson had apparently not been given the same courtesy, despite his status as newly minted knight of the realm.

"Where is my grandfather?" Roland asked. "Are we to present ourselves in his study for review?"

"The duke is occupied." Withers left his answer at that. "If you will follow me, I will show you to your rooms. The footmen will see to your things. Mrs Yardley, can you arrange for a tea tray to be sent up?"

Grace took Roland's arm again, barely resisting the urge to cling to his side. Other than the sprouts, not a single servant had smiled in welcome. At best, the junior staff had studied her and Roland with curious gazes. No matter her intentions, Grace feared she would not find any easy path toward stepping into the role of lady of the house.

The Breaker of Northumberland would set the tone. Snubbing them sent a clear message. Though the law dictated Roland to be his heir, and Grace the future duchess, he was far less certain of their worthiness for the titles.

2

Roland had not been certain what sort of welcome would await them when they arrived at Alnwick, but 'decidedly anticlimactic' had not been one of the possibilities he had considered. A part of him was glad that their arrival was short of drama and fanfare. Grace had been in a nervous flutter for days.

Their pre-wedding meeting with the Breaker during the summer had nearly been a disaster of epic proportions. After the way he had declared a woman's only value lay in her ability to bear heirs, Roland could scarcely blame Grace for not looking forward to spending the winter cloistered with his grandfather.

He looked at the closed adjoining door between their rooms, considering. Grace had claimed travel fatigue shortly after their welcome at the front of the castle, and had gone with Elsie to their room for a short respite.

"Your burgundy coat, my lord."

Jolted out of the mire of his thoughts, Roland's attention turned towards his valet, standing there with one of his least-favourite coats. "Er, thank you, Briggs. Did... did I choose this?"

"No, my lord," Briggs said, keeping a carefully expressionless face. "You seemed to have other things on your mind. I chose it for you."

Roland stared hard at his valet, reminded again that his brother had recommended this particular replacement to him. Perhaps not coincidentally, Briggs had first been Thorne's valet. For only one week. Roland feared the man's tenure in his employ would be similarly short. "I despise this coat."

"But your lady wife adores the way it makes your eyes seem darker and more mysterious. And it is warm. The wind has picked up outside, and the lower halls are rather... draughty."

Blinking, Roland consented to allow himself to be put in the horrid coat. He would have done without a valet on their trip if he had dared, but they had been on a timetable, and Thorne had correctly—if somewhat gleefully—repeated his own words back to him about hiring new hands to keep up with the expectations of his position.

"Has there been word back from my grandfather?" Roland asked, changing the subject. "I was hoping we could find a few minutes to meet privately before supper."

Pursing his lips, Briggs shook his head, lifting his hands to straighten Roland's cravat. "Mr Withers assured me your message had been delivered to the duke, but there's been no response yet, my lord."

"You do not have to call me that so often," Roland gritted out, feeling irritation creeping back.

"You are Lord Roland Percy, Earl Percy, my lord. Only one frail heartbeat separates you from the dukedom, and Sir Nathaniel made it quite clear that I would be doing you the greatest disrespect in being informal with you."

"I suppose my brother was also the person who told you not to let me have an opinion on what to wear?"

He could see Briggs trying to restrain a small smile. "He did imply that allowing you too much choice could be a terrible disservice to everyone."

"That does sound very much like him," Roland said dryly, focusing on Briggs' expression. "It surprises me that the two of you didn't get on better."

"Ah. Well, we perhaps were rather too much alike in some respects. It is said that there is a peculiar charm in contrast."

Peculiar, indeed. The valet was in his early thirties, a handful of years older than Roland and Thorne, a few inches shorter, fair haired, and slender. It was hard to imagine finding more contrast from his strapping, dark-haired, blue eyed brother. But Briggs wasn't entirely wrong that there was a decided similarity in their bearing.

In better humour, Roland allowed Briggs to finish dressing him. "If there has been no word from the duke, has there been any from Thorne?"

"Oh yes," Briggs nodded. "Sir Nathaniel has been out riding, and he will be ready to meet with you and Lady Percy in the drawing room before dinner."

"Out riding! In this cold?"

Briggs' briefly quirked eyebrows were as expressive as a shrug. "He may be downstairs already, my lord. You may castigate him for his rash choices at your leisure."

"Well, now that you have given me your permission, of course," Roland drawled, heading for the door as Briggs gave him another small smile.

As he stepped out into the hallway, Grace's door opened and Elsie poked her head out. "Lord Percy! If you wish to wait a moment, Lady Grace is ready to accompany you downstairs."

Roland's heart lifted, glad to hear Grace was ready to face whatever awaited them below. He didn't even have a chance to acknowledge Elsie's request before the door opened wider, and the maid withdrew to let Grace pass.

"My lady," Roland greeted her, taking her hand and pressing a kiss to it before he flattened her palm against his cheek. "You look better. You seemed so tired earlier."

She smiled at him in response. "Just a bit of travel weariness, love. You look very lordly. I like that coat on you."

Yes, Briggs did kindly inform me he was dressing me solely for your pleasure."

Her smile grew wider. "Did he? Even though you hate this coat?"

"If you knew that, I see I have no hope of keeping any secrets with our servants around. What else do the three of you whisper about when I am not listening?"

He had couched his grumpy words in a teasing tone, but she grew more serious. "Does it bother you? That they... whisper? If it bothers you, I will tell Elsie not to talk to him if you like."

"What? No, I do not care. As long as they are loyal to us, I expect their communication will be a godsend when our duties inevitably drag us apart. Why do you ask?"

Grace paused, as if thinking other thoughts, but then she leaned forward and whispered conspiratorially. "If you are not troubled, that is a relief, because I rather think Elsie fancies Briggs."

"She does?" he stopped, surprised, and the corner of her mouth turned up again. "To think I was just fantasising about dismissing him. I suppose this means I will be stuck with him forever—or at least until Elsie turns her nose up at him."

Grace's hazel eyes sparkled at him, warming him through. "You would really keep him just for Elsie's happiness when Nathaniel sent him packing with us so quickly? I think you are a romantic," she teased.

"Truly, the man is fine as a valet. And it seems heartless to send him off without employment now. He would be stuck in Alnwick until spring with nothing to do."

"Fine as a valet, but... Briggs is not your brother," Grace said shrewdly, identifying the very heart of his discontent. "I think you have been unhappy to be apart."

"A better way to put it might be that I have grown far too accustomed to his endless skulduggery and the jests at my expense. With no one to incessantly batter my ears with nonsense, now, I find myself quite at a loss. Fortunately, that will soon be remedied. He is waiting downstairs as we speak, likely holding his breath, eager to crow about how he has foisted his valet upon me."

His wife laughed at the picture of it. "Then perhaps we should go join him before he faints."

"Yes," he agreed, offering her his arm. "Let us face our enemies—together."

She grew a little pensive despite the humour he used in referencing their last misadventure. He wondered again, as he had many times before, if she was more worried about this reunion than she let on. But he had no time to dwell on those thoughts, because a familiar pair of bright blue eyes locked on theirs the very moment they began to descend the stairs.

"Nathaniel!" Grace greeted him, letting go of Roland's arm to hurry down the stairs.

Thorne's welcoming smile turned to a look of alarm, and he opened his arms to catch her in an embrace as she hurtled towards him in her unsteady descent. "Go carefully, Lady Grace," he chided her softly, looking embarrassed to be the one to do so. "Like a few other things at Alnwick Castle, the steps can be a bit treacherous."

Roland's more sedate pace closed the gap within seconds,

but hearing the caution and painfully mindful of the watching footmen nearby, he quickly shepherded his brother and wife around the corner into the drawing room, waiving off their offers of assistance. Only once the door was shut on them did he feel comfortable enough to clap Thorne on the back. The man answered Roland's first unasked question with a hearty squeeze.

"Your arm is better?" Grace asked him, lightly touching the shoulder he had injured during their summer misadventures.

"Nearly normal again. A little weaker than it was before," he confessed. "And this confounded chill makes it ache. But I hope that will pass soon, otherwise it will be a very bothersome winter. Nevermind that! What of the two of you? Have you any... good tidings to share?"

Tactfully phrased, Roland thought, stifling a small smirk as Grace flushed an unexpectedly deep red when Thorne's eyes glanced at her belly. His grandfather, propriety be damned, would not be nearly as discreet in asking the question.

"Yes, Bath was a lovely destination, thank you for asking," she replied acerbically, but her eyes slid to the side.

Both men frowned, and Roland wondered if she was regretting their decision to delay trying for a child. Their courtship and the wedding had been a forced march to the beat of other people's drums. With his grandfather's ultimatums in securing a woman's hand in marriage satisfied, the danger faced during the season, and Thorne safely out of the Breaker's reach, Roland and Grace had agreed privately to take a little time to enjoy their marriage—and each other—before worrying about any begetting. They would learn the important details about managing Northumberland this winter, and in the spring, they could travel to Ireland, or perhaps Portugal. After that, time would tell.

"Yes. Our lives have been quite dull," Roland said cheerfully, turning the subject. "How much could one say about beautiful countryside, taking the waters, and quaint castles? It would be far more interesting to gossip about you."

"Gossip about me, in front of me?" Thorne smirked. "There is little to tell. Whatever else one might say about Danforth, he chose good people to manage his lands in his absence while he was at court. I also have a letter for the both of you—from my mother. I suppose my tale made for some brief but scintillating gossip for her. She is showing improvement, and sends you her regards."

Before they could talk further, a clatter in the hallway turned their heads towards the door. The three of them turned politely, expecting the Breaker to stride into the room. But when the door to the parlour flew open, however, two small figures tumbled in—wide-eyed and breathless, their cheeks flushed with mischief.

Behind them, Miss Fenton followed. "Come along now, bairns. It's time ye bid your goodnights to his lordship and her ladyship, afore ye're off tae bed."

Grace immediately sat down on the nearest couch, extending a hand to each child and drawing them towards her knees. Roland and Thorne withdrew slightly as they chattered with Grace about their day, lingering and asking if she would be able to read them a bedtime story.

"I cannot read you a book tonight, dear Sprouts, but I promise we will read one soon. How are you settling in with Miss Fenton?" she asked kindly. "Do you like it here at Alnwick Castle so far?"

Wes looked reluctant to answer, but Willa shook her head fiercely. "I don't like it. I hear noises in the hall sometimes. It's scary!"

"Mice, I'm sure," Miss Fenton murmured with quiet reproach when Grace cast an inquiring look her way. "It would be a task indeed to keep them out of an auld castle like this!"

"'Tis not mice!" the boy retorted sharply, before dropping his voice to a whisper. "It might be 'the Snatcher.'"

Wes's voice might have been whispered, but it was still loud enough that Roland heard him quite clearly. "A snatcher! I have heard of the Alnwick Vampire, but never a snatcher."

"My goodness, Roland!" Grace scolded him as the children's eyes grew round. "Are you trying to make sure they do not to sleep at all?"

Thorne smothered a laugh. "Don't worry, sprouts. If he ever existed at all, the angry villagers of Northumberland bur— er, did away with the vampire a very long, long time ago, a hundred years and more before you were born."

Both children looked mollified that they weren't in imminent peril from a vampire, but Wes's face still held an air of uncertainty.

"Here," Roland murmured, sitting on the couch beside Grace. "Tell me why you are so worried about this... man?"

"It's not a man, it's a monster," Wes muttered. "The others in the village say it steals kids from their beds and eats them."

Willa scoffed. "Do you believe it's seven feet tall and has horns, too? There's no such thing as monsters like that. *Or* vampires," she added with a cross look at Roland.

Roland magnanimously ignored Thorne covering his mouth on the far side of the room. "You are as clever as Lady Grace," he told the girl. "There are no such things as monsters and vampires. Most noises have far more mundane causes."

"Like mice," Grace agreed, smiling. "Or perhaps a certain duke wandering the halls late at night?"

"Exactly," Miss Fenton said firmly, taking a child by each hand. "Say yer goodnights, children. We'll go find a bonnie, happy tale tae read."

"Goodnight!" both chorused dutifully, exiting the drawing

room, but the boy's eyebrows were still drawn together in unhappy thought as he left.

"Well!" Grace exclaimed with a sigh. "I suppose with such a large, draughty old castle, it was only a matter of time before little imaginations ran wild."

Roland chuckled and shook his head. "Alnwick's young ones are making up new legends to replace old ones. I suppose each generation must create their own. The duke has not said anything about missing children to you, Thorne?"

"No," he finally said. "Nothing on that topic or anything else, to be honest. I have scarcely seen the Breaker. I have been here nearly two weeks, and he hasn't joined me at the breakfast or the supper table even once. I thought he might be avoiding me after what happened in Brighton, and truthfully, I was glad for it."

Before either of them could reply, a soft knock sounded on the door, and Withers, the duke's ageing butler, let himself in following it. "The dining room is prepared, my lord, my lady. Dinner is now served. His Grace regrets that he will not be joining you this evening."

Though he had been working on tempering his reactions to befit his rank, Roland could still feel his brows drawing together in consternation. "Thank you, Withers. Is His Grace unwell, or is he merely occupied this evening?"

"His Grace asked for some solitude this evening. I believe he simply requires a bit of rest, Lord Percy," the butler temporised. "He will see you instead at breakfast."

"I see. Convey our regards to His Grace. We will follow you shortly, Withers."

The butler gave a respectful nod and exited the room. The door latch barely clicked before his lady wife, tense with suspicious energy, turned to his brother. "You have scarcely seen him... But you *have* seen The Breaker?"

"Aye. A few times," Thorne answered her. "We crossed paths actually, the day before yesterday as he was leaving the library, and he seemed as hale as one might expect a man of his years. But we have exchanged only perhaps five words the entire time I've been waiting for you to arrive."

"How strange," Grace murmured. "That does not sound much like His Grace. I wonder why he is being so insular."

3

Without the Breaker's presence, dinner was a pleasant—if somewhat chilly—affair, and Grace welcomed Roland to share her bed the entire night. "I will freeze otherwise," she had insisted, with an exaggerated shiver for emphasis.

He was more than delighted to be granted such an invitation for any reason, though he could sympathise with that sentiment. It *was* cold. They had arrived at Alnwick only barely ahead of the first plummeting temperatures that had likely made an icy, half-frozen hard muck of the roads. Frost still rimmed the glass panes, even though the sun had been up for about two hours now. Grace had firmly planted herself in the seat nearest the large hearth at the breakfast table, cupping her hands around the delicate porcelain of her teacup for warmth, as close as she could without appearing gauche.

But she didn't make any other complaint. She focused on looking serene and worthy of a countess, though he was sure her thoughts were anything but.

Thorne had already come and gone, and he and Grace had lingered at the table, hoping the duke would eventually make an appearance. Finally, as the clock struck a quarter to eleven, Roland's patience snapped, and he turned to his grandfather's butler. "Tell me, Withers, is His Grace planning to grace us with his presence today, or shall we continue our stay as if he were a ghost haunting his own halls?"

The butler's face was heavily lined with conflict. "His Grace has been indisposed, my lord. I am not privy to his precise plans for the day, but I shall inform him of your inquiry at once."

Withers departed to handle the errand—in relief, Roland thought—and Roland tapped his fingers briefly in irritation on the table before stifling the gesture. Beside him, Grace lay a hand on his wrist and then took the morning paper from him.

That broke the tension. Roland shot her a glance, flicking his eyes towards the footman who remained in the room.

"Let them talk," Grace murmured softly, reading the current affairs.

Roland smirked to himself, knowing that despite the fact that they had agreed to be on their best behaviour, it was too much to expect that she would be able to hide all of her more willful tendencies.

Just as Roland was prepared to assume that they had wasted their morning entirely, he heard raised voices on the upper level, growing louder as they approached the stair. Roland was amused how quickly Grace quickly returned his paper once she recognized the bass rumble of the duke.

"—not a child to be moved around by you and locked out of my things! I asked for privacy, not this constant interference. How am I supposed to manage anything when you are meddling and moving things about?"

"Your Grace," Withers said beseechingly, and then the voices dropped too low to hear.

Roland didn't dare look in Grace's direction as he waited, focused on the door. What the devil was going on at Alnwick?

He had little chance to wonder anything else as the duke carelessly threw the door open in a fit of pique, and only the footman's hasty interference kept it from crashing against the wall. Both of them rose from their seats to acknowledge his rank. Leaning heavily on the head of his cane, the Duke of Northumberland levelled a hard look at Roland and then a longer, more considered one at Grace.

Or rather, her waistline.

"I see the two of you did not die on the roads after all," was his terse greeting. "You certainly left it long enough. Unless you were having... female troubles, in which case I suppose I must forgive it."

Grace had heard far worse things from the crotchety old duke's mouth, so she did not bother gasping in indignation, but her cheeks reddened. "My womanly impositions are not fit for discussion at the breakfast table—or any table, for that matter," she replied just as bluntly.

The Breaker's left eyebrow lifted slightly at her slightly cheeky reply, but he only nodded once, jerkily. "If you lack the refinement, at least you have a spine to benefit the role you have to play. And, I hope, uncommon womanly intelligence in the bargain to learn quickly. You are mistress of the household now, and there are many social obligations to attend to that cannot be put off just because you are unready."

Grace's lips parted slightly in surprise, but the duke turned back towards Roland, ignoring her. "You should accept that as my heir, there are things you cannot leave too late to attend to properly, Lord Percy. Travel plans in the north would be only one of those... things."

Roland decided then and there that discretion might be the better part of valour, else it was bound to be a very long winter. "You are correct, Your Grace. Since I spent so many years farther south, I was somewhat remiss in recalling how quickly it got dark this far north at this time of year. It slowed our progress more than planned, but I did keep you informed of our progress."

His grandfather grunted, and then turned back to Grace, now letting his irritation show on his face. "Perhaps I was being too subtle. *I* need to begin instructing my grandson to make up for this lost time, and *you* should go see the housekeeper. *Now.*"

Grace stifled her instinct to do the exact opposite of what the Breaker ordered. She wanted to spend as little time in his presence as possible, so there was naught to be gained by acting the contrarian. Outside in the hallway, she realised she had no idea where to find the housekeeper. More importantly, the staff would not welcome her wandering around their domain. She turned to the nearest footman and asked him to see if Mrs Yardley could spare her some time.

"Mrs Yardley has made herself available," he confirmed. "If my lady would care to wait in the family sitting room, I will let her know you are ready to see her."

"That will be fine. But before you rush off, would you mind showing me the way to the sitting room? I am still learning my way around."

The footman took the lead, guiding Grace through the corridors and up the stairs. Grace followed blindly, focusing her attention on what would come next. Roland had been able to offer only limited advice about how to interact with Mrs Yardley. She had joined the Duke's household sometime while he was away, giving her enough experience at running the house, but leaving him with no knowledge of what Grace could expect. This meeting was most certainly a test, and Grace did not mean to fail.

However, Grace also knew that she and Roland would not be departing anytime soon. It would be the height of foolishness for Grace to make Mrs Yardley into an enemy. Therefore, it was incumbent that Grace find a safe middle ground until she could get a firm handle on where Mrs Yardley stood.

The footman opened a door on the first floor and welcomed Grace inside. The family sitting room boasted a southern exposure that maximised the available sunlight. It was small, but richly furnished with armchairs and sofas upholstered in floral silk damask. A brocade tapestry depicting a pastoral scene hung on the interior wall, helping to hold the heat from the fireplace in the room.

After the footman closed the door behind himself, Grace allowed her curiosity full rein. This was her room to use as she saw fit. The old duke might even allow her to make changes to it if she asked. She was, after all, the lady of the house. However, the longer she studied the space, the more beauty she found in it.

The legs of the armchairs had been carved into lion's paws, bringing to mind her childhood dreams of far-off lands. She traced the floral scrolls carved into a side table, one perfectly sized to be a writing desk. Across the room, the gilded edges and lacquered finish of a large cabinet called for her to explore. Inside, she found paper, ink and quills along with sealing wax and a stamp. Miniature volumes of poetry bound in fine leather filled another shelf. Though they were not to Grace's taste, she decided she would read them anyway. Perhaps she would find some sweet nothing to whisper in her husband's ear. The next cabinet proved to be half empty, offering space to store books more to Grace's liking.

She was checking her appearance in the ornate overmantle mirror hanging above the fireplace when a sharp rap on the door announced Mrs Yardley's arrival.

"Come in," Grace called.

"Good morning, your ladyship," Mrs Yardley said as she

came into the room. She dropped into a shallow curtsey, as befitted Grace's station as future duchess, but made no friendly overtures. Her face was carved into a mask of polite indifference. Whether she would turn out to be an eventual friend or foe remained unanswered.

"Please, Mrs Yardley, have a seat. We have much to discuss." Grace indicated a pair of carved wooden chairs at a table next to the fireplace. She took the nearest and settled into it, folding her hands in her lap as her mother had taught her.

Mrs Yardley took the opposite chair and sank onto the edge of it. She kept her back straight, not daring to relax in front of her superior, as she unfurled a roll of papers and laid them on the table. "I have brought along a list of the household inventory for your review. You will see that all is in order. Cook has also sent along the menus for the week. If you have any feedback, I will pass it along, but I cannot promise we can make changes at such short notice, particularly given the state of the roads."

Once again, Grace felt pulled in two directions. Her mother would have never stood for a servant dictating any limitations on her control over the household. But Grace was not her mother, and she had no interest in arguing over which dish to serve for the meat course at dinner. Likely, they had prepared the menu based on the duke's preferences, and any changes would only incur his wrath.

Grace chose discretion over valour, turning the conversation toward the events the duke had referenced. "I understand that there are social events in the diary. Might we begin with those? I am sure they must be more pressing than me seeing how many candlesticks Alnwick boasts."

Mrs Yardley nodded her agreement. She shuffled through her notes until she located the right page. "Given the season, we have several annual events planned for the coming weeks. Tomorrow, we will decorate the castle. There are dinner parties with the local gentry, the Christmas and New Year's balls, the village fair this week—"

"Tell me about the fair," Grace said. "Are we to host here in the castle?"

Mrs Yardley cast Grace an askance glance. "No, my lady. His Grace does not want all and sundry traipsing through the hallways. It is in the village hall. The ladies of the village put the event together. It is more of a charity drive than a festival. I have prepared a set of notes on it here."

Grace accepted the proffered piece of paper and skimmed over the housekeeper's neat penmanship. Each letter was clear and carefully formed, but lacked the fanciful flourishes of an upper class woman. Mrs Yardley had helpfully included a timeline for the event, a list of women and men assisting with the preparations, and the donation of the ducal estate.

"We are to provide the food and drink?" Grace asked to make sure she understood.

"Yes, my lady. Cook is already preparing pots of stew. We have ordered extra bread from the local bakery and cheese from the local dairy."

The choices made sense—the stews would be hearty and easily made in large quantities. By sourcing the breads and cheeses elsewhere, the estate would support local businesses. Grace could leave well enough alone, but what if this was the test? Nothing in Mrs Yardley's comportment suggested she wanted Grace to be further involved. However, if Grace remained mum, was she ceding ground she would later regret?

"I would like to make an addition to our contribution."

Grace's words hung in the air. Mrs Yardley froze in her seat, almost as though she was bracing for whatever Grace would say next.

"We shall bring apple pies, or any orchard fruit we have in abundance. I am certain the people of Alnwick will appreciate a sweet treat on such cold days, would they not, Mrs Yardley?"

"I— that is, yes, my lady. But pies?" Mrs Yardley's cheeks flushed. She ventured, "Might a pudding do instead?"

In truth, Grace did not have a preference at all, but now that she had set out on this path, she meant to see it through to the end. If the staff failed to execute her small request, she would know exactly where they stood with regard to her wishes.

"My family always brings pies to the village events. Our cook has quite the reputation, and they go down like a treat. The cook may make hand pies if they are easier to prepare and transport, but I insist they have a fruit filling. Is there any problem with my request?"

Mrs Yardley's eyes darted left and right, but she shook her head. "I will pass along the orders, my lady. In fact, I should go now, so Cook has sufficient time to get organised."

As she watched Mrs Yardley gather her papers and exit the sitting room, Grace could not help but take satisfaction in how their first meeting had gone. So busy was she being proud of herself, she failed to note Mrs Yardley's tense shoulders and furrowed brow.

4

Golden sunlight illuminated the castle windows on the morning of the village fair. Cheered by the sight of the cloudless blue sky, Grace announced they would walk to the village hall.

"Must we, miss?" Elsie asked from her position near the fireplace in Grace's bedroom. She rubbed her hands together and held them closer to the flames to emphasise her already half-frozen state.

"It is but a short walk, Elsie. Given the theme of charity, it is only right that we act in a humble manner so that the focus remains on the community and not us. Besides, you have a fine pair of new gloves and a wool muff. That is far more than many of the attendees will have."

Elsie bobbed her head and disappeared into the dressing room, mumbling under her breath. Grace caught only snippets, but that was enough to understand that it was more than the cold causing Elsie's concern. She followed Elsie into the smaller chamber, all but backing her into a corner.

"What are you mumbling about?"

Elsie gnawed at her lower lip, her eyes firmly focused on the ground. It took another round of prodding before the maid came clean. "The staff has been working nigh round the clock, my lady. Putting their feet up at all, even if only for a few minutes, would be greatly appreciated."

"Around the clock? But how can that be? We have had no guests this week, and the castle staff is more than sufficiently resourced, even if we did. Surely setting out the Christmas decorations did not take so long."

"It's the pies, ma'am."

"Pies?" Grace was certain she had misheard. "The fruit pies for the fair?"

Elsie raised her gaze and gave a single nod of confirmation. "I know you meant well, my lady, but making dozens of pies requires planning, or so Cook has said time and time again this week. She sent the stable boys out to get honey from all the nearby farmsteads. The housemaids were tasked with peeling and slicing fruit, while the footmen found more baking tins. Last night, they were up to the wee hours moving pies in and out of the ovens."

Grace's spirits plummeted the more Elsie went on. "But I thought it was a simple thing. Mama always donates pies to the village fetes."

Elsie stopped biting her lip to give Grace a weak smile. "In a well-run household, her ladyship should remain unaware of the effort things take, and the castle is no exception. Mrs Yardley was most insistent that none of the staff grumble in your presence."

"Making it very clear who was to blame for the added work." Grace's shoulders dropped. "Why did you not say something before now? Surely you are comfortable enough with me to let me know if you are working all hours."

"I was not involved. I'm an upper servant."

Competing emotions roiled in Grace's stomach. Glad as she

was to have not inconvenienced Elsie, whom she thought of as a friend more than a servant, it likely made matters worse belowstairs. "How do I make this right?"

Elsie expressed no surprise at Grace's question. She had served at Grace's side long enough to understand Grace's concerns. Perhaps that was why she had kept the matter to herself for this long. Like Grace, Elsie was also an outsider searching for her place in an unfamiliar household. Undermining Grace would result in less respect accorded to Elsie as well. Their places were tied together, depending on the respect for the lady to carry over to the maid.

"An extra half-day would not go amiss," she ventured.

"A half-day plus a small monetary reward. I will pay it out of my allowance."

Elsie flashed Grace the first full smile of the day. "That will go down well, my lady. I will make sure they know you are funding it yourself."

"Let me tell Mrs Yardley and Withers first," Grace said. "It will be a good reminder that I am not without resources, and I will not stand for being made to look like a fool. Now, gather my warmest dress and sturdy leather boots so that we can be ready to depart on time. On foot," Grace added. "The rest of the staff may travel by carriage and wagon along with our donations to the event."

An hour later, Grace arrived in the castle courtyard, bundled in a fur-lined pelisse and matching muff, with Elsie at her side. She found Mrs Yardley and Cook waiting at the gate. Mrs Yardley's neutral expression gave no hint as to her true sentiments, but Cook tried her best to avoid meeting Grace's eyes.

Before the quartet of women made to depart, Grace asked them to wait a moment. "Cook, I want to personally extend my gratitude for your extraordinary efforts in organising the food for today. Particularly, for handling my last minute request to add pies with such good humour. Our meals thus far are as excellent as any I have eaten elsewhere, so I am confident the treats will be highly valued. They will cheer people, which I am reminded is the spirit of the season. Mrs Yardley, I would like to arrange for everyone involved to receive a reward, yourselves included. Elsie can pass along the details when we return home."

Cook's cheeks pinked with delight at Grace's words. Even Mrs Yardley allowed a small smile to cross her lips as she bobbed her head in agreement.

Grace suggested the local women take the lead, with her and Elsie following behind. Elsie nudged Grace with her elbow and whispered words of praise in a tone too low for the others to hear. Grace, however, was hesitant to consider this any sort of victory. She was no closer to learning where Mrs Yardley's allegiance lay. At best, they were back at a stalemate. But now was not the time for such worries, not when Grace had a village worth of people to meet.

The size of that challenge became clear when the women walked into the village hall. High windows allowed light to flood the space. Someone had strung garland over the doorways. Sprigs of holly with their bright, red berries formed the centrepiece of decoration on every table.

People, predominantly women, bustled around the room, bearing trays of food and piles of clothing. They moved with the order of a well-oiled machine as they designated which wares went in which parts of the room. Even the children present seemed to know how to stay out of the way.

It did not take long for the others to realise that the lady had descended from the castle. Grace caught more than a few curious glances cast her way before a woman approached for an introduction. She was of a similar age to Roland, perhaps a few years older at most. Her modest clothing was well-kept, despite being of simple fabric. It was the knitted shawl on her shoulders that caught Grace's eye.

"Good morning, my lady," she said to Grace, before adding hellos to the rest of their group.

"Countess Percy, may I introduce Miss Whitby? She is the local schoolmistress and has taken the lead in organising today's event," Mrs Yardley said, stepping into the gap before the woman was forced to introduce herself.

Grace beamed at the woman, wanting to make a good impression. "A fine event, indeed, based on what I have seen so far. You are both clever and kind-hearted to donate your time in such a way."

"You are too kind, my lady. His Grace has been most generous this year in offering his support. The pies are an unexpected delight." Miss Whitby studied Grace. "Is that your hand that I see behind their addition?"

"I can only take credit for the idea. Our wonderful cook and her staff deserve full credit for them." Grace pulled her hands free of her muff and passed it to Elsie. "Tell me how I can best help, Miss Whitby. And please, do not stand on ceremony. I can pitch in as well as the next person."

"If I may," Mrs Yardley said, cutting into the conversation. "Her ladyship has yet to meet most of the townspeople. Before assigning her a task, might you see to introductions? Mrs Pattimore, Elsie and I can offer our help right away."

To give Miss Whitby her due, she glanced at Grace to get her permission before executing the housekeeper's instruction. Grace kept her grin in place, though inside she wished Mrs Yardley had held her tongue. It was not that she wanted to avoid the introductions, so much as preferring to encounter people in a more natural way.

Mrs Yardley's suggestion ensured Grace was paraded around like the prized calf, a role she thought she had left behind in her debutante days. Nonetheless, she kept a stiff upper lip in place, making sure to say hello to everyone, no matter where they sat in the social structure. The shopkeeper, midwife, and even a busy mother of four might all soon prove useful, especially if Grace's pregnancy progressed to term.

She spotted Roland and Thorne arriving an hour later. Roland could do little more than to wave hello before he, too, was thrust into the rounds. Seeing the attention turn his way, Grace decided it was time to make her escape.

"Is that warm cider I smell?" she asked. "I would not say no to a mug. Would you like to join me, Miss Whitby? I am keen to learn more about your school."

Miss Whitby was delighted to find a possible new benefactress. She dispatched a pair of young men to fetch a pair of chairs while she procured the cider. In short order, Grace found herself tucked away in a corner. The teacher sat to her right, off to the side so that they could both have a view of the room. The event was picking up pace now that the doors were thrown open in welcome. For a short while, the women watched as villagers and people from the surrounding area came to collect what they needed for their winter stores.

Any children were quick to wave a shy hello at Miss Whitby while they goggled at the fancy lady at her side. Grace hid a grin behind her chipped mug of cider, imagining all the questions the teacher would get come Monday.

"How large is the school?" Grace asked.

"The number of pupils swells and shrinks according to the agricultural seasons, my lady. Now, with the harvest behind us and parents looking for ways to occupy their children during the dark winter days, we have close to one hundred pupils. In the spring and autumn, the number shrinks to half of that at best."

"My word!" Grace was indeed impressed. "You must have several teachers to assist with managing such a large number."

"A couple of local girls help with the youngest ones. I have a single assistant who focuses on literacy, while I teach the children their numbers. It may not sound like much, but up here, there is little need for more."

"It is more than many young women of my set are taught, which is another problem in itself. However, that is a topic for another day." Grace set her empty mug aside and rose from her chair. "I would very much like to support your endeavours, Miss Whitby. When you have a moment of time, please prepare a list of what you need. I will send an invitation for tea, and we can go through it together. I have occupied your attention for long enough. I can see my lady's maid is in need of an extra pair of hands. I will go help her."

Before Grace could walk away, a kerfuffle broke out in front of her. A harried, middle-aged woman wearing a dress made more of patches than original material gave a cry.

"Harry? Harry?" Her voice rose with each utterance of the name. "Where's my Harry? Where's my boy?"

All around, voices dropped low, but there was no missing the vein of worry running through their words. Other villagers stopped what they were doing to help the frantic mother find her missing child. Mere moments later, the crowd parted and a dirt-streaked child ran through.

"Mum? You callin' for me?" he asked in pure innocence. "I was outside playin' with me mates."

The woman threw her arms around her son, caring not one whit for the mud he was getting on her clothes. To Grace's eye, her reaction seemed wildly out of kilter with the situation, but no one around them showed signs of sharing Grace's opinion.

"What was that all about?" Grace asked, leaning close to Miss Whitby. "Does the boy have a history of running off?"

"There have been some problems," she replied, glancing left and right to see if anyone else was listening. "Not here in

Alnwick, but in nearby villages. A child here and there taking off in the middle of the night. I have taken great care to lecture my pupils on the risks of being exposed to the weather, but I fear the other schools have not done the same. You know how these things go—one child sneaks off, another hears about it and latches onto the idea. You need not fear, my lady. Our children are far too sensible to take off into the wilds of Northumberland."

"I should hope so," Grace agreed. Yet, for the rest of the day, despite the gay atmosphere and kindred spirits, a nagging thought vied for Grace's attention.

Were the missing children somehow connected to the tale of the so-called snatcher Wes and Willa had heard? In a large city like London, children went missing all the time. But this far north, surely such events had to be rare exceptions.

Despite her efforts to reassure herself, when Grace climbed into bed that night and closed her eyes, she could still see the panic that had been carved in the lines on that poor mother's face.

5

The duke had spent days harping on the importance of appearances, and now, apparently, that extended to Sir Nathaniel Thorne. If Roland Percy was determined enough to use a royal favour to make a gentleman of his bastard brother, then Gideon Percy, the second Duke of Northumberland, would not put himself at odds with his heir. At least, not in public.

This was how Roland found himself heading to church, crammed into a far-too-small carriage with his grandfather, his wife, and his brother. It was the longest ten minutes of his life.

In an attempt to be diplomatic, Roland had chosen to sit beside his grandfather on the forward-facing bench, leaving Grace and Thorne to sit together. In hindsight, Roland regretted the decision, as it left His Grace free to glare at Thorne the entire ride. Thorne, however, appeared perfectly at ease, returning the duke's glares with a pleasant expression whenever he stopped pretending he was memorising the view outside of the windows.

St. Michael's Church in the village was a squat, imposing piece of old Gothic architecture. Snow had begun to gather in the shadowed corners where stone met earth, making the walls look like they rose from the churchyard like the bleaching, exposed bones of a large animal. To complete the illusion, in the nearby cemetery, a score of ancient gravestones jutted up like crooked teeth.

Roland could hear the two footmen who had been riding on the back scrambling off once they arrived, preparing to assist His Grace on the descent from the carriage. The awkward fuss that everyone had raised during their departure told him clearly that his grandfather had not been stirring himself to leave Alnwick Castle much of late. And as he watched the older man struggling to step onto the carriage stool without leaning on the proffered hands of the footmen, he began to have an inkling why.

His Grace had not seemed nearly as unsteady during the summer. It seemed that the ageing Breaker was being served evidence of his own mortality, and growing infirmity was becoming more difficult to hide.

The yard was cold but sunny, and despite the temperatures, a fair-sized throng of people were tightly clustered in conversational groups as they waited for services to begin. A handful of gentry made up a separate group to one side. Among them, Roland could see Alnwick's bailiff, with whom he had crossed paths on previous visits, and the rector, Reverend Shepherd, with whom he had renewed his acquaintance the day before.

"Your Grace," Reverend Shepherd beamed. "I know I have visited you at Alnwick Castle regularly, but it is such a pleasure to see you at St. Michael's this morning. I think it has been some time since we've had the honour of your presence here—was it truly as long ago as the harvest festival? I trust the estate has kept you well occupied these past months."

The duke inclined his head. "Hmph. Yes, well, the estate

does not manage itself, does it? Seems there's always some matter or another keeping me locked away. A great deal had to be attended to after the trip to Brighton, but I am reminded that does not diminish the importance of being seen and showing face. With my heir and his wife wintering at Alnwick, it seemed an opportune moment to return to proper habits and press younger bones into the duties that will soon be theirs."

"Well said, Your Grace. We were most grateful to have Lord and Lady Percy's assistance with the village charity fair." The reverend turned to include Roland and Grace in his thanks, nodding at them. And then he turned towards Thorne, clearly waiting for an introduction.

After a pause, the duke finally responded gruffly, a faint wash of colour in his cheeks. "Reverend Shepherd, this is Sir Nathaniel Thorne, a *guest* of ours at Alnwick."

"My half brother," Roland added, smiling as the reverend's eyes widened slightly in comprehension.

"Sir Nathaniel, my goodness. Forgive me, it has been so many years since I last saw you, I scarcely recognised you. You have certainly come up in the world since you were a young lad. Welcome back to Alnwick. How does your mother fare? Is she still in Alnmouth? I did not see her the last time I attended a sermon there."

"Thank you, Reverend, it's good to be back," Thorne murmured with only the barest trace of insincerity in his tone. Roland doubted the others would have caught it. "My mother moved to my holdings this summer."

The handful of other aristocrats standing around were still listening politely, and when a small, awkward silence fell again, the reverend smoothly picked up the thread of introductions. "Lord Percy, Lady Percy, Sir Nathaniel, I do not know if you have had the chance to meet everyone else here?"

"Just Mr Harding, who I have met with in past visits, in his capacity as bailiff."

"Then allow me to introduce our magistrate, Colonel Ellesmere, his wife, Mrs Ellesmere, and Mr and Mrs Seymour. If you'll excuse me, Your Grace, my lord, my lady—I must attend to the rest of our congregation. It has been a pleasure speaking with you, and I look forward to continuing our conversation soon."

Roland noticed that his wife's attention seemed to be on the far side of the church yard during the introductions, but when addressed, she smiled at everyone genially. Greetings done, the gentry focused largely upon the duke, and Roland was free to turn his head to see what had previously caught her notice.

Among the rest of the congregation, expressions seemed to be solemn, the chatter hushed and intense. Now and again, they would glance towards the duke and the cluster of gentry. Grace met his eyes when he looked in her direction, and her frown was contemplative.

"Lord Percy," the magistrate said pleasantly, drawing his attention back to the group. "It would be a pleasure to have you and Lady Percy join us for tea one afternoon. My wife and I should very much like the opportunity to get better acquainted, now that you are spending time in Alnwick. Perhaps we can arrange something at your convenience?"

"Of course, Colonel Ellesmere. I shall speak with my wife and find a time that suits us both."

The last few words of Roland's reply were clipped by the ringing of the church bells, but the colonel nodded, having gotten the gist of it.

Mindful of the difficulties His Grace had suffered in getting into and out of the carriage, Roland offered his arm to his grandfather, who gave him a scowl in return and ignored it. Instead the old duke leaned forward slightly, putting more pressure on his cane as he took a slow, deliberate pace inside. The rest of those there to attend services waited to enter.

Since the duke held the highest rank, it was only proper and customary for him to precede the rest. However, there would be a price paid by everyone for their deference. The Duke of Northumberland saw no need to make his way through the front doors with any haste, and so getting the congregation into the church was an uncomfortable production.

Coughs and low murmurs could be heard behind as Alnwick's citizenry shivered in the cold, standing in file. Roland was so distracted by his grandfather's shuffling pace and the tension that resulted from it that his neck itched from the imagined staring.

Once His Grace cleared the entryway, the lower orders obligingly hastened towards the back of the church, keeping clear of the aisle that led towards the front and the Percy family pew on the right hand side. Then the duke promptly settled in the place closest to the brazier, which unfortunately was the first spot inside of the box, blocking egress for everyone else.

One of the footmen hurried up from behind to help wrap several woollen blankets around the duke's body and legs, and Roland circled the bench to sit at the Duke's right hand side, jaw tight with mild embarrassment as his grandfather ordered him to shift the placement of the foot warmer closer to his feet. In the end, the whole congregation was settled before they were, and Roland's annoyance burned within him like a personal stoked fire.

Graciously, the reverend took his time to approach the pulpit so it did not make them feel like they were holding things up. Thorne waited magnanimously while Grace slid closer to Roland along the dark-stained wood and then he sat on her other side.

Exhaling slowly to release some of his ire, Roland finally

recalled the odd looks that he dismissed as awe and curiosity, and he glanced into the congregation again. *No,* he thought to himself, *people are unhappy.* And a few couples looked downright grim and pale, a woman sitting with them looking as though she had been crying not too long ago.

Thorne, seeing where Roland was looking, shook his head slightly. Whatever had happened, he had no more insight to offer.

Reverend Shepherd took his place within the pulpit, and the rustling of bodies settled. "By now, many of you have heard the tragic news that has stricken the Turner and Shaw families. We ask for your prayers for the two young children who left their beds in the night, heedless of the dangers beyond their doorstep. May God keep them safe in His hands and guide them home tonight as the cold and hunger remind them of where they truly belong. And may He grant their grieving families peace in this time of deep sorrow."

Beside him, Grace's hands tightened on her bible, the kid leather wrinkling to show the pressure of her fingers. A chill of foreboding travelled down Roland's spine as he recalled the Sprouts's tall tale, and the news from the schoolmistress. Several children gone astray, supposedly runaways, and all from the hamlets and small villages dotting the area around Alnwick.

As discreetly as he could, Roland let his shoulder press against hers briefly in comfort. He could understand the urge to leave home and find a better life—better, perhaps, than most. Unlike these children, Roland had not left without resources. His stomach roiled at the thought of children out on their own.

Reverend Shepherd spoke at length of duty and what was owed to one's family before segueing into the story of Jonah and how he found himself inside the whale after running away from the command of God. Roland wondered how the rector would have judged his own past. Reverend Shepherd closed with the story of the angel's visit to Mary, and of Joseph's call to remain at her side. It was not for them, people tarnished by sin, to question the ways of the Lord.

Grace was so upset she could barely keep a countenance of indifference, and she fidgeted quietly through the benediction. It took everything within him to not sigh at the earlier procession proceeding in reverse, but eventually they made their farewells to the reverend and exited back into the yard.

Only a few steps away from the door as they walked towards the carriage, Grace caught Roland's arm and pulled sharply. "We cannot go. We have to look for those children."

"Lady Percy," Thorne said soothingly behind her. "Surely they already have people out searching."

"Not many, unfortunately," came a voice from a few steps back, and all turned to see the magistrate, Colonel Ellesmere. Seeing he suddenly had the duke's entire family waiting for him to expound, he rubbed his neck and continued. "My pardon for interrupting, Lady Percy, Sir Nathaniel. Lady Percy... when the first few children disappeared from the nearby villages, we sent men to aid in searching, and never found hide nor hair of them. I understand you hail from a more pleasant climate than Northumberland. Up here, the cold can be deadly. I have sent only people with woodcraft skills and the experience to survive exposure to look. If we cannot find them before nightfall, the odds grow slim they will ever be found."

Found alive, at any rate. But Roland did not want her to contemplate that possibility. Grace had faced more horrors this season than any proper lady should, and if he could help it, he would never permit her to bear the weight of such tragic thoughts. The suffering of innocent children would break her.

He added softly, "These are not city children. They are country hardy. If they were not found during a search, they did not want to be found. Perhaps they are hiding in Shillbottle. Or set down as far as to Newcastle-upon-Tyne to find a better life."

"They are gone, or they are dead," said His Grace bluntly, looking displeased that they were standing around in the cold to discuss missing peasant children. "This land is not for the weak and ignorant. There is fast moving water, wild boars, rugged, rocky areas where scree might break loose and they could break a leg in a fall. Come spring, a few bones always show up in ravines and washes."

"I see, Your Grace. How awful for the families of those victims," Grace said, her face becoming as white as the fallen snow.

Blast and damnation, Roland cursed in his thoughts before he turned away from his grandfather to face Colonel Ellesmere directly. "I, and Sir Nathaniel too, I am certain, would be pleased to help participate in today's search. We are familiar with the lands and have the skills to deal with the rough. I am sure we could find a few other helping hands. It would do our appearances good to participate in such a noble cause as finding a lost child, do you not agree, Your Grace?"

As he was now facing his grandfather, away from Grace and the magistrate, Roland let his anger flash in his eyes, daring the duke to argue. Put on the spot in such a public place, the Breaker inclined his head in both warning and agreement.

Satisfied, Roland returned his attention to the magistrate. "Very well. I beg your pardons for how rude my haste is, Colonel Ellesmere, Mrs Ellesmere, however my lady looks half faint from the cold. Allow me to bring His Grace and my lady back to Alnwick Castle, then my brother and I shall call upon you. You can direct us wherever we may be of greatest assistance."

"That is very gracious of you, Lord Percy," the magistrate agreed quickly, looking at Grace's pallor.

Roland took Grace's arm with solicitousness as they headed towards the carriage, but he pulled her close enough to whisper in her ear. "I will only do this if you stay at the castle, safe and warm."

He was certain she would argue—that she would at least demand to be allowed to wait with the magistrate's wife. Perhaps it said something to the visibility of his temper, however, that not only did Grace acquiesce without a fight, the duke also quietly accepted Thorne's arm and assistance towards the carriage.

6

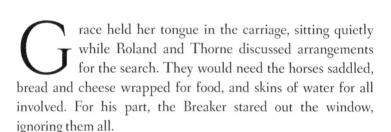

Grace held her tongue in the carriage, sitting quietly while Roland and Thorne discussed arrangements for the search. They would need the horses saddled, bread and cheese wrapped for food, and skins of water for all involved. For his part, the Breaker stared out the window, ignoring them all.

Every now and again, Grace cast a glance at her husband, checking whether he was looking her way. It made sense for her to remain behind in the castle while the men went off to join the search. But Grace was not exactly known for choosing the safest options, particularly not when lives were at risk. A large part of her yearned to offer aid, but the wiser parts of her mind cautioned her to care for the life she cradled in her body. If she set out and something went wrong—even if she found the missing children—she would never forgive herself for putting the life of her future child at risk.

Roland, however, seemed content to accept her acquiescence at face value. Upon their return to the castle, he kissed her goodbye before rushing off to change into his riding clothes.

Withers had disappeared upstairs, following behind the duke, leaving Grace standing alone in the front hall. There was a strong, crisp pine smell from the wreaths hanging, and it mingled pleasantly with the beeswax from the polished bannisters, but the cold stone of Alnwick Castle detracted from the warm feeling of Christmas she had always experienced when decorating with evergreen boughs at her old home. Here, the pine smell was strong and a little wild, like the forest itself encroached upon their doorstep.

In search of company, Grace climbed the stairs to her suite of rooms, thinking she might find Elsie tidying her things. She was keen to learn how the servants had reacted to the news of her reward.

But Elsie was not in her sitting room, nor bedroom, and not in the dressing room, either. Grace had every right to ring for her maid, but how would she frame the request? Elsie had responsibilities enough without Grace adding entertaining the lady of the house as another.

She picked up the book she had been reading, but set it down after ten minutes of staring blankly at the same page. Her mind was too awash with concerns and fears to allow a fictional world to take hold. She gathered her stack of unanswered correspondence and went to work reading the first. It proved to be a letter from her dearest friend Charity, now Duchess Atholl. Having gone from married to widowed within a month, and now conducting her mourning in the wilds of Scotland, Charity had plenty of time to pen long missives to her friend.

For a time, reading the letter lifted Grace's spirits, but when she reached the end, she felt even more alone. Her hand hovered over the page, her mind searching for the right words to share. She could not tell Charity of her most precious news before she had shared it with Roland. Keeping that to herself left her bereft of information to share.

A knock on the door saved her from brooding. Mrs Yardley entered. "Luncheon is ready to be served, my lady. His Grace is taking his meal on a tray. I can have one prepared for you, as well, if you would prefer not to dine in the dining room."

Grace grasped the opportunity to get out of her room, and expressed her desire to dine at the table. At least there, she would have footmen and mayhap even Withers on hand to answer any questions that came to mind.

She followed Mrs Yardley through the hallways and down the stairs until they neared the entrance to the dining room. It, too, was festively decorated with gold ribbon tied around bunches of ivy. But that was the most cheerful thing about the empty room.

A uniformed footman stood tall on either side of the door, their faces perfect masks of indifference. Somehow, their silent presence was more unnerving than being alone. It made little sense, particularly given she had grown up in a house with servants. The fact remained that the staff here were still strangers to her. She did not know which footmen told jokes when belowstairs, nor which housemaid could be relied upon to keep a secret.

The table stretched along the length of the room, with seating for sixteen. A single place, at the foot of the table, had been set for Grace's use, lonely candles jutting from the twined emerald and gold threads of ribbons around the candlestick holder. She walked past the empty chairs, the smoke from the burning candles tickling her nose, and imagined the house filled with guests. It was a foolish thought, but she allowed the picture to grow ever more elaborate. When the footman pushed her chair under the table, the image disappeared.

Withers entered the room, followed by a line of footmen bearing trays. Course after course, they took turns delivering and taking away plates and bowls, topping up her wine, and offering sauce. Each passing further emphasised their difference in station. No matter how much Grace wished it, these people would never truly be her friends. Though Elsie came close, she, too, was in Grace's employ.

Her appetite soured, Grace declined offers of pudding and tea. As she rose from her chair, a footman hurried over with her wrap.

The stylish throws her mother had pressed upon her fell well short of what Grace needed for a northern winter. After watching Grace shiver for a day, Elsie had asked Mrs Yardley to locate something more appropriate. Within a few hours, the housekeeper had delivered a thick, wrapped bundle that smelled of cedar and must, hinting at its age. Elsie aired it out for a day, cleaned away any lingering dust, and returned it good as new.

Though the wrap was a hand-me-down, Grace had grown rather fond of it. Made of damask, lined in velvet, it was heavier than the cashmere wraps popular in London. Metallic threads made it shimmer in the light. Grace was not often one to give into the fanciful tales, but wearing it here, in the ancient halls of Alnwick Castle, allowed her to imagine herself as a princess of Camelot or some other olden time.

She pulled it tight, revelling in the warmth it had gathered while resting near the fireplace. She walked past the stairs leading to her rooms, intent upon exploring other parts of the castle. Elsie had mentioned a second set of winding stairs that led up to the castle walls. Intent upon her destination, Grace turned into a lesser used corridor, one with no windows and only a few flickering torches to light the way.

The swish of her skirts seemed overloud until a shuffling noise reached her ears from behind. Another shuffled step and a thunk of wood on stone called to mind the bumps the Sprouts had heard during the night. She swung around, determined to identify the source of the noise, and saw a distant shadow. It moved closer at a halting pace, until a torch illuminated the hunched form of the Breaker.

"Back again, are you?" he asked in a rough voice.

"I never left," Grace replied. "It is far too cold out."

"Too cold, too dark," he muttered, venturing closer. He peered at her through squinting eyes. "Never seemed to stop you before, but I suppose good sense must eventually prevail."

As far as the Breaker went, that was practically a compliment. His cane slipped on a smooth place on the floor. Though he caught himself, Grace acted on instinct, reaching out a hand to shore him up. She expected him to shove her away, but he latched on, allowing her to bear some of his weight.

For the briefest instant, the fierce facade of the old duke crumbled, leaving behind a weary old man. Grace found herself losing the battle against her heart's desire to soften its stance on the feared Breaker. Her head warned that she would regret spending even a moment longer with him, but her mouth opened and asked him where he was going.

"To the library," he said. "You come along. You can get a book of your own to read."

The honeyed notes of his favourite pipe tickled her nose, and the smell of camphor grew stronger, bringing to mind her great grandmother's ointment she used on her aching hands and knees. The Breaker might think himself invincible, but time weighed on him, pulling his shoulders forward and halting his steps.

She had viewed him for so long as a punishment to be avoided at all costs. Now she questioned her judgement. How much old history might be forgotten if they did not mend their fences? What might she and Roland, and even Thorne, learn from his stories of time long gone? He had wed, fathered children, and suffered through their loss. Might it bring him some measure of peace to recall Roland's father as the child he once was? Roland and Thorne bore no love for the man who had sired them. Grace wondered whether hearing about his early days could cast him in a new light.

The duke, too, seemed inclined to smooth his rough edges. Not once did the old duke chastise Grace, nor question why she was not yet with child. He muttered a complaint or two about her willfulness, but somehow that made her smile rather than frown. For the first time, hope bloomed that he might one day regard her as an individual with her own mind rather than as a vessel to bear the next generation.

He pointed her to the next hallway to the left, and then indicated she should open an unfamiliar door. The handle refused to budge until the duke laid his gnarled fingers over hers and pushed down with his added might. The latch grated as it slid back, but move it did. Grace nudged the door forward, wincing at the creak of the unoiled hinges. She half expected to find a pitch black space, but instead, light spilled into the hallway.

They had arrived in the library, just as the Breaker said they would, though by a different door than the one Grace knew. After the half darkness of the corridor, Grace blinked while her eyes adjusted to the bright lights of the room.

The room was not overlarge, particularly in comparison with the grand drawing room and expansive dining hall. Yet, what it lacked in space it made up for in richness. Fires blazed at either end of the room. Four tables, each topped with candelabra, stood in the centre of the space, providing a work area for those with more to study. Shelves and shelves of books rose from floor to ceiling, lining every wall in the room. Velvet covered settees with elaborately carved legs and matching side tables filled the remaining space, tempting Grace to curl up with a book and a steaming cup of tea.

"Go on over there," the Breaker said, pulling away from her. "I had them shelve your sentimental books in that corner, where hopefully no one will find them."

Grace watched the man hobble away to an overstuffed chair situated beside the lit fireplace. He dropped into the seat with a low groan and leaned over to rub his leg.

Grace was left with the question of what he had meant by his statement. *Her books?* She had procured a volume here and there during their summer and autumn travels, but all those books now had a home in her cosy sitting room. She had arranged them there not two days before. If the duke had demanded the footmen move her private collection into the library, she would not hold her tongue.

She left the man to his ministrations and hurried over to see what he had done. As she walked closer, she let her eyes skim over the book bindings. All she saw was rows of matching deep brown leather with titles stamped in gilt on the sides. Only the very bottom row saw that pattern break. There, the leather varied from brown to blue and to maroon, and the heights varied in size. Grace sank down onto her knees so she could get a closer view. Not a single book was familiar, though she was interested in a few of the titles. She plucked the second volume of Samuel Richardson's *Pamela* from the shelf, but skipped past the books of poetry.

"Hannah?" the duke's gruff voice called out. Grace continued at her task. The duke raised his voice again, this time louder. "Who is there? You cannot hide from me."

Intrigued, Grace tucked the book under her arm and rose to her feet. She glanced around for the housemaid the duke was calling, but found the room empty other than the two of them. Stranger again, the duke was staring directly at her, his mouth twisted in frustration.

"Are you playing tricks on me?" he asked, glowering at her.

"I—" Grace waited to see if someone else would speak up. Perhaps this Hannah, to whom he had called for earlier, but his gaze never shifted. There was no choice but to continue. "I am not up to any ill deeds. Was there something you needed?"

"My book. I left it here, tucked against the side of the cushion, but it is nowhere to be found." He shoved his hand into the space to emphasise its emptiness.

Grace fumbled for a reply. "I did not touch a book of yours. Do you think Hannah moved it? Is she one of the maids?"

The duke gripped the arms of the chair so hard that his shoulders shook. "How *dare* you utter that name to me!"

Confused by his sudden burst of anger, Grace stepped back.

"Withers!" he roared, growing more agitated with every breath. He shifted in the seat, searching for the strength to rise. He knocked into his cane, sending it clattering to the floor and making him shout again in frustration.

On the other end of the room, the main door swung open. Withers hurried inside, moving as swiftly as he could to assist the duke.

"Your Grace, allow me to assist you," he said in a carefully neutral tone. Withers held himself steady, bracing upon the chair as the duke heavily pulled on his butler's arm to lever himself to a standing position.

"What have you done with my book?" the duke demanded to his butler's face, now that he was upright. "Did you move it?"

Wither's eyes darted briefly towards Grace's stock still form. "My apologies. I did move it, Your Grace. It is in your room now. Allow me to accompany you back there. The light is better for reading there and your chair is far more comfortable."

The Breaker stopped and harrumphed, the wind leaving his sails. "How many times must I tell you not to move my things?"

"I am sorry, Your Grace. I was only trying to anticipate your comfort." Withers took great care to avoid meeting Grace's gaze, despite her weighty stare and concerned expression.

It left Grace with a peculiar feeling as Withers closed the door behind him. The sudden silence almost made it feel like the scene that had just happened had never transpired at all.

Grace gripped onto the back of the nearest chair back, not caring that she was crushing the velvet upholstery. Her fingers sank deep, anchoring her to the present. She had not imagined her interaction with the duke. But as for what to make of it, she knew not.

Running through the exchange with the duke in the hallway, Grace could only come to one conclusion. The duke had thought he was talking to someone else. Not the Countess Percy, wife of his grandson, but... Hannah. Whoever she was.

Before she could convince herself to let go of the chair, the door opened again. It was not a servant who entered the room, but her husband. His nose was still red from the cold. He was back from the search.

She studied the shape of his shoulders, searching for clues to the outcome. When he stepped into the light, the pained expression on his face made it abundantly clear that the news would not be good.

7

Seeing no one else in the library, Roland strode across the room to Grace. She met him halfway, tilting her face up to his. He ran a finger under her chin in a gentle caress. "You look a little better than you did in the churchyard," he said, studying her face for the signs of fatigue he had seen in her so often lately. "You went so pale when the duke was being vulgar. Are you all right? You still look upset."

Grace gave him a minatory look before taking his hand away, though she squeezed it briefly before she let it drop. "I am fine. It was just—" she stopped, looking away as her eyes grew a touch shiny. "Nevermind earlier. I was shocked by his callousness, which now in retrospect seems like a funny thing to say. He has always enjoyed being shocking, and I do not know why I should let his behaviour keep catching me unawares. Still... Roland, if you found bodies of children, let me remain ignorant this time, please."

His heart squeezed in sympathy with her fear, but at least her words reassured him that she was not ill. Truly, she did seem more herself. Perhaps the lingering fatigue was just from the days of travel after all.

"We did not find any bodies," he assured her, and she relaxed. "I do not even have to lie to you about that. Thorne, the magistrate, and I went to check the areas around the known caves and places where kids have a penchant for holing up when they play truant. There is no sign of them."

"Thank God," she said, heaving a breath before she caught herself. "Oh, goodness, what am I saying? How can I be so relieved when they are still missing?"

"Because missing means there is still hope they will be found alive," he said, smoothing a damp spot away from the corner of her eye.

"You make a fair point. But... what happens now? And where is Nathaniel?"

"He sent me home like a clucking mother," Roland told her, because he knew that would lighten her mood. "We began visiting some of the neighbouring crofts to see if we could pick up a trail, and he was worried about the hour growing late. 'The heir to the duke should take no such stupid risks,'" he said, emulating his brother's voice. "'Grace would gut me for making her a widow in her first year.'"

She laughed briefly at that. "I would, too. We still have more adventures to have together, Lord Percy."

Her mildly suggestive tone caught Roland's attention immediately. "Indeed," he said, prowling closer to her, but Grace raised a knowing eyebrow at him.

"We are *supposed* to be behaving in front of the duke's servants," she reminded him as he threatened to sweep her into his arms.

"How odd a comment, Lady Percy. I do not see any of them here watching. I think they might forgive us given that we are also *supposed* to be... how did grandfather put it? Spreading legs for the good of the nation and all that?"

"I think that was my part, not yours," Grace said dryly, but the pang of her secrets, and the thought of her strange afternoon with the duke, soured her mood. She consented to press her cheek briefly to his shoulder, whispering in his ear, "Imagine Mrs Yardley walking in upon us like this."

Roland let her go immediately with a mock shudder. "*Ach.* You win this round, fair lady."

"Speaking of your grandfather," Grace said, warming to the subject as she thought back on their conversation. "I had a strange encounter with him just before you got back."

Roland's forehead creased as he listened to Grace relate the tale of what had happened. "I cannot think of who Hannah is. Is she one of the maids?"

She shook her head slightly. "Not that I am aware. I was hoping you might be able to tell me. If she was a maid, I have not met anyone by that name so far."

"You should ask Mrs Yardley if she knows," Roland suggested. "Alnwick Castle is so large you may not have met every servant who works here now. For all we know, she could be a scullery maid, someone who was dismissed, or even the daughter of one of the servants."

"Yes, you are right. Still.. I think... It worries me a little that he might have thought I was Hannah."

"The duke is well on in years..." he said slowly. "I saw no unusual signs of infirmity beyond needing his cane to walk this summer, but maybe his mind is beginning to wander, and you resemble this other person. Did he seem belligerent?" Realising what he said, he began to correct himself.

"You mean, more so than his wont?" Grace said tartly. "I know what you mean. No, he was... quite docile, actually. Which now that I think about it, perhaps that should have been my first clue he was not quite feeling himself."

Frowning slightly, Roland considered the implications, hoping that her concerns were unfounded. Because otherwise, all his carefully laid plans for the coming year—to give Grace the adventures she had always wanted—would lie in ruin.

Grace seemed to sense his distress. "I did not mean to worry you. He returned to his old self quick enough, and chastised me for it."

"I am not worried, love. Knowing the duke, he is more likely to become the next Vampire of Alnwick to spite us. A brief mixing of names is not necessarily a reason for concern."

"Perhaps we should stay once spring arrives, to be certain he is hale," Grace said solemnly, looking conflicted. "Roland, I—"

"No. Let us not go down this dark path, Grace. We will keep an eye on him this winter before borrowing trouble on what this means for our future. One day we will have to settle down—just a little bit," Roland said softly, smiling at her. "I want you to have no regrets. I do not want you to feel trapped here."

"I would never feel trapped as long as we stay together. But, Roland—" Grace began, her words cutting off as a familiar rap sounded on the door. "Nevermind. Perhaps there is news we need to address."

"All right. Come in," Roland said, raising his voice.

The duke's butler glanced around the room before nodding shortly to himself. "My lord, my lady, I beg your pardon for the interruption, but Sir Nathaniel has returned with Mr Harding. They are requesting a moment of your time, if you are available."

"By all means, Withers. Show them in," Roland answered.

Withers left, and Roland glanced back at Grace, but she shook her head. Whatever she had to say that was interrupted before, apparently it would keep. She stayed distant and thoughtful while they waited for Thorne and Mr Harding to arrive.

When they entered, both men still had florid noses and

cheeks, but pinched, pale lips from the cold. Grace immediately pointed to the chairs by the fire, exclaiming, "You both look half frozen. Could you bring tea, Mr Withers?"

"Thank you, Lady Percy," Mr Harding said as he settled, mopping his nose with a plain handkerchief. "I am so sorry. The cold makes my nose run."

"No apologies required," she said with a smile, turning them towards the subject of her burning curiosity. "Please, take a moment to compose yourself. It was kind of you to aid Lord Percy and Sir Nathaniel with the search. You must be very busy."

"Oh, it is my pleasure to be of assistance, Lady Percy. Though, truly, I would have helped search for those children regardless."

He stopped to clear his nose more thoroughly, and by the time he was through, Withers arrived with the tea. Grace poured, looking as though she would die with impatience waiting to hear what news the two had brought.

"Kind as he is, Mr Harding's help is the only reason why we have any clue what has happened to the children at all," Thorne said, rubbing his hands together to bring feeling back into them before he accepted his cup. "Once we completed our reconnoitre with Colonel Ellesmere I was at a loss as to what to do next. Mr Harding was the one who had the idea and the authority—after we sent Lord Percy back, that is—to check with some of the tenants nearest the roads. Well, we had no luck asking about stray, individual children, so we began asking just about anything that might be unusual. Anything at all. And our very last stop, a farmer mentioned he saw what may have been our two children in the morning twilight hours, as he was doing his chores."

"Both," Roland echoed, surprised. "Before dawn? I can see

why he thought that could be unusual. You think it was the missing children? The two children were together?"

Thorne's face looked grim, and Mr Harding wrung his hands. "There is more, Lord Percy. The reason that the farmer noticed them at all was because they were pushing a wagon out of a muddy hole. The farmer hailed and asked if he could help them, but they were able to get free with the help of the driver, so he did not approach."

Roland took a sharp breath through his nose, thinking quickly. "A wagon and a driver changes almost everything we have been thinking. Does the farmer think they were with him voluntarily?"

Thorne shook his head. "We asked, but he could not say one way or another. He did not speak with them, and had thought the boys belonged to the driver, so he paid little mind to them once he saw they were with someone—"

"I would think it does not matter! Two boys gone missing in the dark of night. Whether they went willingly or not, do their parents not deserve the peace of mind of our inquiry?" Grace exclaimed, and Thorne held up his hand, to stay her anger.

"I am of the same mind, Lady Percy. So I asked our farmer a better question, instead. I asked how they were dressed."

"And?" she asked, putting her hands on her hips.

"He had gotten close enough to see one of the lads had rags wrapped around his feet rather than proper shoes."

"Like the boy might have been stolen from his bed after all. Then it was abduction, most likely." Roland gritted his teeth, beginning to pace as he thought aloud. "Kidnapping. And they may have been threatened to stay silent. How *dare* someone abduct children here! This cannot stand."

"There's little we can do now, I'm afraid," Mr Harding said carefully. "But come first light... Perhaps we might employ one of the huntsmen to see if he can track a wagon?"

"No need. Sir Nathaniel and I have some experience in tracking—certainly, enough to follow a line of wagon ruts. We can be out again at dawn." Roland made fists of his hands as his rage built into a fearsome, towering thing.

Thorne left his chair, then, and placed himself directly in the path of Roland's pacing, forcing him to come to a halt both physically and within his racing thoughts. His brother said nothing, but his meaning was clear enough: *Stop. Control yourself.*

He was piqued, but Roland nodded a curt acknowledgment, badly reining in his emotions. "Mr Harding, your assistance today has been invaluable, and I appreciate your time. I regret keeping you from your home and a warm hearth while we investigated this matter. I believe it is best that I let you return now."

Harding set down his empty cup. "Of course, my lord. It's been my duty and my pleasure to assist. If there's anything further you require, you've only to send word. I'll take my leave now and wish you all a pleasant evening."

There was tense silence while Mr Harding departed, and once the door clicked shut, Thorne set his hand on Roland's shoulder without further comment.

Roland's breath left him like air from a smithy's bellows. "Thank you for your interruption. For a moment I was so angry at the sheer audacity of this... this *villain* that I saw red."

Grace smiled thinly at the two of them. "I cannot blame you, Roland. If you had not nearly had an apoplexy, I might have had one in your stead."

"I thought these days were behind us, but it seems that trouble follows you two like a lost pup," Thorne said, letting Roland go once he could see his brother calming down. "So, we have what appears to be abduction, but clearly there have been no ransom demands, else the entire village would not have assumed they ran away. And with the half dozen children missing this fall... forced labour?"

"Few other reasons would make any sense," Roland murmured, drumming his fingers on his folded arm. "But where? If they were headed east, away from Alnwick..."

"Wherever there is a shortage of hands, I would reckon. Newcastle? Berwick-upon-Tweed?" Thorne guessed.

"Goodness... would the kidnapper take them so far?" Grace asked. "At a better time of year, perhaps... But in the winter?"

When no answer was immediately forthcoming, Thorne slapped his gloves against his thigh. "We'll have a clearer picture tomorrow if we can find the wagon's trail. One thing, at least, is certain... Wes's tall tale about a 'Snatcher' was more accurate than we gave him credit for."

"Though let us hope he was mistaken about the horns and the habit of eating children. You both must promise to be careful," Grace said, biting her lip. "As sad as the situation is, I would be beside myself if something happened to either one of you. I will... oversee matters here."

Gooseflesh prickled the back of his neck as comprehension jolted Roland. Grace did not want to involve herself in the mystery of the abducted children. He did not even have to argue that she should pursue safer lines of inquiry.

Why? Had the events of the summer frightened the sense of adventure right out of her? Or was something else more wrong than he imagined?

8

Grace made her excuses not long after dinner, claiming she wanted to curl up under the warm covers of her bed with the book she had taken from the library. In truth, she needed time to come to terms with the reality of her situation.

This matter of the missing children was not going to be solved overnight, no matter how much she wished otherwise. She had witnessed Roland's fiery response to the bailiff's discovery. He was taking the matter personally, and she could not find any reason to disagree. It was an affront to the Percy family, to all the people of the area, that someone felt free to prey upon their young.

Roland and Thorne would follow every thread of suspicion until those missing children were home safe. Grace would not entertain the alternative—that the children might be lost forever.

Her hand drifted closer, coming to a rest on her abdomen. She found firm skin and the slightest beginnings of swelling. No matter how she had denied it, citing the lack of proof, Grace could not find any room to doubt her condition any longer now that her belly had begun to round. Thus far, the changes had not been enough to catch Roland's attention, but soon he would have to be blind to not notice.

Assuming he was not already suspicious. Her offer to stay in the castle had raised his eyebrows. He had not pressed her for details in front of his brother, but Grace would be a fool to assume he would simply let the matter drop. He would know that remaining behind chafed at her heart when she and Roland had always confronted these situations together. Staying behind felt unnatural to a woman who prided herself on being brave.

Brave, but not foolish. In Henry IV, Falstaff said, "the better part of valour is discretion," and for now she understood what he meant, truly. Taking care of herself—of their child—was the best and smartest thing she could do now, even if that meant retreating on another front.

She consoled herself with the fact that she did not have to be useless as she felt; there was another mystery afoot at Alnwick Castle. She could get to the bottom of whatever was happening with the duke.

For she was nearly certain in retrospect that the Breaker had suffered some spell of confusion. Was that an unusual event? Or was it a momentary slip, as sometimes happened when people grew older, and not of yet to be a concern?

Who *was* Hannah, and why did Grace uttering the name send him into such a rage?

And should she mention any of this to Roland, when he was already looking into the missing children? Maladies of the mind could take years to become problems. Was there merit in watching and waiting to see if there was another occurrence?

Pondering the question of loyalty left Grace tied in knots. She eventually abandoned that line of thinking. For now, she would leave things be, because who knew what new information tomorrow might bring to them?

So, Grace was reading in her own bed when Roland knocked on their connecting door.

"May I come in?" he asked.

He was still fully dressed. Despite the fact that she was clothed in a warm winter night rail, his elegance made her state of dishabille feel indecent. He had remained downstairs with a pile of his own correspondence for a long while after she had headed up.

She patted the space on the bed beside her. "Of course. I will always have a place for you."

Normally, Roland would hurry across the room and pull her into an embrace, or at least caress her cheek and drop a kiss her forehead. On this night, he took his time crossing the wooden floor, and settled on the edge of the bed, giving her a wary look. "Is there aught amiss? You would tell me if there was, right?"

Her hands stilled. If something were truly wrong, Grace would have of course told him. But all her recent musings fell into the grey space. She had only unfounded suspicions about the duke, and with him being so unhappy right now, she was unsure whether her news about her expectant condition would be welcome or not.

Roland had been so quick to assure her they could stick to their plans when she asked about staying, and he already seemed eager to leave. He did not want to be in Alnwick or in the Breaker's company any longer than required.

Now, both her child and the duke might demand it. She studied the lace on her coverlet, not able to meet his eyes. "I am fine, Roland. Truly."

Roland's jaw tightened, and he got up to pace. "You are not yourself, Grace. I have never known you to willingly sit back." He rose from his seat and paced around the room. "And it is not just this. During the last weeks of our journey here, you were either gritting your teeth over the ruts in the road or collapsing against me in exhaustion. Here you are now, in bed long before we usually turn in. If you are unwell—"

"I am the picture of health," Grace said, cutting in before he could veer any closer to the truth. "I am not accustomed to such long and arduous travel. It took more out of me than I expected. But look at me now. Are my cheeks not pink? Have I swooned? I have hardly sat still these last days."

Roland came closer and shifted the light of her candle so that it would illuminate her face. "I cannot shake the sense that there is more than your words say to me. Nailing your own front door shut would not have managed to keep you at home, safe in your house, when we were dealing with the murdered guardsman. It makes me worry that you would ask to stay behind now."

She wished he would stop asking, because her resolve would not stand this for long. Grace felt the truth burning the back of her throat. She swallowed, nearly choking on it. Her mind raced, her eyes darting left and right in search of some explanation he would buy. She did not want to lie outright.

No, Roland would be satisfied only by the truth, and therein lay the solution to her quandary. She would give him a truth, of lesser importance to be sure.

Grace lifted her gaze, meeting her husband's suspicious stare, but still letting regret and shame colour her face. "I did not want to trouble you with my worries. We both have our duties, but unlike you, I am still learning the breadth of what mine are. I did not grasp the complexities of running a house this size and challenges of engaging with the community. I am making foolish mistakes, and it is embarrassing."

Roland stilled. "We have only just arrived, Grace. You cannot have done anything wrong."

"I have, though." Grace told Roland of her request for pies for the fair, and the unexpected way it had rippled through the household. "Even now, I do not know for sure whether I fell into a trap set out for me, or into one of my own making."

"I—" Roland's voice trailed off. He ran his fingers through his dark hair and shook his head. "I see. Surely they cannot hold such a small misstep against you, especially when you tried to set it right."

"They might, if I do not learn quickly. I feel like a dunce with a frustrated tutor. The Breaker already undermined me to the staff before we arrived, and the longer it takes me to gain my footing, the more he looks correct. In these circumstances, I should not go gallivanting around the countryside, even though my heart shouts for me to help. They will see me shirk my duties, and because they do not know me as you do, they will not understand."

Roland's eyes narrowed. "You have never let societal expectations dictate your actions. That is why you stay home now? You are the woman of the house, and their employment is at your discretion. No. I think something has cowed you. Something has made you cautious. I wish you would trust me with the truth about what it is."

Grace's face flushed as her husband called her out for dancing around the truth. She longed to confess everything, but now was not the right time. Not when he had more important matters to occupy his thoughts. She blinked back the tears threatening to spill and took a deep breath. "You are right. There is something else, but it is not a problem you can solve— that anyone can solve other than time itself. I promise I will tell you all, when the time is right. Until then, please trust that I am fine. There is nothing for you to worry about other than finding the missing children."

Roland let his hand drop to his side. He studied his wife, his deep brown eyes scouring every inch of her, brow creased in concentration. Grace did not dare move an inch for fear of giving it all away. He had to believe she was telling the whole story.

After a long pause, he rose from the bed and straightened the covers he had rumpled. "As you will."

"You do not have to go. You may stay, if you want to," Grace offered quickly.

"Not tonight. I will stay in my room. I must rise early, and there is no need for you to lose your sleep. Get your rest so that you may focus on your duties." The slightest emphasis on these words stung.

Grace cursed herself for the way the conversation with Roland had ended, though she had no one to blame but herself. He was angry. She saw it in his cold manner and the lines of his back during his stilted departure from her room.

She was doing the right thing in keeping the pregnancy to herself. He would not thank her for adding to his burdens when so many others were depending upon him. She was fine, she reminded herself. Elsie was keeping watch over her. All Grace had to do was bide her time a little longer. Once the children had been found, he would be in a better state of mind. He would be ready, surely, then, to hear that they would have to stay in Alnwick.

Despite the assurances of her twisted logic, Grace tossed and turned that night. Finally, in the wee hours of the night, she gave up and lay on her back in bed, praying for some guidance— or at least wisdom—in how to approach things without making a complete muddle of it. That was when she felt the tiniest flutter of movement, low inside her belly.

—-

Elsie woke Grace, clattering into the room with a breakfast tray in hand. The maid was perfectly capable of moving silently, but evidently she had decided it was time for Grace to rise.

"Separate rooms again, my lady?" she asked as she

positioned the tray on the empty side of the bed. And then she looked at Grace's face. "You have been upset."

"I felt it last night."

The maid understood immediately. She hurried over and sat down on the edge of Grace's bed, taking her hands. "But that's wonderful news, my lady! Come summer, you'll have a lovely baby to hold in your arms."

"Lord Percy and I argued before bed."

"About expecting?" Elsie looked shocked, but then she keenly looked at her again. "No, you've still not told him."

Grace gave a shake of her head. Almost by rote, she said, "It is not the right time. He has much on his mind, and I cannot add more to his burdens."

Elsie rarely spoke out of turn, but in this instance, she straightened up and put her hands on her hips. "I may not understand the ways of you toffs, but in this I am certain I have the right of it. That man loves you, miss. He wouldn't place any other cause above you."

Grace crossed her arms over her chest. "I am waiting for the right moment."

Elsie rolled her eyes and then swung around, intent upon her morning duties. But she did not try too hard to hide the mumbling under her breath.

"You have not held your tongue around me so far this morning," Grace called. "Out with it. Though it may not seem as such, I do value your countenance, Elsie. You are one of the few people here I trust."

Elsie narrowed her gaze and studied her ladyship's face, searching for any hint of falsehood. She huffed and finally said, "There's no right time for anything, especially not between you and his lordship. Once you two get involved in a matter, it has a way of taking over your lives. Until those children are found,

Lord Percy and Sir Nathaniel will ride over every square mile of their lands."

"As they should."

"Mayhap, my lady. But what if something happens to you while they're away? Do you think Lord Percy will thank you for causing him to leave you to suffer alone? Would you thank him if the circumstances were reversed?"

A chill wracked Grace's body at the thought of either happening. She took a deep breath and willed her heart to calm. "He will be careful."

Elsie, however, was not done. "Will he? I saw his lordship and Sir Nathaniel depart this morning. They took weapons with them. What they do, they do believing it is dangerous, and you've let him leave while impassioned. You've turned your face from risky tasks because you might be carrying his child. Lord Percy won't start doing the same until you tell him what you are hiding."

The memory of Roland, beaten and bloodied, standing with a gun to the back of his head flashed into Grace's mind. If someone kidnapped those kids, they would hardly throw their hands up in surrender. Only one thing would prevent Roland from walking into harm's way. Grace had to give him a reason to stay safe.

"But those children—" Grace said, feeling a terrible twinge of guilt.

"Will be found," Elsie said firmly. "If not by your husband, then by your people. You are a countess now, and soon to be a duchess. *Of these people.* You do not have to do everything yourselves. You can command the aid you need."

Blinking at her maid, Grace nodded. Come evening, one way or the other, she would bring him into her confidence, telling him of the changes coming in their lives.

"I am fortunate to have such wise counsel. I will tell him

tonight, you may be assured of it," she promised her maid. That decided, Grace swung her legs over the side of the bed and felt around for her slippers. "While he is away, I need your help with another matter."

"Oh?" Elsie glanced over from the dressing table where she had been setting out Grace's things.

"Have you noticed if anything might be... amiss with the duke?" Grace skimmed over the highlights of her interaction with him the day before. "Is there a Hannah belowstairs? Or Anna?"

Elsie shook her head, equally mystified. "No name even close. He's an old man, my lady. We had an old woman in our village. She lived well into her ninth decade, and stayed mostly as sharp as a tack. Still, even she muddled names from time to time. Just because he got confused doesn't mean he's lost his wits."

Roland had said much the same thing, but Grace's doubts refused to fade. "He has been staying here in the castle, locked away from everyone. His movements have slowed compared to when we saw him this summer. And what of him making an excuse at every mealtime?"

"I suppose you could be right," Elsie admitted. "But how are we going to find out? Withers doesn't move a finger without the duke's permission. He won't tell."

Elsie was right about Withers. The butler had been part of the duke's household longer than anyone else there. He was well past the age of retirement, but was determined to remain for as long as the duke breathed.

They needed someone younger, someone who might fear losing their position when the title changed hands. Grace outlined her thoughts to Elsie and asked for where she should start.

"Your best bet is Mrs Yardley, ma'am. She's fair with the

staff, and she'll have a hard time finding another position of this calibre this far north."

"Is that enough to convince her to break her silence on a matter of such significance?"

"I hope so," Elsie murmured. "For all our sakes. You're with child, his lordship's on the hunt, and the duke might be losing his grasp upon his mind, for all we know. If there was ever a time when we needed our allies, as Lord Percy says, this is it."

9

It didn't take the two men long to find the muddy hole in which the wagon had gotten stuck. The track had been half-frozen early yesterday morning, so the ground had broken raggedly around the footprints that circled what was now a large, ice-rimmed puddle. A long rut where a wheel had dragged through heavily was well preserved.

While movement in the winter wasn't altogether unheard of, looking at their trail, Roland understood why the farmer had thought a wagon travelling in the dark on such a treacherous path seemed peculiar.

"He was lucky he didn't break an axle in this," Thorne commented, and Roland grunted.

"Or you could say we were unlucky. If he had gotten stuck a little harder, perhaps we would have more to go on. Or the kids could have escaped."

They walked back to where they left Horse and Arion, who stood together, head to tail, scratching each other's rumps with their teeth. Thorne slapped Horse's side gently, indicating it was time to let them mount up, and the horse whickered a complaint.

"I can scratch your arse just as well as Arion can. Git over," he said, rubbing the itchy place on the horse's back.

The horses finally sidled apart a few steps, and both men got back on, turning them to follow the main wagon rut to the northeast. They picked their way slowly, as the ground had hardened considerably, and the path was not smooth. Neither one wanted to risk the horses foundering.

Before they had set out, with the rough bearing to guide them, the Colonel's small group of searchers had decided to split their efforts. With nearly a day on them, the wagon was likely long gone. But given the farmer's position, which had been northwest of Alnwick and not far from an area where the river wound like a backwards S, and also given the wagon's easterly bearing, one might make a few assumptions about destinations.

This veritable sheep track of a path would eventually cross a road that took them east, southeast towards Denwick, and so some of the searchers had gone ahead there to ask questions. But the kidnapper could have also decided to head towards the main road. North and west from that point, there were a number of small areas one might want to bring a child for labour. South, the road went past the abbey as it headed to the bridge across the river. It wouldn't be impossible for the villain to skirt along the west edge of Alnwick.

So Roland and Thorne had opted to follow the trail as long as they were able. Or perhaps as long as Thorne was able, since Roland had been almost too preoccupied to be useful.

"A penny for your thoughts," Thorne said as they rode side by side, his voice slightly muffled by the scarf covering his mouth and nose. "I would be willing to wager double that it concerns your lady."

"Are you wagering the same penny you plan to pay? I suppose that would make it a draw." Roland said nothing more, not certain how to articulate the entirety of his thoughts on the whole matter.

"Grace does not seem to be acting much herself. Is she having nightmares? I could scarcely blame her if she was having bouts of melancholy after the incident on the Black Hawk, but she appeared well enough at your wedding."

"A few times, early on, she had bad dreams—about Danforth holding the gun to my head," Roland confessed, and Thorne closed his eyes briefly in sympathy. "But those tapered off months ago. Grace seems possessed of a hardy spirit, which is fortunate given her penchant to stumble into events of such mortal terror. So... I do not think that is what is troubling her. But on the other hand, I still have no answers, because she will not talk to me about them."

"Ah. Then I understand why you are so vexed. Unlike her, you don't seem to care for mysteries, and she is sitting upon one that she won't discuss."

"You have a knack for reading me, far better than I have for reading my own wife, then," Roland said, jaw tightening.

"Of course. We're men, and men are simple creatures," Thorne jested. "But in seriousness, I do not believe Grace would be withholding something from you out of malice."

"Agreed. I have no worries on that score. It's just... Something is clearly the matter. Is it ridiculous that I am piqued because I know *she* is worried about something, and she will not trust me with what it is? However big or small it is."

Ahead of them, they could see a marking post, and Thorne began to scan the ground to ensure he could still make out the trail. "No, I would feel much the same, if I were you. But have faith. I am sure she will confess the truth to you eventually."

Roland wished he could be as certain.

Thorne leaned backwards in the stirrups as they drew up to the fork, and Horse, sensing the change in position, came to a stop. Roland drew up his reins. Though the gelding was of no special breeding, Horse had turned out to be a sensitive and solid choice when they had purchased their mounts. Thorne was also a natural at training. The pair barely needed a bridle at all, Thorne signalling the horse more often with light touches on the neck and sides, or his position in the seat.

It only took a moment to discern that if Denwick was the eventual destination, it was not a direct one. They followed the ruts as they meandered towards the southeast, a course that would take them to the road.

"Denwick would have been too easy, I suppose," his brother murmured under his breath as they carried on. "If you will not let it rest, then what seems to have been on your lady's mind? Perhaps that would give you some clue."

Roland grunted. "My grandfather. Being lady of the house. The cold. Half-truths, at best."

"Or perhaps the fallen crumbs around the bigger piece of cheese that so far she's unhappy here in Alnwick. She's struggling to find her footing. Give her some leeway to find her place. I could see Lady Grace being reluctant to add to your burdens while you're learning from the duke. Is the Breaker giving her a great deal of trouble?"

"The opposite, actually," Roland said shortly. "Which, perhaps ironically, somehow adds to my burdens even more, because now I have to find the time to contemplate the small possibility that the duke may be unwell. So..."

They rode in silence for a few heartbeats, and then Thorne drew a breath to say something more. Roland waved his hand to cut him off.

"Honestly, brother. I do not wish to speak about it anymore. Not unless you want to drive me into losing my temper." His voice was a touch too loud in the wintry silence, and Roland cursed as Thorne flinched slightly. He tried to put more humour into his words as he apologised. "I am sorry. But, you see? My nerves are already shot."

"Truly," Thorne said dryly. "Perhaps it's just as well I packed this to ward against the cold." He reached into the breast pocket of his coat to withdraw a leather-wrapped silver flask, and offered it to Roland, who seized it like a starving man offered food.

Uncapping the flask, Roland pulled down his scarf and tipped it back, expecting brandy. Instead, a sharp, peaty liquid burned his throat as he swallowed, eyes watering. "Oh, it's whisky," he said hoarsely, coughing briefly before pulling the cloth back over his face, and Thorne grinned sunnily at him. Not that Roland could see his brother's mouth underneath the scarf, but Thorne's blue eyes crinkled in that way they always did when giving him a mocking grin. "You could have warned me."

"And miss out on your surprise? Never."

"You could at least cultivate a taste for the lowland stuff," Roland took another long swig, figuring it would serve him right if he drained the flask, and expected Thorne to protest. But his canny brother simply pulled a second flask out of his other jacket pocket, taking his own swig. "I am sick of swimming in the swamps of my own thoughts. Tell me something else." For there was another nagging worry on his mind, one that he had not voiced even to Grace. "Did you get back to London after the wedding?"

"Only for a brief stop to inspect the house," Thorne admitted. "They did not want me travelling much until they were certain the arm was well on its way to mending."

"That would have only taken a month, and here we are in December. What did you get up to in the other months between? I also notice that *your* valet—who has been causing me no end of grief, thank you very much—has not been replaced."

Thorne was silent for a long moment—so long that, in the end, Roland voiced his suspicion. Thorne's new title was weighing on his shoulders. "Grace and I thought we were giving you a gift by raising your status, but instead, it is a burden."

"No," Thorne's answer was immediate. "No. That isn't it."

"Are you quite sure?" Because Roland had read and burned the brief, badly written letter from Dolly Thorne, his father's once mistress, and had been plagued by doubt ever since.

I have learned the truth of what you have done. You wish to do well by him, but the only way you can is to let him be. Your world is not ours, and it is improper to aspire to greatness. We who have been born to the lower classes need to remember our place. Let my son live a life of his own choosing. You will only harm him if you force him to rise above it.

Thorne let his brother see his whole face. "Tell me, brother. How did you feel when you were pulled from the front and thrust so directly into polite society?"

Blinking, Roland let the corner of his mouth curl in unhappiness. "Like a pig dressed up in fine clothing and paraded in front of a bunch of dandies."

Thorne smiled faintly and took another swig before he pulled up his scarf. "Aye, just so. It is too much change. Too fast. But... hopefully I will eventually find my place in it. Just as your lady will find her place in Alnwick."

But he didn't sound much convinced, and Roland leaned over from the saddle to grab his brother's arm. "I may have disdained polite society, but I never once doubted I belonged to it. And what right should I have had to that certainty? My blood is not what should make a man fine. Just like the knights of old, one's character is where greatness and nobility shows. Make no mistake, brother—*you are worthy of this.*"

Startled blue eyes stared back at him, and sensing his rider's confusion, Horse came to a halt. Roland let his arm fall so he wouldn't be pulled from the saddle, and he took up the reins to wheel Arion around after his horse kept plodding forward.

"You believe it, Roland, but not everyone does."

Including, apparently, his brother. That was when he understood what must have happened. When Thorne had gone back to take care of his mother, Dolly had spent her efforts trying to drag him back to where she thought he belonged. And perhaps his brother had even more than half believed she had the right of it.

Even water, over time, would wear a stone down.

But that influence was limited. Dolly Thorne was dying. She had consumption—a long and lingering case of it. And even though Thorne could not be formally recognised as a Percy, the members of the ton would neither overlook the Regent's favour nor the truth of his bloodline. Thorne didn't have to rise above his station—he only needed to have the confidence to reach out to claim what was already his by right.

"That is their burden. It should not be yours." The atmosphere between them now felt strange, and Roland regretted taking this particular moment to say the words, no matter how much Thorne apparently needed to be told them. He rubbed the back of his neck, and then sat straighter in realisation. "You *foisted* your valet on me because you were afraid to have him with you when you went to see your mother."

Thorne ducked his head, and Roland scoffed.

It said much that he had felt his elevation would cause enough strife. He had met Thorne's mother twice, and she had refused any support or charity from the Percy family out of hand. His misbegotten sense of duty had extended to ensuring that, even when his grandfather had kept his hand closed tight around the purse strings, Roland managed to find a way to support Thorne well enough that his bastard brother could send his wages on.

But this was intolerable. Roland would have to make sure to orchestrate something so that Briggs ended up back in Thorne's employ right before he needed to pay another visit. The cheeky servant would handle her spectacularly.

"Aye. I leased a small place for her in Swanage and contracted a charwoman to do her laundry and cleaning. It seemed like it might be easier to manage her without an entourage."

"Swanage? I thought you would move her to your own estate."

Thorne hitched his shoulder uncomfortably looking down at the ground again. "Besides the use of Danforth's London house, the Regent gave me lands in Dumfriesshire and Cumberland. I will have to build a place of my own eventually. In the meantime, none of them are good for someone ailing with her condition. The weather on the south shore is better for her. I did try to talk her into Weymouth, but Swanage is... less grand..."

Roland began to open his mouth again but paused as Thorne began circling Horse, looking for something.

"The wheel track," Thorne shouted over his shoulder. "We lost sight of it!"

Roland set his heels to Arion's sides, kicking the horse forward into a canter to catch up, and as he glanced around, he spotted their quarry. "There!"

They had passed a place on the trail where a thick copse of trees grew tall, almost entirely obscuring the banks of one of the small nameless creeks that fed into the larger river. Where the edges of the embankments were fairly steep, a small cart had been abandoned there among the trees, no sign remaining of the horse that had pulled it.

The creek was fast enough to have kept from freezing yet, though ice glazed the rocks somewhat and frosted the edges. A deep furrow in the mud of the bank, and one small footprint still untouched in the dirt, told them everything.

"They took to the water. Probably to get past Alnwick quickly, without being noticed," Roland murmured. "There's a few villages right along the bank of the River Aln east of here."

Thorne nodded. "And we know the two children are together. It should help with questioning. We can ride out and inquire if anyone has seen a man and two children come in from the river."

10

By rights, Grace could have demanded Mrs Yardley come to her room. However, she decided she would be better off extending an olive branch instead. She asked Elsie for a recommendation.

"When is Mrs Yardley most likely to be free of her duties? Late morning?"

Elsie wrinkled her nose. "She'll be run off her feet until luncheon, my lady, given how many housemaids there are to keep watch over during morning duties. If you want her to be able to sit down and have a proper natter, I'd say to ask her for a meeting in the early afternoon."

Elsie's suggestion had merit, but risked the housekeeper spending the morning wondering what Grace wanted. Grace did not want to tip her hand. The time of day worked, but she needed an excuse for her request. She glanced around her room, searching for inspiration, but found nothing unusual. After all, Grace had passed much time in her quarters since her arrival.

And therein lay the solution. Grace sent Elsie belowstairs with a request for Mrs Yardley to show her around the rest of the castle. She spent the remainder of her morning thinking of ways to tell Roland her news. *Their news*, she reminded herself. She still did not want to add to his worries, but Elsie had convinced her to speak up, lest Roland do something rash.

Step one was to find out as much as she could about the Breaker's health. If his condition required them to remain in Alnwick for an extended stay, the news of her pregnancy would be a blessing in disguise. After all, she and Roland had always planned to have a family, whenever the time was right. Though right now was not part of their discussions, it did otherwise fit their thoughts on the subject. The impending arrival of a child would be a welcome distraction from dealing with the Breaker. It might even bring the Breaker some joy in his last days.

Heartened by that thought, Grace rested her hands on her abdomen and whispered her first words to her unborn child. "You are wanted, my darling baby." The faint flutter in reply sent her heart soaring.

Grace enjoyed her lunch meal with a newfound appetite and was ready and waiting when Mrs Yardley rapped on her bedroom door.

She entered at Grace's command and bobbed a respectfully half-curtsey. "Elsie said you wanted to see me, my lady?"

"I would like to review the rooms of the castle. Lord Percy and I may wish to entertain, and I realised I am not familiar with the disposition of the guest chambers, nor of their current state. Can you spare time to accompany me?"

"Of course, my lady. Elsie indicated your plans and I have cleared my schedule accordingly. Where would you like to begin?"

Roland's quarters were, of course, adjoining Grace's suite. Thorne should have been, by rights, in the same wing as the rest of the family. However, that would have put him near the Duke, a situation neither wanted. Instead, he had a room one floor up in the rooms set aside for guests.

As Grace hadn't entered the other family rooms yet, she suggested they start there. Mrs. Yardley moved briskly to the one on the other side of the hall.

Like Roland's, this room was draped in masculine shades, with white cloths hiding the furniture beneath. Grace, feeling a tad curious, lifted the edge of one. Beneath it? Nothing but a barren side table. Hardly worth noting.

She meandered further into the room, her eyes landing on what appeared to be a small desk by the window. More light, she decided. After drawing back the curtain, she set her hand to lift the sheet covering the desk.

Something tickled her fingers.

Grace recoiled, shaking her hand like she'd been struck by lightning. "No, no, no!" she muttered under her breath, quickly inspecting her palm. She saw nothing but smooth skin, much to her relief.

Then, from the corner of her eye, she spotted it. Something dark, something terrible, something with far too many legs. The creature scuttled across her sleeve, moving as if it had all the time in the world.

And, of course, it was a spider.

Grace's mind flashed back to that day with her brother, the one who had thought slipping a spider into her bed was the height of humour. The way Nanny had dismissed her terror. The horde of baby spiders weeks later that had come spilling from behind the wardrobe. It was all too much.

It was the memory of that nightmare of legs and eyes that made her squeak—a sharp, piercing sound that sent Mrs. Yardley spinning on her heel.

"Good heavens, my lady!" Mrs. Yardley dashed across the room with surprising speed, her arms swinging like she might tackle Grace to the ground. Instead, she swatted at Grace's back, her hands moving with the vigour of a woman trying to rid herself of a dozen wasps. Finally, with a triumphant stomp, she put an end to the spider's reign of terror.

Grace stood frozen for a beat, still horrified by the sensation of spider legs trailing down her back. Mrs. Yardley, however, was the picture of professionalism. Or she was, until she caught Grace's eye.

"My lady, I..." Mrs. Yardley's voice cracked. She bit her lip. The corners of her mouth quivered. She sucked in a breath, fighting with everything in her to hold her composure, but then—

A snort. A tiny, betraying snort of laughter escaped.

Grace blinked at her, startled. Mrs. Yardley's eyes went wide with horror as she clamped a hand over her mouth, but it was no use. She was losing the battle. Another giggle bubbled up, followed by a full, helpless laugh.

Grace stared in stunned silence for a moment. Then, all at once, the ridiculousness of the situation hit her.

Her bark of laughter echoed in the room.

"Oh, do stop!" she gasped, holding onto her abdomen, "or I'll never recover!" But neither could stop. They laughed until tears welled up, until Grace had to grip the back of a chair for support.

Finally, wiping at her eyes, Grace looked at Mrs. Yardley, who was catching her breath. "You've saved me from a fate worse than death."

Mrs. Yardley grinned. "It was my pleasure, my lady."

The two women, for all their differences in station, shared a look of pure camaraderie. Something unspoken passed between them—something human.

The awkwardness that had previously hung between them melted away, leaving behind a shared moment of hilarity and a newfound common ground.

Mrs Yardley pointed at the door. "If my lady is ready to move on, we may proceed to the duchess suite."

"Yes, please, if we will not disturb the duke."

Mrs Yardley assured her the Breaker would be none the wiser. She pulled a key from the chain at her waist to unlock the door, but when she inserted it into the lock, she found the door was open.

Inside the room, a single lit candle in a simple brass candlestick sat atop a sheet covered table. The flame flickered at the wind coming through the open door and nearly guttered out. The wick was burned down nearly to the bottom, casting barely enough light to illuminate the space around it.

Mrs Yardley hurried over to retrieve the item, exclaiming over the drips of wax staining the sheet.

"Has someone else been in here?" Grace asked. "A maid or a footman?"

Mrs Yardley lifted the candlestick and hurried over to the window. She pulled the curtains open wide enough to allow sunlight to brighten the space and then she blew the candle out. "We tidy these rooms once a fortnight. They are not due to be cleaned for another week."

Grace entered the room and took the candle from Mrs Yardley. It smelled of beeswax, much like the candles in Grace's room. Based on the diameter of the remaining bit, Grace determined it was one of the larger ones designed to last until the wee hours of the morning. For it to still be burning now, burnt down as it was, it must have been lit well before dawn.

When the household would have been sleeping.

————

From Mrs Yardley's worried expression, Grace presumed the woman had made the same calculations. The housekeeper met Grace's eyes.

"The duke keeps unusual hours. Some nights he barely

sleeps, instead walking the halls like a ghost in his white nightshirt," she confessed.

Grace recalled how unsteady the duke's gait had been the day before. No matter her feelings for him, she did not like the idea of him wandering in the dark. Alone.

"Perhaps Withers could assign a footman to keep watch—"

Mrs Yardley gave a firm shake of her head. "The duke was very adamant on that point, my lady."

Grace's gaze slipped to the candle and then to the white sheet. "We are lucky that spilled wax is our only damage. Had it caught fire..." She stopped there, her throat growing tight with fear.

Grace's plans to ease into the conversation with Mrs Yardley blew away with the last hint of smoke from the candle. She put the candlestick back down where they had found it and then turned to block Mrs Yardley from leaving the room.

"We have barely crossed paths with the duke since our arrival last week. When we ventured to the church for Sunday service, Reverend Shepherd commented on how long it had been since he had last seen the duke. Is there something Lord Percy should know?"

Mrs Yardley shifted around, turning her back on Grace while she pretended to brush dust off the back of a wooden chair. "Some days are better than others for His Grace."

"How long has he been this way?"

The housekeeper shrugged her shoulders, her arms brushing against the ring of keys tied at her waist. "He does not travel much anymore, my lady. The trip south took much out of him. I am sure he will recover in good time. He always has."

Had Mrs Yardley been able to meet Grace's gaze even once, her statement might have gone some way toward alleviating Grace's concerns. But the woman was steadfast in her attempts to look anywhere else. She leapt into the silence with a suggestion they move upstairs.

"Would you like to see the nursery?" she asked. "There are some old toys and books in storage in the rooms nearby."

Grace was familiar enough with the nursery rooms, as she made her way to them at least twice a day to visit the twins. Yet, she feared she would do more damage to the burgeoning camaraderie with Mrs Yardley if she continued to question her. Thus, she agreed to the housekeeper's suggestion. "Miss Fenton will likely welcome a respite from her duties overseeing the children. We can invite them to come along to look with us."

The women exited the room, pausing long enough for Mrs Yardley to secure the lock on the suite's door. Then, the housekeeper stepped aside to allow Grace to lead the way up the stairs. Grace took care not to slip on the smooth wooden boards. When she reached the landing, she stopped to wait for Mrs Yardley to catch up. The woman moved with ease, her steps sure in her practical leather half-boots. Her stern expression gave no hint of her discomfort around Grace.

The part of Grace which fought hardest against society's senseless regulations wanted to crack the housekeeper's composure.

"Mrs Yardley, do we have a Hannah on staff?"

Mrs Yardley's forehead pinched in confusion. "No, my lady. Did someone introduce themselves as such?"

"What about Anna? Or Annie?" Grace persisted.

Mrs Yardley paused on the stairs. "There was an Annie, Annie Meadows. She was a scullery maid, my lady. She left two years ago to marry a local farmer."

Grace laid that information over the duke's strange behaviour. Would he know the name of a scullery maid? Would he expect to see her in the library in the middle of the day? Mrs

Yardley was equally mystified by Grace's seemingly random questions.

Grace took some amount of satisfaction in leaving the housekeeper wondering what was amiss. She pivoted and strode down the corridor to the doorway to the nursery. Before she reached it, she heard the children's voices raised in anger. The part she could half hear suggested the children were squabbling over what game to play next.

Grace twisted the handle and swung open the door without giving any warning. Wes and Willa were both on their feet, facing off against one another with matching determined expressions. Miss Fenton sighed in relief at seeing the cavalry arrive, and then flushed as the implications of Grace's arrival hit her.

"I'm sae sorry, my lady. The children have been cooped up indoors for tae long today. I'll take them straight outside tae get some air."

"There's no need," Grace hurried to reassure her. "Mrs Yardley and I are here to ask the Sprouts for help with an exploration."

"An exploration of what?" Wes asked, eyeing Grace in suspicion. "It ain't of the baths or laundry, is it?"

Grace bit back a laugh. "There is no cleaning involved, I promise. Mrs Yardley has informed me there are some old toys and books stored away. Would you two like to accompany us as we go to see what is there and what condition things are in? There might be something left from when Lord Percy was a child."

"Cor!" Willa sighed. "What do you think his toys were made out of? Gold? Silver?"

Grace imagined they were made of wood or some other sturdy material, just as her own toys had been, but she would let

Willa and Wes see for themselves. "Does that mean you wish to come?"

The twins dropped their argument and nearly knocked Grace over in their hurry to exit to the hallway. Mrs Yardley gave them a tight-lipped, narrow gaze and hushed them before leading them to a door at the other end of the hall. Grace told Miss Fenton to enjoy a cup of tea and a rest before returning to her post.

Grace was the last to enter the room Mrs Yardley had unlocked. Unlike the rooms below, this one was far from ready to host anyone. What must have once been a child's bedroom had been turned into a storeroom of sorts. Large trunks and stacks of wooden crates filled much of the space.

Mrs Yardley moved around with a certain familiarity, ignoring the crates in favour of the trunks. She pulled the ring of keys from her waist and set to unlocking each one in turn. Wes screwed up his face into a grimace when he saw that all it contained were folded clothes.

"I thought you said we'd find some games," he grumbled. "What about that one over there? You forgot to unlock it."

"I don't have the key for that one," Mrs Yardley explained, earning a sullen stare from Wes. She took pity on him and accompanied him to the next trunk in line, this time finding dozens of oddly shaped wrapped items. He lifted one without waiting for permission and shucked the wrap free with no care for saving it. He gave a small cheer when the item revealed itself to be a wooden toy soldier. "Can I keep it?"

Mrs Yardley opened her mouth to reply but then thought better of it. She looked to Grace as lady of the house to give an answer.

"See what else is in there. When Lord Percy returns, you may ask him which of the items you can borrow during our stay." Grace glanced at Mrs Yardley and was pleased to see the woman give a nod of approval at Grace's response.

Willa tugged on Grace's skirt until she had her attention. "I'm sick of playing soldiers all the time, miss. Do you think there's anything else in here? Even a ball would be a welcome change."

"If there is not a ball, I will ask Miss Fenton to procure you one from the village. In the meantime, let us look through here and see if there is anything stored beneath all these clothes."

Much like the old wrap Grace wore to keep warm, the cotton baby clothes smelled of lavender with a hint of old mustiness. Willa was just as entranced as Grace at the tiny shirts and woollen leggings sized for a newborn child. Grace held one up in the light, already imagining she was pulling it out for her own child.

"What's that?' Willa asked, pulling Grace from her reverie. She pointed at a faded pink ribbon poking up from underneath.

Grace pulled up the edges of the baby clothes, taking care not to rip anything. Willa threaded her small hand into the gap and tugged free a painted figurine in a pink gown. She lifted it up and stared at it in awe.

"She's beautiful," Willa cooed, turning the doll left and right as she admired it. She fingered the curls poking out from underneath the bonnet. "She's got real hair! And look at her cheeks! Her eyes almost look real!"

Grace held out her hand for the doll. Willa relinquished it, but not without a sigh of disappointment. Had Willa had a doll before her parents died, leaving her and her brother orphans? Grace had got so accustomed to thinking of the girl in unison with her brother that she had not stopped to consider whether she might like some more feminine toys of her own.

Grace studied the doll, taking note of its condition. The glass eyes seemed firmly fixed. The bonnet and gown were still in good condition, barring the faded colour. Perhaps Willa would be interested in learning to sew if she could make more clothing for the doll. With that in mind, Grace flipped it over to see if the dress could be removed. The buttons slid free with the ease borne of hours of youthful play, revealing a line of letters inked onto the doll's torso.

Grace let out a gasp of her own. "Hannah!"

"Who's Hannah?" Willa asked, shoving in to get a closer look. "Do you think that's the doll's name, miss?"

"I have no idea," Grace replied, her mind awhirl with thoughts. Who was Hannah and how was she connected with the duke? Did Roland have an aunt somewhere? Or had the Breaker lost yet another child before adulthood?

Grace longed to carry the doll back to her room, but one glance at the covetous expression on Willa's face had her second-guessing her thoughts. "Would you like to keep her?"

Willa's eyes grew round as porcelain saucers. She nodded, too surprised to form words of thanks. Grace knew somewhat of how she felt. While Willa now had a doll, Grace had her first real clue into who the mysterious Hannah might be.

A cough from the doorway drew her attention. Grace laid the doll on Willa's outstretched hands and turned to acknowledge the footman waiting in the doorway.

"Pardon me, my lady, but Reverend Shepherd is asking to see you."

Grace wrinkled her brow, but could not recall any requests for a visit. Why was the rector showing up unexpectedly, and asking to see her, of all people.

Roland! Grace's vision dimmed as her worst fears reared to the surface. She had waited too long to tell him her secret. And now, the reverend was here to deliver bad news.

11

The two men pushed the horses as quickly as they dared on the way back to Alnwick, which was fortunately not too far a distance. As they clattered down Canongate in the direction of the castle, Roland spared a brief thought about Grace, feeling anger rise up again before he ruthlessly pushed all considerations of this to the side.

Not now. Not soon. He would see his wife again at some point, and he could press her for details on what secrets she was keeping from him then at his leisure. Roland ignored the front entrance of the castle, instead heading to find the bailiff while Thorne took care of their horses.

"Mr Harding," Roland said, stepping into the man's office. "I am sorry to be in a rush, however, I need you to send a runner on to Denwick and Colonel Ellesmere."

Harding's eyebrows lifted in relief. "Have you found the trail then, Lord Percy?"

"We did. We found the wagon by a riverbank upstream of Alnwick."

Harding paused to consider that and then scribbled a hasty note as he moved to the door to call for a footman. "It hardly makes sense to ride downstream to row back upstream, and there's precious little in that direction. Alnmouth, Hipsburn, Lesbury and Hawkhill lie to the east, not far from the river, which considerably narrows the field of search."

"I agree with you," Roland said with a slight smile. "Thorne and I plan to continue scouting east. Hawkhill is too small a settlement to support any industry. But Lesbury and Alnmouth are a different matter. If the farmer spotted them during his morning chores, they could have traversed the river even as far as Alnmouth and left the water by daybreak. So I think we should cover both sides of the Aln and ask questions."

"Do you want to take the north side of the river, or the south, my lord? I will have Colonel Ellesmere recalled and we can traverse the side opposite of you."

He deliberated, looking at one of the maps of the area Harding pushed towards him. "Sir Nathaniel and I will take the north and Lesbury. You take south and Hipsburn. With the daylight hours growing so short, I am not certain there will be enough to conduct a proper search the entire distance to Alnmouth."

"If I might suggest a course of action, my lord, we can check up to these villages and then come together again this evening. If needs must, we'll go on towards Alnmouth tomorrow. Do you intend to head out again straight away?" When Roland nodded an affirmative, Mr Hawkhill asked, "Are there any other messages you wish me to pass on?"

Roland thought about sending a message to Grace. Thought about it, and let the urge fall away. "If my lady asks before you depart, you may tell her the search proceeds apace. But do not trouble yourself to seek her out to relay this information. She will be unable to help us anyhow, and I believe my lady has other business to attend to."

They had not bothered with much in the way of breakfast when they left at dawn, so Roland was glad Thorne had the forethought to refill their flasks and snatch some bread and cheese during their brief stop back at Alnwick.

"It need only tide us until we reach Lesbury," Thorne said in apology for the quick rations. "We can stop at the inn there to kill two birds with one stone, giving the horses a rest while we eat and ask questions."

It was a solid plan. As the crow flew, Alnmouth and the sea coast were only a handful of miles away. But they would be following a less direct path along the river's edge, seeking signs of the boat's passage. The normal journey to Lesbury was not a long one, perhaps three quarters of an hour, but by Roland's best guess, it could take as long as two hours if they had to ask many questions of tenants along the way.

"I am only relieved that you thought of it at all, because I certainly neglected to."

Thorne looked over at his brother as they crossed the river again, this time by way of the Lion Bridge, and could see the way Roland sat stiffly, almost angry. "It wouldn't be the first time you've been distracted into being particularly single minded."

Roland grunted an agreement and chewed his piece of bread, giving his tense jaw something more productive to do.

The tenants closest to Alnwick had fallow cereal fields, and they passed these by quickly. While there was always much for a farmer to do, even in December, most of that work would be indoors in threshing barns or outbuildings as they separated grain and maintained their equipment and livestock. The likelihood of one of these farmers spotting someone at the river would be minimal.

The treeline at the river's edge didn't provide much cover, and it wouldn't conceal an abandoned boat well. Not even a small one. So they made it to Lesbury in good time, shortly after one o'clock.

Lesbury was what one might generously describe as a single road that ran from the bridge past St. Mary's Church. Small stone buildings lined the packed earth that made up the street, advertising the local smithy and a few other services. There was one lone structure that seemed to serve as both a coaching inn and tavern, whimsically named "Inn" to judge by the sign.

The proprietor was a man whose stocky body resembled the kegs he had stacked in one corner, and he stretched his eyes to see Thorne and Roland enter in riding outfits several cuts more fancy than his usual. Together, they approached the counter, watching the man's cautious appraisal of them.

"Good man, a word, if you please," Roland said, and the innkeeper nodded, wiping his hands on a wet cloth. "My brother and I would appreciate a meal—whatever you have on hand is fine—and a chance to ask you a few questions if you could spare us a moment."

"I've got mutton and barley stew on the fire, and bread and cheese. We're not too fancy here, m'lord," the stout innkeeper said, a bit uncertain. "If ye'd rather wait for a proper meal, I could have me wife fetch a chicken."

"No, a hot bowl of stew sounds perfect." Roland assured him, and the innkeeper nodded, waving them to a table near the fireplace.

Within a few minutes, the man returned with a heavily laden tray. He set out two wooden bowls of stew, spooned heavily from the bottom of the kettle if Roland had to judge by the chunks of meat and root vegetables, two mugs of pale ale, and several thick slices of oat bread and butter.

"'Tis my own recipe, m'lords," the innkeeper murmured as

he set the mugs before them. "I hope it suits." He waited, fidgeting slightly, for their questions. "What else can I get ye?"

Thorne gave the man an appreciative nod to put him at ease. "Thank you, good innkeeper. Lord Percy and I have been travelling slowly from Alnwick, and this will warm us through to carry on."

"Lord Percy!" The innkeeper's eyes widened. "Beg pardon, m'lord, for not recognisin' ye."

Roland cast a baleful eye at his brother. He would have been happy remaining an anonymous lord. "No harm done by it. I know I have not spent much time in Northumberland for a long while. Would you be gracious enough to answer a few questions for Sir Nathaniel and I?"

"Of course, Lord Percy. Of course." The man bobbed nervously, including Thorne now in the bobbing.

"We are on the trail of a pair of children who went missing from Alnwick two days ago, and we were wondering if you have seen or heard anything suspicious."

"Children missing from Alnwick! Oh." The innkeeper paused as if his mind was an ox lumbering on the wrong track that had to be hauled into a new direction.

"You haven't heard about that, then?" Thorne prodded.

"Nay," the innkeeper said brusquely. "Not this last disappearance, anyhow. But there's been talk before. Five or six gone missin', I reckon?"

"You seem surprised by our inquiry. What did you think we were here to ask about?"

The stout man fidgeted again. "I wondered if you two might be here on behalf of His Grace to follow up on Mr Harding's reports—though that didn't make much sense to me either, m'lord, Sir Nathaniel," he added quickly.

Thorne's brows drew together as he looked across the table at Roland, and Roland closed his eyes briefly in acknowledgement, wishing he could pinch the bridge of his nose to relieve the building pressure behind his eyes. Another problem?

"I confess I am not aware of any reports from Mr Harding in the area... But I will be seeing him this afternoon and you can be sure I will ask him about it."

"Very gracious of ye, Lord Percy. I'm sure Mr. Harding's a busy man with plenty to look after. He fixed me chimney this spring when a brick came loose in the flue. But the mill's roof is in a bad way, and Murphy's beside himself. A lot of farmers have flour to process in these winter months."

"But about the children," Thorne added, lifting a hand in oblique apology. "You did say you've heard stories?"

"Aye, m'lord. Sad business, that is. Been the talk of the village, how many kids have supposedly gone up and run off. I can tell you what I know, but... there ain't much to go on."

"Have you seen a man travelling down the river with two children sometime these last days? Or through town?"

"T'wards Alnmouth?" The innkeeper scratched his side idly, thinking. "Can't say I have, Sir Nathaniel. Haven't seen any new faces I didn't ken in the last sevenday." He paused, a small gleam of anger in his eye. "D'ye think they were kidnapped, then? I can spread the word, keep a lookout if ye like."

Thorne shifted uncomfortably at the man's obsequiousness towards him. "That would be kind of you. I assume everyone's river craft is spoken for. Does anyone here hire boats?"

"Here? Nah. There's a couple skiffs and a punt now and then to move things to the port, but it's slowin' down for the winter."

"You're saying that the river is quiet this time of year?"

The innkeeper looked from one man to the other, unsure what they were asking. "There's a man down in Alnmouth with a couple shallops and wherries ye might be able to hire, assumin' they're not already spoken for... if that's what ye'd be needin'?"

"We will check with him," Roland added gravely. "But we're more curious to know how heavy the movement on the river is."

The innkeeper sensed what he was getting at. "Aye, quite a bit of travel, Lord Percy. When the ground turns to muck, but before the river ices over, it's a better way to travel. But they're mostly one-man crafts, ferryin' goods to and fro. None I've seen with two bairns."

"Thank you, I appreciate your time," Roland murmured, sighing inwardly. A dead end. They would have to carry on towards Alnmouth, hoping that either the others would find a clue, or that there would be one to be found within the port village itself.

"Yer welcome, m'lord. If there's aught else I can do, just ask. Enjoy yer meals."

The stew was plain, but hearty enough, and Roland and Thorne ate in good spirit, not talking much. Soon, they were collecting their mounts, ready to push on towards Alnmouth. But after he mounted, Roland circled Arion, thinking.

A number of the thatched roofs that Roland could see along the main street were sagging—including the mills', which sported a dark, rotting hole in one place. Thorne, taking his cue from his brother, also looked closer at the buildings and general state of the hamlet.

"Thorne," Roland murmured. "Hold Arion for me, a moment."

Handing his brother the reins, Roland marched back inside the inn to find the innkeeper over at a farther table, whispering furtively. When the man at the table pointed in Roland's direction, the innkeeper straightened up, looking guilty.

"You said that Mr Murphy reached out to Mr Harding about the state of the mill?" Roland queried.

"Aye, m'lord. Just after Easter, when the rains made the roof start leakin' terribly."

"What was Mr Harding's response?"

"Mr. Harding sent an apologetic note, sayin' there were many repairs that needed doin' that summer, and he'd do what he could. Murphy's sent several messages since to both Mr. Harding and His Grace, but they've gone unanswered."

"But your chimney was repaired promptly?"

"Well," the innkeeper hedged, "might've taken a couple letters, now that I think on it. But Mr Harding came through in the end. His Grace had to approve the work, he said, and I reckon that took time."

Roland paused, wording this last question carefully. "Do you know roughly when was the last time that the duke toured the holdings?"

"Just after Michaelmas, I think, beggin' yer pardon, m'lord," said the man sitting at the table when the innkeeper grasped for dates. He looked at the innkeeper, who nodded, satisfied that was the truth.

"Aye! The gossip was that His Grace was at the harvest festival in Alnmouth. That would've been October."

Tilting his head in acknowledgement, Roland pulled on his gloves. "Thank you both. I will look into things. Good day." Striding firmly to the front of the inn, Roland let himself out and took his horse from Thorne.

"What else have you learned?" Thorne asked him.

"One of two possibilities. That my grandfather may be growing remiss in his duties," Roland said shortly, feeling tension building in his shoulders, "or the dukedom is running terribly short of funds."

12

Though Grace longed to rush down the stairs, the presence of the children prevented her from doing so. She could hardly leave them on their own, yet if the rector was there to deliver bad news, she did not want the children to hear it. Fear prevented her normally nimble mind from working through the situation logically.

Mrs Yardley spoke up, offering a solution. "Children, would you like to come to the kitchen with me? I believe Cook made a fresh batch of biscuits. We might find Miss Fenton while we are there. If that is amenable to you, my lady."

Grace gave a sharp nod of agreement, promising herself to better show her thanks later. She left the housekeeper and the children to the tidying and told the footman that she would see the reverend in the drawing room. The need to know the purpose of his visit warred with her desire to keep bad news at arm's length. She took a moment to compose herself and to clean any dust off her face before taking her time descending the staircases.

Though the castle was large by any measure, Grace saw the light from the drawing room doorway spilling into the hallway far too quickly. She forced one foot in front of the other, demanded her body turn and enter the room. She lifted her gaze and found Reverend Shepherd's friendly face smiling back at her, with his wife at his side.

"Good afternoon, my lady. Mrs Shepherd and I feared you were all alone and thought to come by and keep you company." He motioned to the woman at his side. "I believe you met my wife at the charity fair."

Grace had a vague memory of the woman's face among the crowd, but little beyond that. She was a wisp of a woman, with hair that was a shade too light to be brown, yet lacking the golden shade of blonde so popular in London. Her nose had a slight hook on the end, though it took Grace a moment to notice. The woman had a habit of keeping her head tilted somewhat down to disguise the feature. Her eyes were a watery blue grey of a faded old gown.

Within ten minutes of the trio sitting down to chat, Grace understood why she had failed to remember the woman. Mrs Shepherd was colourless in both appearance and opinion. She played the role of dutiful wife so perfectly that it could only be a true representation of her personality.

For his part, Reverend Shepherd filled in the gaps. "I was so pleased to see His Grace join us in church. The people of Alnwick take great comfort from knowing he is in our midst. You must agree, my lady."

Grace pinched her leg to keep from pulling a face. The Breaker had been accused of many things in his lifetime, but being caring was not one of them. She chose her words carefully. "Yes, the duke is certainly a force in the world."

Mrs Shepherd bobbed her head in agreement, her vacant, placid smile unmoved.

Reverend Shepherd carried on. "I am only sorry that your

first visit to our hallowed sanctuary had to come on such a sorrowful day for the community."

On this at least, Grace could agree. "We are all very worried about the missing children. Did you form part of the search party yesterday?"

Reverend Shepherd's smile drooped. "Alas, I felt called to serve those families in a different way. Mrs Shepherd and I spent many hours with them yesterday and today, reading passages from the scriptures to keep their spirits up."

Again, Grace pinched her leg. Those parents would have likely preferred that every able-bodied man in the area joined the search instead of offering well-meant words. Though, perhaps not everyone thought as Grace did. She reminded herself not to be so quick to judge.

Reverend Shepherd was still talking. "I heard tell that Lord Percy and Sir Nathaniel are continuing the efforts today. Though they mean well, unless our Lord has kept watch over his lost sheep last night, I fear we will only find bad tidings. Had they a reason to head out again this morning?"

"A farmer caught sight of a pair of boys riding in a wagon in the early morning hours," Grace explained. "They fit the description of the missing children. Lord Percy and Sir Nathaniel planned to follow the trail. They have not yet returned. Let us all hope they will bring good news."

"Amen," Mrs Shepherd said, speaking for the first time.

"My wife is right, we must pray on this. In fact, I will host daily prayer sessions in the church until we have word of the boys. I must speak with Lord Percy on this," the reverend said.

"If you like, you may speak with me now," a deep voice said from the doorway.

Grace turned and found her dearest love standing there, unharmed other than a red nose and wind-burned cheeks. She sprang to her feet and hurried over to greet him, only managing to stop herself from pulling him into an embrace when she remembered they had guests.

"Any news?" she asked, to cover up for her hurry. "Please, come by the fire and warm yourself as you tell us what you found."

"Very little," Roland replied, unwrapping the scarf from around his neck. "We followed the trail until we reached the Aln. From there, we believe they went downriver... perhaps to Alnmouth."

Grace and Reverend Shepherd peppered Roland for more details, but he kept his answers brief—so much so that Grace began to suspect he wanted the rector gone. After several minutes, their guests finally got the message.

Reverend Shepherd rose from his chair and offered his wife his arm. He faced Roland. "I was telling your wife of my intention to host daily prayer sessions in the church. If you do not mind, my lord, I would greatly appreciate it if you kept me apprised of your progress. Though our Lord knows and sees all, I have found that our prayers stand a better chance of being answered when we are specific with our requests."

Roland promised to share anything he discovered and then sent their guests on their way.

Grace could bear the burden of her secret no longer. She closed the door to the drawing room and rushed over to Roland. He allowed her to kiss his cheek, but he set his hands upon her waist, keeping her from embracing him fully.

"I am sorry to have to leave your side again so soon, but I found another matter that requires my attention."

"Oh?" Grace kept a tight hold on his lapels, unwilling to let him go so soon. His dissatisfaction only deepened.

Roland stepped closer to her, touching her face so she would understand the magnitude of the trouble. "I must speak with Mr Harding, and I must do so alone."

He had thought he had let the previous night's events pass, but it seemed he was still holding something of a grudge. Grace looked so shocked by his asking her to leave that Roland knew he had to soften the edges of his request. "There are so many tenants in a state of disrepair that it makes me suspicious that something is deeply wrong."

"Is there?" she asked him, narrowing her eyes. "Or are you still wroth with me?"

"Unfortunately, it is quite true. I find it difficult to believe, but some of the residents of Lesbury say the duke and Mr Harding have stopped responding to their requests for assistance."

She finally dropped her hands from his lapels. "That does sound quite serious. After all this summer, are you sure that I cannot help you?"

"No. I am about to give him a dressing down, and no man would be comfortable about having an audience for that. An audience that consists of my wife would be doubly humiliating."

Her eyes widened in surprise, but she stood down. "All right. Will you tell me later?" Grace asked, resting her hand atop his. "I also wish to speak with you... about things."

Roland barked a short laugh. "Yes. I think we really must have a talk."

He knew that sounded ominous, but he left her standing there as he headed back to the hallway. Just outside of the drawing room, a footman waited.

"You," Roland said, and the footman straightened up. "Withers mentioned at one point he had taken the liberty of setting up a place to become my study. Do you know where it is?"

"Er, yes of course, my lord. It's actually just the room over here." The footman was indicating the next door down from the drawing room.

"Fine. Be so good as to fetch Mr Harding at once. I imagine he has had time to return from Hipsburn by now. Inform him that his presence is required in my study immediately."

"At once, my lord."

The footman departed, and Roland let himself into the study, lighting the candles against the failing evening light. He hadn't yet set foot in the place once, but he discovered Withers had anticipated all of Roland's needs—paper, ink, and even Roland's preferred brandy.

Roland paused and let his hand linger on the glass decanter as he contemplated. There seemed more than a temporary courtesy implied to the eventual heir in this. He poured himself a generous glass and sat at the desk, rubbing his temples.

Mr Harding's arrival was swift—so swift, actually, that either he had already been coming to find Roland, or the footman had abandoned all pretence of decorum and had pelted through the castle to the bailiff like a boy of nine. Roland could not be sure what was more likely.

All he was certain of was that there were far too many secrets being kept in Castle Alnwick, and he was through playing the fool. So he did not invite Mr Harding to sit.

"I had noticed that there were signs of disrepair when Thorne and I made our way to Lesbury, but it did not cross my thoughts that there was something so truly wrong here at Alnwick until the innkeep asked me if I was there to finally—*finally*—inspect and approve work to be done on the mill's roof."

Roland paused, leaning back in his chair as he was trying to keep from gripping the glass in his hand too hard. Mr Harding waited in front of his desk, pale, and Roland's temper came to a head.

"I say, Mr Harding. Do you have nothing to say about this? *At all?*"

"Lord Percy," Mr Harding stammered. "I am sorry. I should have brought things up to you sooner but there have been so many other matters—"

"Stop," commanded Roland. "I do not want to hear vapid words and pale excuses. I require you to tell me what in the hell is happening here in Northumberland. I want to hear nothing more out of you, unless it is your confession of wrongdoing."

"My lord!" Mr Harding gasped, turning first white and then red. "May I speak frankly with you, Lord Percy?"

"By all means. In fact, I insist."

"I would not dare steal from the hand of the duke." The bailiff met Roland's eyes squarely, in earnest, and Roland waited for him to go on. "Can I claim no wrongdoing? Well... you may have me on this. As I have said, I should have approached you much sooner. The duke..." Harding trailed off, hesitating to say anything that might seem a slight to the Breaker. "The funds allocated to me early in the spring for repairs have long since run dry, and I have not been able to secure a meeting for more."

Roland's forehead furrowed. "There is more neglect showing here than a few months, Mr Harding."

And then the man's shoulders fell as he hung his head, spreading his hands in surrender. "You are not mistaken, Lord Percy. In truth, it was your father who had handled the disbursement of these previous funds and..."

"And my father is now dead," he interrupted succinctly, taking a breath as he wondered how much—how long— Thaddius had likely been skimming from these disbursements. "I believe I see what you are reluctant to say, I think. However, if the funds were depleted, why have you been unable to secure more? The mill's roof might collapse by spring."

"I have tried, Lord Percy. I have been requesting meetings

with His Grace to request more even before he went to Brighton. I paid for the innkeeper's chimney myself, lest all of Lesbury burn to the ground because of the risk of fire. And now I must make a terrible confession—the situation has gotten to the point that I did keep a very small portion of the funds from the last quarter to address what would not wait until Christmas. But you must believe me, my lord, I have kept the most exacting records for all of it, to the very penny. You must believe I had only the most honourable intentions."

Roland did believe him, however this made the situation no easier. Standing up, Roland ran a hand over the back of his neck as he paced, thinking. "I would like to see your records for the last year—no, make it the last two. I assume that you requested meetings with the duke through Mr Withers." Harding nodded. "And?"

"In the early spring, Withers told me that His Grace was in mourning and was unavailable. After Easter, I was informed that His Grace was dealing with more pressing issues and would send me word as soon as he was able to attend." Harding hesitated, adding, "After he returned from Brighton, my requests went ignored."

His headache worsened. Not only did he have to find missing children, it seemed as though all of Alnwick was collapsing around his ears, and he could not tell which disaster was most pressing. How had things gotten to such a state? "You may go for now, Mr Harding, but rest assured I am not finished discussing this matter with you."

Harding wobbled, swallowing with difficulty, and fled as if Roland might decide to set hounds upon him. Roland did not even wait to get up before he bellowed, "Withers!" as Harding opened the door. "I require Mr Wither's presence, *forthwith!*"

He followed Mr Harding to the hallway to ensure that there was someone who heard, and as he did so, the drawing room door opened. Grace emerged, her eyes wide and her face pale. Roland suspected she had had her ear pressed to the wall and had heard every word.

This clearly was no time for beating about bush, and he was suddenly keenly aware that his wife had chosen to observe his grandfather. How much did she know? "You may as well come in, too," he told Grace, his heart aching in his chest at the idea that Grace may have been withholding such important information.

Both were still standing in the hall, facing one another, as Withers trotted in as quickly as his old feet would bring him.

"What," Roland began, struggling to form words around the distraught lump growing in his throat, "have the two of you been concealing from me?"

Grace was shaking her head lightly, looking stunned, but the butler's old head bowed over his hands. "Your lady bears no fault, my lord. She knows little more than you. His Grace's infirmity is increasing," he began slowly. "At first it was mostly palsy. He lost his balance. Feeding himself gracefully became an issue. I am sure you noticed his tendency to take meals privately."

Roland's jaw might have been carved of marble, it felt so hard.

The old butler covered his eyes in shame. "My lord, I have been serving His Grace since before his own father passed. When the first signs of this malady began to take the duke's mind... I pretended I did not see. They were so fleeting, in the beginning. But I cannot pretend any longer. He is no longer merely occasionally forgetful or mistaking faces. He may be slowly slipping into madness, and I did not wish—I did not know how—" he trailed off. "Please, forgive me."

13

The butler's words were like a great, shadowy beast that settled its weight on his shoulders, and Roland turned on his heel to go back into his study. Privacy. Discretion. What terrible things had been happening in Northumberland because of the fear of telling the truth?

Grace must have dismissed Withers. He did not hear the man depart, or Grace as she approached him. But he felt her hands upon him as he was guided to his chair, and a glass of brandy pressed into his hand.

He reminded himself that this was not, after all, more than they were beginning to suspect at any rate. But what had before simply been a disturbing spectre had now been given strength and body.

Looking at the glass of brandy, he set it aside on one of the tables, dropping his head into his hands as his mind began to deal with the many implications.

"Are you all right?" his wife asked him softly.

"I am fine," he said, and laughed shortly. "I do not know why this was such a surprise, to find our worst fears about the duke coming true."

"That is because you hoped it would not be." She knelt by his side, brushing her hand over the side of his face.

He was still vexed with her for keeping secrets. He caught her hand in his and held it, searching her face with his piercing eyes. "How much did you suspect about the duke's state of mind? I need the truth from my wife, Grace."

Grace did not shrink away. "Withers was correct. I had no real sense anything was wrong until I took him to the library and he called me Hannah," she said. "I had only a vague notion to look into it more deeply, which I confess, I did not have much chance to do because I was feeling sorry for myself."

"Because we argued," he commented. And she nodded slightly.

"That would be a rather large part of it, yes."

Finally, she was being more forthcoming, which was both more in character and a mighty relief. He did not want to be dealing with these obstacles, thinking she might withhold something he needed to know. He relaxed his grip on her hand, pressing it to his cheek. Taking comfort in it.

"Did you hear all of the conversation with Mr Harding after all, then?"

"Of course," Grace said tartly. "I set a glass upon the wall to listen."

Roland snorted in amusement. "*That* sounds more like my Grace."

"Before you give me too much credit," Grace added, "it was not something that I really needed to. You had raised your voice quite a bit."

"Well, it seems you had the right of things. The duke is unwell. If my grandfather had set my father, of all people, to handle some of the duties, then he must have been concerned about his health for some time. This, atop the news that children are being kidnapped from their beds and villages are crumbling from neglect. This visit to Northumberland has been one nightmarish revelation after another."

"Might I remind you, he travelled to Brighton and concealed the indications of his illness from everyone as well as he did. Had he been anyone else, we might have suspected he was ailing sooner. His sheer perversity kept everyone at such a distance it was hard to see. But the very fact he was able to muster that perversity in character... he is not necessarily at death's doorstep, but the duke *is* an old man, Roland," she said kindly. "It is somewhat understandable that neither one of us anticipated the need to step in."

"Or perhaps I was willfully blind. I was so desperate to avoid letting the duke get a hold on Thorne and me that I did not see what was there to be deduced simply by being present. Not sooner with the ill-advised passing of monetary duties to my father, or later when I was living in the same house with him this summer.

"I plan to check the books to make sure, but I would not be surprised in the least to discover that Thaddius had been shorting the bailiff of necessary monies to fund his vices. What I saw in Lesbury and some of the farms..." Roland swallowed his ire. "I should have noticed sooner. It was there, plain as day. I could not see the forest for the trees."

"You have had a few other things to occupy your mind, my love."

Roland looked away, guiltily. "I am the heir to the Duke of Northumberland. I need to recall that fact. The tenants' well being is part of that duty, and it should not be superseded entirely by my marriage."

"I do not think it is something you have forgotten," Grace murmured wryly. "As I recall, you were most incensed by the idea of someone stealing children from their families. Your speech was most stirring. And quite possessive."

It had been, at that. His lip curled faintly, before smoothing out.

"You may find that the duke will require more assistance, but Elsie reminded me that we do not need to bear our burdens of the role alone. We can command the additional help we need for endeavours without risking yourself. Roofs can be rebuilt, and searchers conscripted. I can even help you with the books, if you like. We will sort out Northumberland."

He glanced sideways at her, at the challenge in her voice. "You think you can help with the books, do you?"

"Lord Percy," she mocked. "Do you think I cannot add and subtract?"

"Well, you are a mere woman," he replied jestingly, pulling her into his lap and winding his arms around her waist. "I have been told that women's heads are not built for the strain of such things." She looked down her nose at him, and grinning, he pressed a brief kiss to her lips. "I am sorry for how we left things last night."

"I am too," she said quietly. "Although I suppose we are both stubborn people, so it will not likely be the last time we bicker. Perhaps we should promise not to go to bed angry with one another."

"That would be wise. And Thorne reminded me that everyone was entitled to keep some worries in their private thoughts. I will respect your wishes, if that is how you feel about it, as long as you promise me that you would never keep such a worry to yourself simply because you do not want to trouble me. There is no issue so trivial I would not wish to know it. No burden I would not shoulder, happily, if I knew it eased your mind."

Grace stilled, one hand on his chest, as she studied him. Roland let her look, let her see the truth of it upon his face.

"Speaking of worries, however," he continued, his chin

dropping as he looked off into the distance, thinking. "I must confess, I believe you when you say we will manage to set this dukedom to rights, but... it will take some time. You wanted adventure, and I will happily grant you that journey. However, it would be selfish of me to demand I must experience it with you. If Withers is correct, and the duke's mind is failing, I must be prepared to shoulder his responsibilities sooner than his death."

"It is all right. I know," Grace said softly, her breath catching. "You would not be happy if you felt you were derelict in your duty. And I would not be able to bear suggesting it to you."

"While I attend to the needful, what will you, my lady? If you still desire to travel, I can send you to Portugal after all, with an escort."

"I would rather wait to go with you," Grace told him, poking him in the chest gently with one finger, and he smiled. "We will have years to travel, after things are settled. But, Roland..."

"But, country living is tedious, Grace, and this castle is rather dreary. Did you not say that Charity would be in London this year? We can send you back to the townhouse for the season. I can likely have things well underway and join you as people prepare to leave for Brighton. Surely I can justify a small trip to check on the southern holdings."

"No—I cannot go to London—"

"What?" he interrupted, ignoring Grace's look of exasperation. "Whyever not?"

"If you will simply let me get a word in, my lord," she said caustically, putting her hands on her hips, "I am prepared to tell you why."

Or so she claimed. Roland stilled, mystified at Grace's reaction, because even though now he gave her the space to speak her thoughts, she was clearly tongue-tied, and there was a long silence.

Finally, she said, "By the time the roads are passable, I would have to stay here with you anyway." She picked up his hand and laid it against her belly, to explain all the words she could not seem to find.

"You—" he sucked in a breath, his mind a perfect blank as his thoughts struggled to cope with this new information. "How?"

Grace laughed somewhat bitterly. "Believe me, husband, I spent a good many weeks asking myself the same question. I believe we both know the answer."

Stunned, Roland let his fingers press more firmly against her, finding the barest curve beginning beneath his hand. Grace was carrying his child? And clearly, for some time, too. Had he somehow been so thick headed that he missed all the signs?

"I had no sickness in the mornings," she added. Apparently the trajectory of his thoughts were clear. "Just fatigue. I let you believe that I closed the door to you during my courses. I am so sorry, Roland. For the longest time, the signs were so vague, and I was uncertain. And then I could not bring myself to dash your hopes for leaving Alnwick as soon as we were able. After that, I did not want to add to the list of things that you would be worried about. I kept hinting… hoping there would be a time the news would be welcome instead of another burden."

"Oh, Grace," he sighed, letting his hands slide around her again. He pulled her close to him, letting some of the worries he had been holding slip away as new ones jockeyed for attention.

"Are you angry with me? I know you wished to wait," she asked softly.

"No, dearest," he murmured, pressing their cheeks together, his gaze travelling down what he could see of the length of her body. He wondered how they would reckon with this newest development. How soon she would begin to show. Whether the duke would live to see his great grandson. Somehow, they would see it through. "I am a muddle of surprise and relief. And joy. Annoyance, too, because I am wondering how I managed to be so blind that I somehow missed... *this*."

His emphasis was so pointed, Grace looked to see what had caught his notice, and realised that in this position, he had a clear view of her neckline and chest. Her belly was not the only thing that had been beginning to swell against the hems of her clothing.

Grace's face flushed.

14

Roland did not carry Grace down the stairs to dinner, but it was a near thing. Though her intention had been to convince Roland to take care with his own safety, she had not managed to convey more than she would be passing her confinement in Alnwick. Meanwhile, Roland seemed to think she had been possessed of sudden fragility. He had insisted Grace take his arm on the stairs, and even when they reached the bottom, he did not relinquish his hold.

Grace bit back the urge to pull away, for she despised being treated like a frail creature. Roland could not help himself. As an only child, the poor man had no experience with younger siblings, nephews, or cousins. He had not met his half-brother until he was near grown.

In time, she was certain he would settle down. Even if he did not, she would not hold it against him. She had heard far too many tales of men who sent their wives to the country house, to bear the burdens of pregnancy and childbirth on their own. Roland would never leave her.

And so, as they made their way to the drawing room for pre-dinner drinks, Grace leaned closer to her husband. She was going to cherish every moment of their new, unexpected but welcome, adventure.

Joyous children's voices spilled into the hallway. Roland and Grace entered the drawing room to find the Sprouts clamouring for Thorne's attention. They each had a new toy in hand and were desperate to show their finds to him. With the holiday decorations on the mantle and candles burning bright around the room, one could have been forgiven for thinking it was Christmas morning. Even Grace's emerald wool gown was holiday appropriate.

The children, however, were in much less a charitable mood. Willa was the first to hear their footsteps. She turned to see who was coming, providing Wes the chance to bump her out of his way. The young girl careened backwards, nearly tumbling into Grace.

"Sorry, miss," she mumbled, her head turned the other way to stick her tongue out at her brother.

"Are you hurt?" Roland asked, his hands skimming over Grace's side.

"I am fine, dearest," she assured him, speaking only the truth.

Roland was not listening. He shifted one way and then the other in his effort to see her safely settled out of further harm's way. "Sit down over here. Wait, let me get a cushion."

"Is aught amiss?' Thorne asked, taking the children in hand. He tugged them back to give Roland more room. "Lady Grace, have you hurt yourself?"

Roland froze in place, his eyes darting her way. Though they had not discussed when to share their news, it was obvious that the secret would soon out itself. If her changing shape did not give it away, Roland's strange behaviour certainly would.

Grace offered her hand to Roland and gave him a nod of encouragement. His breathing eased as he settled beside her, his face beaming with pride. He cleared his voice and then made his announcement to the room.

"Grace and I are delighted to share the joyous news that we are expecting an addition to our family. God willing, we shall welcome our child in the early summer."

"Truly?" Thorne asked, looking to Grace for confirmation.

"Yes, and before you ask, I am fine. I have been spared the usual litany of ill-effects. There is no need to treat me any differently," she said, casting a glance at her husband.

"So. You are breeding after all," a gruff voice called from the doorway. With a thump of his cane, the Breaker came into the room. He studied Grace through a narrow-eyed gaze. "Good. I wondered."

Grace stiffened, preparing herself for some further remark, but for once, the old man had nothing else to say. He sniffed and then carried on to the other side of the room, where his favourite chair and a glass of golden sherry awaited him. The room was so large, they could almost forget he was there.

Roland held out his hands to invite the Sprouts to come closer. Like the duke, the children also seemed to have lost their tongues. "Come, children, surely you must have some interest in our news. Will you welcome a new occupant into the nursery?"

The twins exchanged weighted glances. They carried on an entire conversation in silence, being of such a shared mind as twins that they had no need of words. Willa clung tight to the doll she and Grace had found upstairs. Wes scuffed his shoes on the carpet, refusing to meet Roland's questioning gaze.

"We haven't been there for long, sir. We won't make any trouble."

"Trouble?" Roland reared back and then turned his mystified gaze on his wife. Grace could not make sense of it either.

It was Thorne who came to their rescue. "The Sprouts think you mean to move them out."

"We ain't family," Wes mumbled half under his breath.

Grace's stomach clenched at the pain in his little voice. This poor child, orphaned, abandoned, and fearful of finding himself back on the street. Grace shifted forward, her hands stretched out, urging the boy to come closer. "We do not share a bloodline, but you both will forever have a place in our hearts."

"And in our home," Roland added.

Wes abandoned his stilted posture and threw himself into Grace's open arms. She hugged the child tight and patted his back. He stayed still for only a few moments, practically an age for a child so young, before he righted himself and stepped clear. Grace let him go, crossing the room to repeat the same action with Willa. Both children thus reassured that they were not going anywhere before they were ready, Grace suggested they turn the conversation on to a happier topic.

"Sir Nathaniel will be an uncle. Will you help us decide how he should be called? Sir Uncle? Uncle Nathaniel?" she asked.

"Uncle Bastard," Roland murmured with a grin fit to crack his face.

"Roland!" Grace gasped, spinning around, with her hands on her hips, to glare at her husband. "Not in front of the children!"

"Perhaps I might get a vote?" Thorne asked drolly.

The children took the game just as Grace had imagined. The scene was so sweet, so unexpected, and so emblematic of her married life, that tears threatened to spill. They would be tears of joy, but Roland would no doubt act first to rush to her aid and ask for an explanation later. Grace eased away, moving closer to the fireplace on the far side of the room. There, she pretended to warm her hands to give herself time to blink any hint of moisture from her eyes.

The side of her face began to burn, not from the heat of the flames, but from the weight of someone's gaze. She adjusted her stance and found the duke staring at her, only a few feet from her side. She had not meant to stray so far from the others, nor to infringe on his privacy. Yet, now that she was there, she could hardly run away.

As before, he remained mute. Their eyes met for only a moment before he shifted his to look in the other direction.

She should have left well enough alone. but she suddenly had a pang of sympathy for the old duke. He was alone. Both his sons dead before him. Isolated from friendship by power. Despite the shared name, despite his presence, he was not truly part of this celebration. Nathaniel, Roland, and even the Sprouts had become a family. He stood upon the threshold of their warmth, neither accepted nor spurned, watching as the chance to become a part of it passed unheeded.

She wandered closer, taking her time so as not to catch the attention of the others. The duke was not more than a half dozen steps away. She stopped shy of his chair, leaning against the tall back of another nearby.

"You are welcome to join us and talk," she said quietly. "You are a part of our family."

The duke remained quiet, and Grace wondered if he heard. He did not so much as glance her way. "Look at them."

From here, the similarities between Roland and Thorne were evident. It went beyond their shared broad shoulders and wide foreheads. When they laughed, their shoulders shook in near unison. They both cocked their heads to the side at the same angle. It was more than learned. It was innate.

Grace turned to make a remark, but noticed that the duke's focus was elsewhere. He was studying Willa, who had climbed into a chair and was cuddling her baby doll in her lap. She whispered quiet words to her doll, lost in her own imagination.

They were too far away to hear Willa's whispers, but Grace did not mind. Seeing the child behaving in such an unguarded manner was like having a window into both her soul and future.

The duke was equally entranced by the scene. For a moment, his stance softened. He rested his chin on his hand, seemingly lost in the view of the little girl sitting in his midst... or at the doll she held in her hands.

No one else was paying attention to them. Grace kept her voice pitched purposely low to keep from pulling him from his reverie. "Your Grace, who was Hannah?"

"My sister. Sometimes you remind me of her."

Grace could hardly contain her shock that he had answered her at all. Perhaps that is why she dared to ask. "You had a sister? Where is she now?"

Those words, however well meant, broke the spell. He shook his head to clear his thoughts, then swung around to glare up at her.

"Dead. Dead and forgotten, by all but me." He grabbed his cane and struggled to rise from his chair. He waved off Grace's hand with a growl, finding the strength to do it on his own. Or the stubbornness, Grace thought.

He left the room without a backwards glance, his heavy tread alternating with the thumps of the cane, growing more and more distant.

Roland's gaze met Grace's from across the room. He raised his eyebrows, querying what had happened and whether she was well. She found herself at a loss for a reply. Though she was unharmed in both body and spirit, it would be a long while before she stopped hearing the raw pain in the Breaker's voice.

15

Roland wished he could split himself in two. Between the tenants, Grace, and the missing children, he could scarcely be everywhere at once. There had been another minor disagreement between them this morning. He had wanted to leave Thorne behind with her. But she had, correctly, pointed out that Thorne would not have been able to assist with any of the other issues plaguing Northumberland, and she would be perfectly fine in the company of her maid and housekeeper.

So he instructed Mrs Yardley and Elsie to stick to the countess like thistles on the hem of her skirts, and left Mr Harding with the money he could scrape up on short notice to try to secure whatever repairs might be done at this time of year. If there was an issue with the countess, they would let Mr Harding know immediately. Mr Harding knew where he would be able to locate the search party.

So he, Thorne, and Colonel Ellesmere left at first light for Alnmouth.

All the signs had been pointing to the kidnapped children being moved to—or through—Alnmouth. It had been a long time since Roland had felt such a strong urge towards committing violence with his bare hands, but there was not yet a known perpetrator to focus his frustrated anger on.

He tried to release the feeling. He did not want to be like his grandfather, surrounded by men who feared him and his temper. But for the moment, he could not summon a convincing farce of an aristocrat's bored indifference, and enough of his state of mind oozed from his posture that all three men rode in silence. Even Arion's ears flattened back, picking up his master's mood.

Alnmouth was, perhaps, a little larger than Lesbury all told, with upwards of five hundred souls living there. But the residents of Lesbury were mostly farmers, and Alnmouth's population varied a little more widely with the port nearby. There were still many farmers, but the villagers were also sailors, traders, and fishermen.

Perhaps more significantly, at least to Colonel Ellesmere's point of view, Alnmouth was a wealthier place. A handful of shipowners and merchants numbered among the well-to-do.

Since the Lesbury mill's roof was still very much on Roland's mind, he couldn't help but notice one could not see nearly the same amount of marked degradation. How interesting. Had repairs been completed here before Mr Harding had run out of funds, or had some of the locals merely decided to take the matter into their own hands?

"I think it would be fruitful to begin questioning around the docks," Roland said to the magistrate riding beside him. "If the children are being smuggled out of Alnmouth to work elsewhere, someone there may have seen evidence of it."

Colonel Ellesmere looked uncomfortable. "Lord Percy, I understand the sense of urgency that grips you. I, too, would like to see the villain apprehended. It may yet come to this, that we must put questions to some of the rabble directly, but to do so before we speak with any of the gentry would not be proper."

"Of course, magistrate," Roland said stiffly. "I do not know any of the local men of standing. Perhaps you can take the lead and direct me to where we might find the most prominent merchant or shipowner first."

Roland did not need to glance Thorne's way to know the man's thoughts. Thorne had always cared more for Roland's sense of propriety than Roland himself did, but he also knew the value in not beating around the bush when one was rather certain where the most profitable source of information lay.

So many kidnapped children implied an operation that had profit at stake. Their villain was, most probably, *among* the gentry himself, and would therefore have little incentive to speak truth. If they wished to capture him, they would need evidence.

"While you meet with the respectable people," Thorne said, his voice absolutely neutral, "I will pose questions to a few shopkeepers."

It was a fair course of action for Thorne's standing, and the colonel nodded brusquely in agreement. Roland turned in the saddle to meet Thorne's eyes squarely.

Thorne's blue eyes were dancing with malicious amusement, and Roland knew that his brother would instead head directly to the docks. Judging by the clothes he wore, Thorne had strategically dressed for this excursion. His outfit, while well made and somewhat new, lacked any of the ornamentation or ostentation of the upper class. He most likely wished to be perceived as no better than a man of business.

Roland was glad now that Grace had spoken sense to him in bringing him along. Despite his elevation, Thorne would continue to be his right hand in these matters. He was a man straddling the two worlds, and Thorne wasn't likely to have any new rumours formed about him by the gentry that hadn't already been uttered. But that didn't mean Thorne intended to court the gentry's opinions directly.

Roland let a half smile lift the corner of his mouth and he nodded slightly. His brother nodded back—almost a salute of sorts—and wheeled Horse around to head vaguely in the direction of a line of shops.

Mr Thomas Dacre ended up being Ellesmere's first stop. The man was a seasoned trader, owning several ships that traversed up and down the coast from Edinburgh to Newcastle. While he initially seemed wary, perhaps due to their unannounced arrival, he welcomed Roland and Colonel Ellesmere into his parlour.

Mr Dacre served them whisky, although this time, Roland's glass was filled with the lowland sort that was more floral and delicate than the kind Thorne had accosted him with. "I do much of my trade in the north in whisky," Dacre explained. "Whisky for tobacco and salt. South, the route is mostly wool for coal. The war has been a most profitable event for people who know what is in demand." The man's eyes glinted as he drummed his finger on his glass.

They exchanged the bare minimum of pleasantries before Roland eased Mr Dacre towards the matter at hand. "Have any of your captains found children aboard heading for the south?"

"Ah, you are inquiring about those peasant children," Mr Dacre said, looking completely unconcerned. "No, my ships do not deal in passengers of that ilk."

"No stowaways?"

"Definitely not. But Lord Percy, I thought you were given to believe those rodents were kidnapped deliberately."

Roland spread his hands so he would not give his reaction to that callous statement away by making them into fists. "Indications from the latest two missing are such, but there remains a small possibility that some of the other children that disappeared this fall were enticed with the promise of apprenticeship elsewhere."

"I am sorry I cannot be of more assistance, Lord Percy. But no businessman or captain worth his salt would trade in human flesh, legitimately or otherwise. Not when wool is worth ten times as much by weight—and requires no feeding besides."

They made small talk for a while longer. Well, Ellesmere made small talk, and Roland asked some few questions to help him gauge how Alnmouth fared in the absence of the duke's presence. It sounded as though the locals might be exploiting a lack of greater oversight.

Dacre's estate sprawled on a large section of the Aln, not too far from the shipping yard. So it was not too surprising that as Roland and the magistrate departed, they found a small delegation waiting on the main thoroughfare.

"Lord Percy, this is farmer Robson, who is serving as parish constable this year, and Mr Treadwell, Curate of Alnmouth," Colonel Ellesmere said smoothly. "Mr Treadwell was good enough to take the pulpit after the old curate took ill and died this spring."

"Wasn't much trouble at all to relocate from Warkworth. 'Tis important to ensure the Lord's work is not interrupted, Colonel Ellesmere," Mr Treadwell said piously, though a glimmer of humour sparkled in the man's faded green eyes.

He seemed a genial man, perhaps ten years younger than the parish constable standing beside him. Roland imagined he had been serving the congregations of Warkworth beneath the rector; the empty post allowed him to spread his wings.

Mr Robson was assessing Roland rather frankly, and Roland, sensing only curiosity, returned the appraisal. Robson was whippet-lean, his face full of hard angles and his hair silvering at the temples. "The heir of the infamous Breaker,"

Robson said after a moment, but his tone implied no disrespect. "It's good to put a face to the name, Lord Percy."

"And I am pleased to meet you both," he replied. "What may Colonel Ellesmere and I do for you?"

"We thought of putting that question to you, Lord Percy." Mr Robson said, rubbing an itch alongside his nose. "It's most gracious for you to visit yourself, but a man of your stature surely must have more pressing issues to attend to. Please. Mr Treadwell and I are at your service."

Colonel Ellesmere nodded approvingly. "Constable Robson, if you could, please let us know whether any search efforts for missing children in the area have taken place so far?"

"None of the children went missing from our area," Robson said apologetically, "and until these last, we believed as the others did—that these children were runaways. I've done some looking, but to mount an effective search in these parts, we would need to conscript some of the townsfolk. Treadwell—well, he has had more luck so far than I in convincing people it ought to be their duty."

"But you are the arm of the law here, Mr Robson," Ellesmere chided. "Surely people would want to do their part."

Robson flushed slightly. "Magistrate, as you well know, we farmers and tradesmen have our hands full. My own appointment came only because no one else was willing to manage the business of dealing with sotted fishermen. Asking half the town to abandon their work to search for missing children is a difficult matter."

"I know, Mr Robson," Roland cut in gently. "That is a part of why I have been participating myself. We are all in this matter, together, and rank should be no excuse for allowing such harm to another to go unaddressed."

Robson gave Roland a long look, and Roland thought the man might be attempting to squash exasperation with him, but finally, the constable nodded. "I can respect that opinion, Lord Percy. If you truly mean it."

Colonel Ellesmere did not like Mr Robson's response, but Roland held out a hand to stay his rebuke. Those of means in Northumberland had abided—even prospered—under poor stewardship from Alnwick, but Roland knew that would not be true for everyone. Grace had been finding her footing because of the long spell since the last duchess. It seemed Roland also needed to improve the image of the Percy men.

"I do, Mr Robson," he said simply, holding the man's eyes for a moment before looking for acceptance from Mr Treadwell also.

"Perhaps we should take further conversation to the inn," Treadwell volunteered, indicating the building nearby. "The weather is fair today, but the breeze is frigid. "

Over Treadwell's shoulder, Roland could see Thorne standing a short distance away, waiting. Turning to the magistrate, Roland encouraged them to go. "Warm yourself, Colonel, and please take the liberty of arranging any matters required with Mr Robson and Mr Treadwell. I will join you shortly."

As they left, Roland strode towards his brother. "You are back sooner than I expected. Did you find something?"

Thorne shifted to make sure no one was too close. "I found you a smuggler. Well, a former one."

"I suppose he saw the error of his ways and repented?" He let his brother lead him swiftly towards one of the warehouses near the docks. "Brother, if we get robbed—"

Thorne pulled him into the building and out of sight, after a quick glance to ensure no one was watching. A strong odour of fish and brine assailed Roland's nostrils, and he stifled a shudder, recalling the damp, reeking nets in the hold of the

Black Hawk. In the shadowed back of the warehouse was a man half hidden by a line of crates.

"Mr..." Thorne trailed off, waiting for the grizzled man to produce his name, but the old smuggler shook his head.

"Ah dinna reckon ye need me name, just what ah ken, aye? Ye're the lords lookin' for the bairns."

Thorne nodded, folding his arms over his chest, and Roland added, "My friend here says you used to be... a purveyor of certain fine goods."

The man squinted, his eyes nearly getting lost in the weathered folds of his face. "Ah'll hold me tongue on that, 'til ah ken whether answerin'll see me clapped in irons, me lord. How bad d'ye want the truth?"

"I have met men who one might call honourable smugglers. Fishermen hedging against poor hauls and the like. I am willing to forgive goods—not trading in flesh," cautioned Roland, unwilling to bend on that point. Not even for more information on the missing children. "You have my word as Lord Percy."

The smuggler goggled briefly at Roland, as if he did not know who he had been talking to. "If that's how it is, ah reckon that'll do. Aye, ah was a smuggler, but ah doubt ye'd call me honourable. Ah didn't do it for hunger or home. You and yer sort live yer fancy lives, me lord, and the only thing standin' 'twixt your houses and folk like me is ye've made 'em believe they don't deserve what ye have."

He hurled those words like a gauntlet, as if the old man was waiting to see if he could upset them, but Roland was unmoved. "You said '*was.*' I assume you are a smuggler no longer."

"The profits ain't worth the risk no more—not when ships are headin' out wi' proper goods, lining the pockets o' the captain and crew. War's been good business up here, y'see, what wi' the price o' wool these days. Soldiers need their uniforms."

Roland rubbed his chin. "Mr Dacre said something like wool is worth ten times as much by weight as a child."

"An' Mr Dacre'd have the right o' it."

"You extracted a promise from me to only tell me what I already knew?"

The smuggler rubbed his cheek. "I wouldn't want to be tellin' any *yarns* about what's goin' on at the docks, m'lord, but some folk might be *spinning* tales about what's really going out in some o' the sacks o' grain." The gaffer spoke the words like a riddle, one he clearly didn't intend to answer for them.

Thorne was frowning, absentmindedly rubbing the spot on his arm where the bones had broken. It must be aching from the cold, Roland thought, despite the heavy wool... cloth.

Digging into his pockets, Roland found a half crown, and he tossed it to the old codger. "I reckon you have earned a good meal tonight."

Roland strode quickly in the direction of the inn, and only Thorne's inability to catch up without looking ridiculous slowed his pace. The two men found the magistrate still sitting with Mr Robson and Mr Treadwell. Everyone looked up from the table, surprised at the intensity of his arrival.

"Mr Robson, Mr Treadwell, forgive me for asking you directly, because I must confess that my knowledge of the industry in Alnmouth is sorely out of date. To your knowledge, is someone in Alnmouth spinning or carding wool in quantity?"

All three men at the table blinked at him as though he had suddenly sprouted horns.

"Er, no, Lord Percy," Mr Treadwell answered. "At least, not to my knowledge. Sheep farmers there are aplenty, but... Well, perhaps Mr Robson would know better. He has lived here longer."

Robson's forehead creased heavily, his face growing solemn. "There are no wool mills here. Most farmers ship the raw wool elsewhere."

The magistrate's face was set in a heavy frown. "Explain the direction of your thoughts, Lord Percy."

Roland glanced at his brother, fudging the truth a bit. "Sir Nathaniel discovered that someone is exporting more than just raw wool from Alnmouth. An odd circumstance indeed, especially if there are no mills in the area. And Constable, I would appreciate your help in determining where this wool appears to be coming from. I am possessed of a strong suspicion that if we find this missing wool, we might also find some missing children."

Mr Robson's mouth parted in surprise. Judging the faces around the table, he was not the only one aghast at the idea. "I will look into it at once, Lord Percy."

16

Grace and Mrs Yardley exited the castle grounds and stood in companionable silence, surveying the village streets. It was briskly cold, even for a December morning, though the sun was doing its best to ease the chill. Grace headed into the street, her mind full of all she needed to do rather than watching her step. Thus, she failed to notice the faint sheen spotting the cobblestones. One foot slid forward. The other went back. Grace gave an unladylike shriek, fearing the worst, but a firm grip pulled her to safety.

"Perhaps my lady would consent to taking my arm," Mrs Yardley said once they were back on safe ground, taking great care not to show even a hint of emotion. "I am well familiar with which areas are most likely to ice over. Given your circumstances, I suggest we take no unnecessary risks."

Grace took Mrs Yardley's proffered arm, having no desire to repeat her near miss. "Thank you, Mrs Yardley. I will do so in exchange for you speaking nothing of this to Lord Percy. He is desperate to keep me off my feet. While some women would relish the idea of sitting still for weeks on end, I am most certainly not one of them."

"You are not ill, my lady, though most men fail to understand the difference. I shall remain mum, though do not expect me to countenance anything that might truly put you in harm's way."

The housekeeper's statement was fair enough, so Grace opted to move the conversation along to more interesting matters—namely, their plans for the day.

"I would like to visit the shops. All of them," she added. "We will purchase Christmas gifts and spread some holiday cheer through acts of charity." Grace kept the other purpose of their outing to herself. She and Roland were now aware of the shortfalls in spending and delays in approvals. The missing children only added to local pain and suffering. Correcting all of these matters would take time. Grace intended to find out which individuals were in the most dire need of assistance.

"Shall we start with the milliner's shop?" Mrs Yardley asked, pointing at a doorway across the street. "Perhaps young Miss Willa would appreciate a new ribbon for her doll, and we could buy a second to donate to the school."

Grace had a different starting point in mind. "Let us start with the shops farthest away and work our way back toward the castle. That way, if the weather turns, we will not have so far to go."

The main street was quiet, the morning shoppers having already finished their errands and returned home to see to lunch. The sun was nearing its zenith, the bright rays providing at least the illusion of heat. Symbols of Christmas spirit were all around them. Grace glanced left and right, noting the wreaths adorning the doors and candles in the windows. The confectioner's shop boasted a colourful display of sweets. From marzipan to sugar plums to fruit jellies, there was more than enough to satisfy both the children and the young at heart.

Mrs Yardley bid hello to a few people as they went past.

The villagers nodded respectfully, gazing on Grace with great curiosity. Grace longed to tell them all that they were not so different, no matter their stations, but her expensive clothing and weighty title proclaimed otherwise. In time, the walls between her and the people of Alnwick would lower, but she was not so foolish as to imagine they would disappear entirely.

In the village green, someone had hung a kissing bough from the bare branches of the lone tree. The deep green of the waxy leaves intertwined with red ribbons drew both the eye and the heart. Grace made a note to tell Elsie so that she might take advantage of the excuse to coax a kiss from Briggs.

At long last, they reached the cobbler at the end of the row. There, Grace ordered sturdy boots for the twins and a new pair of slippers for herself. The cobbler, an older man with rosy cheeks, a rotund paunch, and a welcoming smile, promised to deliver them all well before Christmas.

Grace added extra coins to the stack before passing them over.

"This is too much," he protested.

"Please, I insist. There must be some family in the area who is in need of patching or new shoes. Allow me to help bear the cost of the repairs." Grace hurried to add, "Tell them you have extra materials or someone cancelled an order. The people here are proud, and rightly so. It shall be our secret."

Each shop visit went on in much the same manner. Grace bought a porcelain dish for Elsie, scented soaps for the housemaids, and silver snuff boxes for Roland and Thorne, imagining their delight on Christmas morning. She spent ages in the toy shop, selecting treats for the twins with great care. This would be their first holiday without their parents, a fact that would doubtless weigh on their minds. Though she could not buy them happiness, the toys would at least be a welcome distraction. Love they had in abundance.

To every shop owner, Grace handed over more coins than were requested, each time asking that the funds be directed to those most in need.

Soon, Grace's stomach grumblings grew too loud for her to ignore. On their way back to the castle, the women happened past the village school just as Miss Whitby, the schoolmistress, was locking the door. Though Grace had enjoyed her conversation with the woman during the charity fair, with all else that had occurred, she had forgotten about her in the days since. Miss Whitby struck Grace as someone who could become a friend, in time. That, at least, was something Grace now possessed in abundance. She nudged Mrs Yardley in the direction of the school and called a friendly hello to the other woman.

"Miss Whitby, what a delightful coincidence to cross paths with you. I have had the children of Alnwick on my mind, as you might imagine." Grace took a package from Mrs Yardley's basket and passed it over. "I picked out a few items I thought might be useful to the school."

Miss Whitby took the package and clutched it against her middle. She stared down at it, but Grace had the sense the woman was not seeing it. When the schoolmistress sniffled, Grace realised the woman was crying.

"Oh dear, have I done something wrong?" Grace whispered to Mrs Yardley.

Miss Whitby lifted her gaze and sniffled back her tears. "Not at all, my lady. The children will appreciate whatever you have given, of that I am certain. Goodness knows they have far too little joy in their lives right now, and far more fear than is healthy."

Though speaking with Miss Whitby had not formed part of Grace's plan, she decided there and then to make time for her. Grace remembered all too well, from both her own experience and spending time with younger cousins, that children rarely watched their words. Miss Whitby likely heard a litany of secrets, large and small, pass through the mouths of her students. If anyone would know how the villagers were getting on, the schoolmistress would.

"I know this is terribly short notice, Miss Whitby, but would you care to accompany me to the Wild Hart for a cup of hot cider?" Grace motioned toward the village inn standing on the opposite side of the town green.

"Oh, I would not like to impose..."

"You would be doing nothing of the sort," Grace reassured her. "Mrs Yardley has suffered through a morning of shopping with me. I am sure she would welcome the chance to drop our packages off at the castle. Is that not right, Mrs Yardley?"

"Of course, my lady. I will send a footman around to collect the remaining parcels and find somewhere to store them until they are wrapped." Mrs Yardley refrained from adding a warning to Grace to take care, earning her an extra notch of appreciation from the future duchess.

Grace had seen her fair share of village inns during her autumn travels. Some had boasted cosy interiors and tasty food. Others proved to be so dire that Roland refused to allow either her or Elsie to move around unescorted. The exterior did not often tell the tale, but the windows offered more than a view inside. Polished glass rubbed clean of soot almost always revealed clean interiors. The Wild Hart was no exception.

The door stood in the middle of the building front, opening into a small vestibule. The door on the right led into the pub. Miss Whitby went left. Grace found herself in a small parlour that smelled of cinnamon and ginger. Candles flickered on the tables and in the lanterns on the wall. Fire roared in the fireplace, beckoning Grace closer.

There was no one else in the room, the weather chasing

away travellers and the hour sending the locals home for luncheon. A grey-haired woman entered from the other side of the room. She wore a white apron over her red dress and a cap on her head. She hurried over to sweep invisible crumbs from a table and beckoned the women to take a seat.

"My lady, it's an honour tae have you here," she said. Her voice carried a hint of an accent, bringing the Sprouts' nanny to mind.

"Are you related to our Miss Fenton, by any chance?" Grace asked.

The woman's face flushed in joy. "Aye, she's my niece, my lady. A fine girl she is, and a more caring soul you won't find."

"There is no shortage of generous hearts here in Alnwick, including our schoolmistress, Miss Whitby. I have promised her a mug of hot cider. Might you have some pastries to go with it?"

The publican promised to return in a trice with the drinks and a selection of her fresh baked goods. Grace and Miss Whitby divested themselves of their layers of outerwear before settling in the wooden chairs around the small table nearest the fireplace. Grace kept the conversation light until the food and drink arrived. Only when she was certain Miss Whitby had grown comfortable around her did she turn the talk toward her topic of interest.

"I must apologise for letting my emotions get the better of me, my lady," Miss Whitby said. "It is a trying time for our children, both those I have seen and those who have remained at home."

"What do you mean?" Grace asked.

"Parents are fearful that their child might be the next to disappear. Some refuse to let them out of their sight, others demand they walk in groups. I have set my lesson plans by the wayside, instead indulging the children in some whimsical play.

The longer we go without word of the missing, the worse it is. I can only pray we will have news soon."

Grace promised Roland and Thorne were doing their best to solve the matter, but she was not sure that her words got through to Miss Whitby. Too many children had gone missing, and hopes were dwindling. Though the duke and Roland were not to blame, their inability to put a stop to the kidnappings was souring everyone's opinions.

When it was time to leave, Grace found herself reluctant to return to the castle. She needed a quiet space to put her thoughts to rights, somewhere more grounded than a gilded room fit for royalty. Her feet carried her across the way to the entrance of St Michael's Church.

The heavy wooden door was unlocked, though it took some effort to push it open. It closed behind Grace with a thud, leaving her in a darkened, hushed interior. The sun's path through the sky had carried its beams away from the stained glass windows. Grace walked up the central aisle, not stopping until she reached the bench where the family had sat during the Sunday service. She slid onto the wooden pew and crossed her hands over her lap, lifting her face upward as though seeking guidance from the divine. They needed all the help they could get.

Unfortunately, no answers came. After a while, she lowered her gaze and shivered against the cold of the unheated church. She shivered again, thinking of the poor children who had been ripped from their beds and made to march to who knew where. Were they cold even now? Had anyone seen to food and shelter for them? She whispered a prayer for their safety, her breathing growing ragged as despondency sank its claws into her.

The echoing bang of the door pulled Grace back to the present. She dashed the tears from her cheeks. Footsteps drew closer, until a voice called her name.

"Lady Percy, is that you?" Reverend Shepherd hurried forward to greet her. "What are you doing here on your own? Where is your escort?"

His tone brought Grace up short. She had not done anything wrong, per se, but she realised now how strange her singular presence must seem. She gave a sigh of relief that it was him and not a parishioner.

"I was on my way back to the castle when I felt myself drawn in. We must answer when called, is that not right?"

Reverend Shepherd rocked back in surprise, but recovered quickly. "You are right, my lady. I can see you are upset. Has there been news of the children?"

Grace shook her head. "No, and that is what weighs on me. Lord Percy and Sir Nathaniel have gone to Alnmouth today. Let us both pray they will find some further clue as to the children's whereabouts."

"Alnmouth?" The rector gave a worried shake of his head and wrung his hands. "If they have passed through the port, I fear for their lives. I have heard tales from my brethren in larger cities of children pressed into workhouses... and worse. Lord Percy must not let word of this get out."

Grace cocked her head to the side, unable to follow his logic.

"In many respects, the loss of the children was easier when we believed them to have run away. A stern lecture and a close eye was all that was required to protect those still here. Now we must visualise children being ripped from their beds and dragged into neverending horrors. The people are terrorised, my lady. If Lord Percy cannot find those children, it would be better for all of us for him to say the man who witnessed the wagon was mistaken. Let the families mourn their children."

"You cannot expect us to lie," Grace countered, her ire rising at the mere suggestion.

"It is for everyone's good— yours and theirs. His Grace is

supposed to protect the people. Their requests for repairs go unheeded, their plans unapproved. Lord Percy is concentrating entirely on the two missing children, and ignoring everyone else here who is in equal need of attention. If you truly want to help the people—all of them—I suggest you remind his lordship of the many issues requiring his time."

17

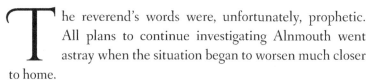

The reverend's words were, unfortunately, prophetic. All plans to continue investigating Alnmouth went astray when the situation began to worsen much closer to home.

Late in the evening, after Roland, Ellesmere and Thorne got back from Alnmouth, Mr Shaw, the father of one of the missing children, went to the local tavern to drink his sorrows away. There, he and a few others got drunk as David's sow, and they decided the next best course of action was to break into the warehouses of Farnsworth Carriers by the edge of the river, looking for clues of their own.

They found nothing untoward. However, men who were falling-down drunk were not especially careful with their lanterns, and the fire that resulted not only burned down the Farnsworth warehouse, but another beside it that had winter stores of grain and roots.

By midmorning the next day, there was a tense standoff between Shaw's sobering troublemakers and a cluster of the unhappy tradesmen whose shipments and storage had gone up in smoke. Before Colonel Ellesmere could successfully diffuse the situation, it escalated into a brawl that left three men nursing broken bones.

"Call for Mr Harding," Grace insisted.

"I think I must," Roland agreed. "Alnwick is besieged from without and within. I hardly know where to begin in sorting out this disaster, but one thing is certain... we need to keep matters from getting worse."

Thorne was sitting at the desk, writing furiously. "Hopefully Mr Robson can deal with investigating wool shipments on his own for the moment. Shall I send him a message as well?"

Roland waved his hand in tacit permission as he went to tell a footman to summon Mr Harding once more. "Be my guest. And my right hand. We have to deal with this first."

"What can I do to help?" Grace asked him. "Shall I go help soothe the tradesmen and see what we can do to arrange compensation?"

"No. Absolutely not," Roland said. "If the people are unsettled, letting you go abroad would be like setting the cat among the pigeons. It would not be good for you to be available as a target for their frustrations."

Grace reluctantly conceded his point, and twiddled her fingers. "Withers has told the maids to stay away from His Grace. Why?"

Roland set his fingertips to his temples. "Since shortly before Thaddius died, Withers has been managing His Grace's worst spells with draughts, keeping him abed."

With the unrest in the village, it was imperative that the Percy household step in to restore a sense of order, backing Ellesmere's efforts and helping soothe discontent with the tradesmen. Roland had made the mistake of seeking his grandfather's assistance in dealing with the brush fires happening in Alnwick, but it seemed whatever condition his grandfather had, agitation worsened the possibility of his having fits.

He had flown into a muddled rage at the impudence of the local peasantry that intensified into hallucinations of persecution by Alnwick's citizenry. It took Withers a half of an hour to calm the duke into a semblance of rationality, and by then Roland understood the full magnitude of his grandfather's unstable state.

Her eyebrows drew together, and Roland could see her calculating as he had, the number of times that the duke had been unavailable when they sought him directly. "How often is this happening?"

"Before the summer, perhaps once or twice a month. It was rare enough that it could be easily overlooked. But by the harvest season, it was apparent to Withers that his spells were being brought on by high emotion, and it was growing worse quickly. This morning, he was nearly combative in his confusion after he found out about the fire," Roland confessed quietly.

"Goodness. You... will you be going out to continue searching?"

"I think I cannot, my love. If His Grace is unfit, then it falls to me to start wheels in motion that no one else can. I must reach out to the solicitor in Newcastle-upon-Tyne—"

"I have already drafted that letter, Roland," Thorne interrupted from the desk, and Grace touched her fingers to her lips to hide a small smile, though her eyes were slightly downcast.

"You were right. We must draw on the assistance of others to accomplish our ends," Roland added drolly. "I must now be a politician and a steward, but at least I have the satisfaction of knowing Thorne has been drafted into the position of my secretary. You need not do anything but rest and take care of yourself."

"Well... all right, it seems you have things well in hand..." she said, glancing around. "I should find somewhere else to be so I am not underfoot."

Roland wished he could keep her nearby, even though it would be a dull afternoon. "It would be less tedious for you. But know you are always here," he consoled her, pressing her hand to his chest.

She nodded and slipped out of his study as Mr Harding arrived with an armload of ledgers. The man saw Thorne sitting at the desk and turned to Roland, perplexed.

"Congratulations, Harding," Roland told him. "I am appointing you as Alnwick's steward, effective immediately."

"Er," Mr Harding stammered, dropping one of the books.

Striding closer to Mr Harding, Roland picked it up and plucked the ledgers from Mr Harding's hands, depositing them on a nearby table. "I trust this gives you sufficient authority to handle the issues related to the tenants, yes?"

"Er," Mr Harding said again. "Does that mean I will be able to withdraw funds for repairs?"

"Yes," Roland said succinctly as he shot a look at Thorne. "Perhaps it is best for me to assume handling payroll for the moment until things are caught up. Shall I increase your compensation to 100 for now, Mr Harding?"

"I'll write the bank next," muttered Thorne, shaking out the cramp in his hand as he blew on the current page.

"Lord Percy! I—that would be extremely generous—"

"Good. When you take over the other disbursements in a few months, you can grant yourself another 50. Thank you for removing this issue of the tenant repairs from my plate."

"It is my privilege, my lord, I assure you." Harding gave a nervous bow. "Thank you for granting me another chance to prove my loyalty to the Percy family. Your trust will not be misplaced."

"I expect not. No good deed goes unpunished, Harding. You probably will rescind your thanks when I raid the duke's desk and find out what other paperwork has been languishing. Feel free to conduct your work here, for now, in case you need my approval with anything."

Feeling a keen need to move, Roland abandoned his own office to the men and went to conduct his raid. Withers, predictably, showed up the moment Roland went to turn the doorknob of his grandfather's study.

"Lord Percy," Withers said, wringing his hands. "Are you certain that this is necessary to enter His Grace's sanctuary like this?"

Roland tried to hold his temper and deal with the old butler gently. Perhaps the duke was not the only elderly resident of Alnwick Castle who was slipping in good sense. "Unfortunately, I believe the answer to that would have to be a yes, Withers. I do not want to violate my grandfather's privacy, but the lapse in oversight has gone on for too long. I simply wish to ensure that nothing crucial has been left unattended. It is in the estate's best interest."

The butler reluctantly nodded. "Yes, of course, my lord."

"Come. I know you have been assisting the duke. I also know that Mr Harding has been forwarding requests that were beyond his capacity for nearly an entire year, and many have not been dealt with. Where are they? With your assistance, my need to disturb the duke's space will be at a minimum."

As Roland sat behind his grandfather's heavy desk, Withers directed his hands to a drawer on the right. Opening it, Roland inwardly cursed as he found a sheaf of papers. Mr Harding's requests for funds. Orders for repairs to the fencing. Petitions for reductions in rent. Requests for grazing rights and subletting.

My god, Roland thought, resting his head upon one hand. When was Withers going to bring this to his attention?

"Please take this to Mr Harding immediately." Roland gave the stack of papers to Withers, and closed the drawer with a thump. Then he checked the drawer above. The duke's signet ring glinted dully in the drawer next to a stick of sealing wax. Roland withdrew the ring, examining the smooth face with the reversed image of the Percy lion carved into its face.

Sighing, Roland closed the drawer, pocketing the ring. It would not be his to wear until the duke died. But while Roland had to act in His Grace's name, he would need to use the seal to show that the ducal approval was granted.

Leaving the duke's study, Roland ruthlessly suppressed an urge to find Arion and go ride out to meet Mr Robson. He did not want to be here, dealing with paper and propriety. The mantle of the duke's responsibilities pulled him in two directions, and as he heard footsteps approaching from behind him, he gritted his teeth in anticipation of another urgent issue, pretending he did not hear.

"Lord Percy, I beg your pardon."

Roland turned at the sound of Brigg's voice and found himself pressed against the wall like he was the victim of a mugging. He certainly hadn't expected to be accosted by his own valet, and he nearly stumbled as the man laid his hands on Roland to straighten his cravat, and then his hair. He was shocked at first, and then chagrined at the length of time it took Briggs to restore order to Roland's appearance.

"There, now you look a little less like a wild thing. *Don't—*" Briggs insisted, "run your hands through your hair, my lord!"

Blinking at him, Roland uttered the first words that came to mind. "Yes, *mama.*"

Briggs gave Roland a toothy grin, and leaned in to whisper.

"I mean it. Don't muss your hair. The footmen here are terrible gossips."

"Duly noted, Briggs. Was that all that you needed to tell me or was there somewhat else?" Roland inched away.

"Colonel Ellesmere has brought the tradesmen by. Since Withers and the duke were unavailable, I've settled them in the drawing room next to your study. Shall I bring tea?"

Roland began to lift one hand in an urge to pull his hair again. Briggs cleared his throat loudly, giving him a look Roland hadn't seen since he misbehaved in school. "Right. Yes, tea. And possibly some of that swill my brother likes to drink—but send that to my study for afterward."

The tradesmen put on a show of disgruntlement, but they were quickly mollified by the talk of compensation for the loss of their goods. All too soon, the light began to fade outside of the windows, and Roland sent the tradesmen on their way.

"You need to work on your face of indifference, Lord Percy," Colonel Ellesmere remarked. "Or perhaps I am wrong, and you should continue cultivating your fearsome visage. It certainly kept the fussing from Farnsworth to a minimum."

"Would that being fearsome could solve other tasks so handily. Have you had any luck investigating the path of the wool?"

"No, I am sorry to say. I haven't even had a chance to start to look into it," Ellesmere murmured. "Hopefully things are quieter tomorrow, because I have even fewer searchers to look after today, even if you and I were available to ride."

"What do you mean?" Roland asked. "Has something happened to the searchers?"

"No, Lord Percy. But like Mr Robson, Alnwick's few constables are just farmers serving their appointed year." Ellesmere grimaced, tossing back the remains of his cold tea. "I requested more hands from the area when we began the search, and they have other duties to go back to. You don't happen to have something stronger than this, do you?"

"My brother's rot-gut is next door," Roland said, inviting Ellesmere into his study.

"That'll do." Colonel Ellesmere nodded in greeting to Mr Harding and Thorne, and Thorne, reading his mind, poured four glasses of whisky.

"To our current problems that not all the money in the world can solve," Roland said mildly, lifting his glass in a sardonic salute. "Perhaps we shall need to find the money for a few permanent lawmen so we never again have an issue arising from conscripted farmers."

Thorne, Roland and the Colonel drank to that, but Mr Harding fingered his glass for a moment. "Lord Percy, if I might suggest something boldly..."

"Please."

"Money *might* solve your problem. You might have a thousand willing searchers if you put a reward at stake. Something sufficiently lucrative that every rock will be turned in search for the villain. Perhaps, say, a percentage of next year's sheep shearing?"

Roland and Ellesmere stared at Mr Harding, but Thorne broke into a chuckle. "A reward from the sheep? That would be a nice bit of irony, Mr Harding."

Pondering the idea, Roland refilled the rest of their glasses, waiting pointedly until Mr Harding downed his first one before he filled it again and set down the bottle. "Perhaps we could. We could send out criers. Have Reverend Shepherd and the clergy spread the word."

Finally, Roland felt as though there might be hope. "I will require all of your help. We will, doubtless, be inundated with false leads. But at least the leads will come to us, and there will be no safe haven for the kidnapper."

18

The four walls of Grace's sitting room were closing in on her. Nevermind that the stones of Castle Alnwick were strong enough to resist even the fiercest of attackers, Grace was certain they were shifting closer together. It was the only explanation she could find for why her throat grew tight when she sat, safe from all harm, in her private quarters.

Deep inside, she was aware of just how absurd her thoughts were. She did not dare speak them out loud, not even to herself. Everyone in the castle was hard at work, starting from dawn and not ending until late in the night. Roland commanded their every movement from his study.

Everyone except Grace, that was.

For perhaps the first time in her adult life, Grace was completely useless. Roland had assured her time and again that she had the most important task of all—carrying their child. But when she sat in the utter quiet of her sitting room, with naught to entertain her but her half-hearted efforts at embroidery, she felt as though she served no purpose at all.

She glared at the snarled thread marring the pristine surface of the white handkerchief stretched across the wooden frame in her lap. Yet another task she could not get right. She had offered to venture into town to help Miss Whitby with the school. Roland had countered that it was not safe, nor wise given the icy ground, for her to venture out. Mr Harding gave her a similar shake of the head when she asked if she could help with the business side of the estate while Roland was speaking with the tradesmen.

"As much as I'd welcome the help, my lady, it would take me more time to explain everything than it would to do it myself. My lady is not familiar enough with the area or the tenants to know which complaints are urgent."

"I am certain I could do something, Mr Harding," Grace had replied, undaunted. "A broken chimney is more timely than a broken door latch, etcetera, etcetera."

"Perhaps so, my lady," Harding said, shifting uncomfortably in his chair. "But the requests themselves are only part of the story. Mrs Smitherton, for example, always says her chimney is clogged, when in truth all it needs is for her husband to sweep it out. If I put her at the bottom of the list, Mr Smitherton will eventually get round to it. Do you see what I mean, my lady?"

Indeed, Grace did. She had left the good man to his work and ventured belowstairs. Mrs Yardley gave a look of such horror at her setting foot in her domain, Grace had hurried back up the stairs, claiming she had got turned around and never meant to be there in the first place.

No matter what Grace wanted to do, Lady Percy, esteemed countess and future duchess, was very much in the way.

Resigned to her confinement, Grace tugged on the knot of thread. It stretched taut and then snapped, leaving the mess of the knot behind and a useless bit of string dangling from her needle. She jabbed it into the cotton cloth, penting her frustration, and ended up stabbing the finger she had failed to move out of the way. Blood stained the back of the cloth, rendering it fit only for the fireplace.

"Drat, bother, and blast," she growled, savouring the way the words felt in her mouth. She loosed the screw holding the wooden frame together and pulled the cloth free. With great satisfaction, she balled it into her fist and launched it into the red-gold flames. For the first time in days, she experienced the satisfaction of accomplishing at least one thing to which she had put her mind.

Her childhood self longed to toss another item in, perhaps a scrap of foolscap or a spool of thread. Those items, however, would be hard to come by in the depths of winter. The action had at least given her some idea for putting her time to better use. She had energy to spare. So, too, did the Sprouts.

Much relieved to have something new to focus upon, Grace marched out of her sitting room and up the stairs to the nursery. As usual, she heard the children's voices before she saw them. This time, at least, when she opened the door she found they were getting along.

"A sea monster!" Willa screamed in mock horror. She dove behind the doll house and shouted for Wes to light his cannons.

"Hold yer fire!" Miss Fenton called, wading into the mix with a white flag in her hand. "Sorry, my lady. The children have been pretending tae be pirates on the high seas ever since Sir Nathaniel told them the story of Calico Jack."

Grace drew up short, her mind going blank on the name.

"He was fearless," Wes said. "Sailing the high seas, flying the Jolly Roger, he used his wits to lay claim to all the plunder."

"I see," Grace said, giving every impression of being impressed. "And was he a Robin Hood type, robbing the rich to feed the poor?"

Wes shook his head. "No, ma'am, he was not. That's why the government tossed him in jail, sentenced him to death, and then hung his corpse on display to serve as a message to the other criminals."

Willa bobbed her head in agreement, the old doll still tucked close to her side.

Grace could not imagine why Thorne would find such a story an appropriate story for two rambunctious children. Determined to change the conversation, Grace asked Willa about her dolly. "Have you given her a name?"

"Anne," Willa said, beaming with pride.

"A nice, solid name," Grace said, but she didn't get further than that.

"Like Anne Bonny! She left her husband to sail off with Calico Jack. She didn't die with him though. No one knows what happened to her. I've decided she's still out sailing. That's why we started playing pirates. He's Calico Jack and I'm Anne Bonny."

Grace gave a moment of consideration to suggesting more appropriate role models for the children, but decided to leave well enough alone. They were healthy, happy, and far enough away from open water to eliminate the risk they might sail off into the night. She waved for them to go back to their playing and went over to have a word with their nanny.

"Hello Miss Fenton, I hope the Sprouts have not made you walk the plank."

"Only a time or two," she replied. "They soon found that those they sent into the sea had a tendency tae return as multi-tentacled monsters. Monsters, I should add, who reminded them tae practise their letters and sums."

The women paused as the children's voices rose again, making chat impossible. If there was one positive thing about Alnwick Castle, it was the distance between the nursery and the family rooms, and the extra thick walls. Though their voices echoed off the hard surfaces, Grace did not worry they might disturb either Roland or the Breaker.

Grace cast a glance at Miss Fenton. The woman was eyeing the children with a fond smile, none the worse for her time spent corralling them.

"I would never have predicted it, but Willa loves that doll something fierce. I've had tae repair the stitching on the body twice. At the rate she's going, she'll need a replacement by Christmas morning."

"Bless you for putting the doll to rights—and for taking such great care of the Sprouts. If you will ring for tea, I will see if they will settle down long enough to listen to a story."

The Sprouts were not keen to call an end to their game, but the arrival of a plate of iced biscuits brought them around. Grace and Miss Fenton laid claim to a settee near the window, while the children sat at their feet. After several sips of restorative tea, Grace felt up to the task of entertaining.

"Would you two be interested in a new story? Perhaps something that might inspire a different game?" she asked.

"I dunno, my lady," Wes replied, his nose wrinkled. "We've got soldiers fighting battles, pirates sailing along the coasts. I don't want some yarn about a princess. That's boring."

"Not if the princess is dead," Willa countered. "And a ghost! Maybe the ghost haunting this castle is a princess or even a queen. Did a queen ever live here?"

"Not that I am aware of...." Grace halted there.

"But there is a ghost, right?" Wes asked, his eyes gone wide. "Willa and I've heard plenty of scraping and shuffling noises. It ain't mice, no matter what Miss Fenton says."

"It's nae a ghost either," the woman countered.

Wes dropped his biscuit onto his plate and leapt to his feet to defend his statement. While he carried on about hearing a door open and close, unexplained footsteps, and strange apparitions, Grace wondered why the duke would wander so far from his room. Was he in search of someone? Or something? Perhaps he sought the sister he had lost so long ago.

Grace pulled her mind back to the matter at hand and noticed Willa had gone awfully quiet. "What do you think?" Grace asked her when Wes paused to catch his breath.

Willa glanced over at her doll and studied it, as though engaging in an imaginary conversation. After a moment, she turned back to Grace. "Anne says ghosts aren't real."

"What about you, Willa? Do you agree with your doll?"

Willa nodded her head once, but then shook it. She scrunched her mouth up and shrugged her shoulders. "I want Anne to be right, but Wes isn't lying about the noises."

Somehow, Grace knew that telling the children it was likely the old duke stalking the corridors would not put a stop to their concerns, or their interest. He was worse than any imaginary monster. They had seen him shout and raise his fist in anger more than once since their arrival in Northumberland.

Yet, it would be equally unfair to dismiss their concerns out of hand. It was not important for them to know who it was so much as to understand that the noises were entirely human.

"I promise there is no ghost. How about I tell you a story from when I was a child? Would you be interested in that? I know it is not a fairytale, but you might enjoy it nonetheless." She offered them another biscuit from the plate and waited for them to get settled again. "Do you two remember my brother Felix?"

"He came to the wedding," Willa replied. "Mrs Archer told us he'll be an earl one day, like Lord Percy is now."

"He will, indeed, but not for a very long time, I hope. Though his title sounds very fancy, I assure you he was just as rambunctious a child as the two of you are now. I was his younger sister and he took no end of delight from causing me trouble."

"I know what that's like," Willa mumbled. Her brother responded with a blistering glare that made Grace bite back a laugh. Both Wes and Willa were equally likely to get up to no good.

"As I was saying, when I was a much younger child, younger than the two of you now, I had a problem with disappearing ink pots. My governess chastised me time and again for losing track of mine, no matter how many times I said I was not to blame. My brother told me I was slowly losing my mind, and would soon have to be locked away for everyone else's safety." Grace checked to make sure the children were paying attention.

"Something about his tone made me question whether he was telling the truth. I was certain there had to be a perfectly logical explanation. All I had to do was look for the clues to find it. The ink pots always disappeared on the days I had my piano lessons. I cried off sick at the start of one, and then hurried to my room. My ink pot was still there. I slid under my bed and kept watch to see what would happen. Not twenty minutes later, Felix crept in. He had been taking the pots and hiding them in an unused cupboard. I caught him red handed and made him confess to our governess. He ended up being the one locked up —for a week, that was—writing lines promising not to do it again. So you see, children, you should not let your imagination get away from you. Do you understand the point of my story?"

"We got it, my lady, but I won't lie. It was boring, miss, no offence intended. Couldn't you have included at least a highwayman?" Wes asked. He got to his feet and went over to the bookshelf, and then returned with an old leather-bound book in hand. "Miss Fenton's been reading us these. Maybe you can find a better idea here."

Grace did not take his criticism to heart, for her story had been designed to educate more than anything else. She opened the book at the page marked. The bookmark was made of a narrow strip of cloth, with a key attached to it with a swirl of red wax. It was a curious marker, to say the least. Grace used her finger to make the place and then went back to look at the first pages. A single name was written inside the front, the letters printed by a childish hand.

"Hannah Percy," she whispered. She flipped back to the key, studying it more closely.

"It looks like Mrs Yardley's keys," Wes said. "When we asked her, she said she didn't know what it was meant to open."

Had anyone else made the comment, Grace might not have made the connection. But she recalled, quite vividly, Wes complaining about the trunk he could not unlock.

Grace pulled the key free from the wax and closed it in her hand. She passed the book over to Miss Fenton. "I am sorry. I have just remembered something I need to do. Would you mind taking over?"

19

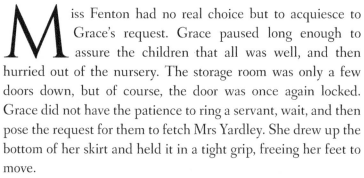

Miss Fenton had no real choice but to acquiesce to Grace's request. Grace paused long enough to assure the children that all was well, and then hurried out of the nursery. The storage room was only a few doors down, but of course, the door was once again locked. Grace did not have the patience to ring a servant, wait, and then pose the request for them to fetch Mrs Yardley. She drew up the bottom of her skirt and held it in a tight grip, freeing her feet to move.

Grace found the housekeeper on the ground floor, bustling between rooms as she checked items off the daily cleaning list. She yielded the relevant key without a single question, telling Grace only to pass it along to a footman to return to her when she was done.

Back up the stairs Grace went, her chest growing tight from the exertion. It was not the pregnancy slowing her so much as the inactivity of the previous weeks. Without her daily rides and walks, her stamina was falling short. With the weather such as it was, she was unlikely to be able to change that.

Grace took a candle from the hallway and carried it into the now unlocked room. She lifted the candle high and studied the contents. Said trunk was still in the same spot, the metal lock darkened by the patina of old age. It had to be a half a century old, perhaps even more. She lit a few more candles around the room until she had plenty of light to see. After cleaning the last remnants of wax from the key she had found in the book, she slid it into the keyhole and held her breath.

The locking mechanism fought her attempts to enter, but it was clear that the key did indeed fit. Grace was not to be deterred. She pulled the key free and gave it a final polish with the wool of her skirt. She slid it back in and wiggled it, coaxing the lock into submission. With a final grate of metal on metal, it turned over and the lock clicked free.

The creak of the hinges sent a shiver down Grace's spine, though there was nothing immediately visible to give her any concern. Much like the other trunks they had opened, this too seemed full of fabric. She pulled the top item free, filling the room with the scent of lilac, and unfolded it. It was a gown in a style long out of fashion. She held it against her body to get a better sense of the shape. The delicate colour and neckline suggested something a young woman would wear.

A debutante, Grace thought, remembering her own days this summer.

The picture of a young woman, one with dark hair and eyes, sprang into her mind. It was so far from the young girl she had imagined as Hannah that Grace could not hold onto the image. She draped the gown over a nearby trunk. When she looked again in the trunk, Grace spied the familiar ivory of foolscap.

It was a small bundle, wrapped and tied with a piece of ribbon. It was a wonder it had survived all these years. Assuming they belonged to the mysterious Hannah, had the young woman packed them away while she was still alive? Or had a maid tucked them in after her death?

There was only one way to find out.

Grace untied the ribbon and let it drop to the floor. There were three pages in total, written in a swirling, feminine hand with little regard for the cost of the material. Grace checked the name at the bottom and found exactly what she expected. Hannah had been the sender.

The answer to why Hannah had her own letters lay in the margins of the paper. The recipient had written his responses on the same pages, penning them in narrow letters written so close together that at first, they seemed like a decorative hand-drawn border.

Grace needed more light to read the small print, a cushioned chair and a roaring fire to keep her limbs from growing stiff. She made a last check of the trunk, searching for anything else unusual. Once assured she had the only item of real interest to her, she closed the trunk, clicked the latch, and left it sitting in the silent confines of the locked storage room.

She handed the door key off to a passing footman and went into her bedroom suite on the first floor. In her favourite chair, placed near the fire, she used the light of a full candelabra to read the old letters.

Hannah's parts were the easiest to read. She began with the oldest letter, judging by the date on the top.

May 25, 1765

My Darling John,

In the grey and shadowed days of Alnwick, you are the light that pierces through, the only joy that stirs my heart. When we are together, I feel alive, as if the whole world has brightened just for us. But when we are apart, it is as though all the warmth of the sun has vanished, leaving me in a cold, unending twilight. I live only in the moments we share, and all else feels like a cruel prelude to an empty eternity without you.

I have pleaded with His Grace, begged him to see the truth of our love, but he remains as immovable as the castle walls that keep me here. He speaks of duty and propriety, but it is nothing but pride that bars us. What more can I say, John? What more can I do to melt his heart? My spirit weakens with each passing day we are denied. If he cannot be swayed, I fear we will have no choice but to part forever, and that thought alone is enough to shatter me.

Yours in anguish,

Hannah

Grace could understand how trapped Hannah must have felt. Grace was a married woman, with responsibilities aplenty and a child on the way, yet even she had more hours in the day that she could fill. For Hannah, Alnwick must have been dreadfully boring. Yet, she had obviously crossed paths with this John, to whom she wrote. She was desperate for him to take her away.

But what had John thought about the matter? Grace had been warned of bad actors who would pledge their love and then leave the woman, unwed and ruined, to face the consequences on her own. She shifted the first letter closer to the candles and leaned in, with her eyes squinted, as she struggled to make out the words. Slowly, but surely, the script came into focus and she was able to mouth the words as she read them.

My Dearest Hannah,

I beg you, once again, to speak with your brother. Our love is true, and I cannot bear the thought of living without you. Surely he will see reason and grant us the blessing we need to marry. Do not lose hope—our future rests on his mercy.

Yours always,

John

Hannah's second letter, dated in early July of what she assumed was the same year, continued on in the same vein, lamenting how much time passed between their stolen hours. She begged him to run away with her.

In response to her pleas for an elopement, he cautioned her to wait. He said they should bide their time, lest risk being left to make their own way in the world. He did not have her wealth, and he feared she would regret her choice to leave it all behind.

Hannah's last letter was more cryptic.

Beloved John,

I was too overcome with joy yesterday to properly express myself. I had lived in such fear of your response to my news. I had prepared myself for the worst, and all you showed was love. You are right. We are not to be ashamed. I must find the courage to speak with the duke. He cannot deny us. Not now.

Yours, always,

Hannah

Once again, Grace recognised something of her own experiences in the letter. Could it be that Hannah had faced the same trial? She turned the page sideways to read John's response.

Dearest Hannah,

If ever there was a time to approach him, it is now. I have faith he will see things differently once you share our news.

With all my heart,

John

Something had indeed changed in their relationship, something that should have offered Hannah some sort of leverage.

Something like a child, Grace thought, resting her hand on her midsection. A child, conceived out of wedlock, the product of a love affair between a highborn lady and a poor man with few prospects. Of course Hannah would feel shame and fear. John had encouraged her to rise above that and push for what they wanted.

Had the duke refused to help his sister? Or had he done all he could, but lost her in childbirth? It was not such an unusual outcome, even if Grace firmly blocked the possibility from her mind.

But what of the child?

Grace thought of Roland, growing up alone in those large houses. Of Thorne, abandoned along with his mother. Was there yet another child of the ducal line living in the world?

Grace folded the letters and slipped them into her pocket. She checked the time. Roland would still be in his study. She set off once again at pace, barely stopping long enough to knock. Roland glanced up when she stepped inside. He was alone.

Secrets had done enough damage to the Percy family. So, she told him everything.

Hannah's letters in hand, Roland strode down the hallway towards his grandfather's suite of rooms, Grace following a step behind. The footman stationed there looked startled to see them both approaching, but to his credit, he recovered quickly.

"My lord, my lady. Would you like me to see if the duke is available?" the man asked.

"Tell him to make himself available," Roland declared stiffly, but not rudely to the footman. "If he must make himself presentable, we will wait."

But the duke was in his sitting room already, and the footman ushered them in quickly. Roland hesitated briefly in the threshold as he took in the scene—his grandfather sitting by his fireplace, without book or cup, a blanket over his lap, as if he had been staring into the fire.

"Your Grace," Roland said into the silence, uncertain about the duke's state of mind.

"What do you want, Roland?" the duke asked in a surprisingly soft, casual manner, not bothering to turn to face his grandson or the countess. His voice was steady, but distant, as if his body were here, but his thoughts were elsewhere.

Was he was lucid then? He did not seem insensible from whatever Withers had given him earlier. But as he opened his mouth to speak, the duke turned to them and his face blanked further.

"Hannah?" he asked Grace.

"No," she murmured, looking wary. "I am Grace. Your grandson's wife. Do you remember?"

The duke blinked and squinted at her. Like the break of dawn over the horizon, Roland could see recollection in the duke's face as his memory ordered itself again. "Of course, I remember," he growled, sounding much more like himself. "What do the two of you want from me at this hour?"

All of the annoyance and certainty Roland had felt rushed out in the next breath. Was there any merit in disturbing proverbial graves? The duke had told Grace Hannah was dead.

Discarding all of the rehearsed, angry lines in his head, Roland thought for a moment. "I never knew," he began instead, "you once had a sister. Hannah. You have never mentioned her. *No one* has mentioned her."

The duke lifted his chin slightly, turning back to the fire. "Only Withers might have remembered. It was a very long time ago."

Roland turned the letters over in his hands. He had skimmed just a few lines from them. It felt, somehow, almost sacrilegious to read such private words of love when they had been intended for another. But an awful suspicion lingered in his mind as the broken pieces began to fit together in his mind. A young girl who had been in love, gone from the family records without a trace?

"She was not just sent away. She was disowned. Excluded from the family." Roland was rather certain of that deduction.

The Breaker made a sound in his throat that was nearly a growl. "She was a willful, disobedient simpleton—"

"Because she fell in love?" Roland interrupted.

"Because *he* was the son of a bloody sheep farmer!" the duke roared, banging his cane against the wood for emphasis.

"Distancing yourself from scandal, sending her to the country, that I could understand. It is another matter entirely to sever things so completely—"

Grace touched Roland's arm, her brows drawing together. "Hannah was not cast out simply because she loved a sheep farmer. She was cast out because she was enceinte."

The duke's face grew grim. "She was cut off because she refused to be sent away for the birth. She refused to be sent away from *him*. And because she did not want to give the bastard up. It was an intolerable situation."

A river of emotion ran deep beneath the duke's words, but he wouldn't let it touch his face. Frowning, Roland looked at the date on the final letter, doing a quick bit of maths in his head. Gideon Percy would have been twenty and seven at the time. The same age Roland was now. "Your father was dead. *You* were the duke who pruned Hannah from the family tree."

His grandfather did not bother to deny it. Instead he gave Roland a level look. "I warned her. I told her if she insisted on going to him, that she would be dead to the line. There would be no money. I would not recognise her progeny or look after her. I tried to give her every reason to stay. To make the right choice. She chose to leave anyway."

Roland's lips parted at such coldness. "And after that, you never once looked into her situation? Her welfare?"

"Not once. Hannah died the night she skulked out, as far as I was concerned."

His grandfather clearly did not like Roland's weighted silence, for he continued, "Your great grandfather, the man who was the first Duke of Northumberland I will remind you, asked me to swear upon my own life that I would protect the title and ensure the Percy line. That I would make certain it became a force to be reckoned with. I loved my baby sister." His gaze grew hard, and he snatched at Roland's hand to pull him closer. "*I loved her*! But after our father died, Hannah became a liability to everything we had built. To willingly submit ourselves to that level of scandal... It could have cost us *everything*."

For most of his life, Roland had considered His Grace the same way everyone else did. He was the Breaker—practically a force of nature. But as he looked down upon his grandfather, he saw past the carefully cultivated, prickly facade to the tired, old man that lay beneath. The one who had sat alone at the impromptu celebration after Roland's announcement of his wife's pregnancy, and who had withdrawn when Grace had tried to draw him in.

Gideon Percy was no longer quite so fearsome. In fact, Roland pitied him.

"It seems, Grandfather, that it cost you everything important anyway," Roland said quietly. "I hope you still think it was worth the price." And he took Grace's arm to depart, leaving the duke sitting by the fireplace.

20

Urgent knocking woke Roland and Grace just before dawn.

A tad bleary, Roland collected his wits as he looked around the unfamiliar room. His wife's room. They had seldom slept separately early in their marriage, and he was happy that, with Grace's secret come to light, she was willing to go back to sharing a bed—even if she had started to snore now that her pregnancy was progressing.

Grace was slower to rise, so Roland found his banyan and opened the bedroom door a crack to find Elsie and Briggs just on the other side. "What is it?" he asked them, sensing a problem.

Briggs answered, "Miss Fenton is in a state. Your young girl, Willa, seems to be missing."

That woke Roland up entirely, and he could hear Grace struggle to a sitting position in bed. "What! Willa is missing?"

"Perhaps my lord would like to return through the adjoining door so we can... handle a discussion without bothering my lady?" Briggs suggested dryly.

"My lady is already bothered," Grace said loudly, struggling with the tangle of the sheets.

Briggs did not let out a long suffering sigh but his face clearly implied it, and he mouthed the word 'propriety' at Roland over Elsie's head.

"Yes, of course," Roland said, giving Elsie an apologetic glance as he closed the door in her face. Elsie would give him a few seconds to depart before she opened it again, and he wasted no time in moving over to his room.

Briggs strode in and began selecting new clothing, disregarding the outfit lying on the bed. One that must have been previously selected for a different sort of day's events, Roland assumed. The clothes Briggs pulled now were among the older ones Roland owned.

"I imagine you will at some point be rooting around in the darker, less kept holes of the castle," Briggs remarked in explanation. "No sense ruining a nice coat."

"Perhaps I should wear the burgundy coat then," Roland suggested, and Briggs gave him a look out of the corner of his eye. "No?"

"No."

Fortunately, Briggs did not slap Roland's hands away when Roland addressed his own hair to expedite his toilette. Small victories, he supposed.

"Miss Fenton and Wes are in the drawing room, waiting to speak with you when you are ready. I also took the liberty of rousing Sir Nathaniel. He should be joining you there to assist in anything. Hopefully you do not object."

"You did exactly as I would want," Roland assured his valet, as Briggs dusted off his shoulders and smoothed the fall of his coat. "Tell my lady where we will be."

When Briggs stepped away, indicating he was finished, Roland did not wait for Grace. He strode directly to the drawing room, opening the door to find his brother had beaten him there. Thorne was ruffling the hair of the miserable-looking Wes, clearly offering some comfort.

Roland took to a knee in front of the lad to put their faces closer to being on the level. "You must tell Thorne and me everything you can about where Willa might have gone, Wes. I promise we will not be angry with you."

Somewhat amusingly, Wes looked to Thorne for confirmation, but Roland did not take umbrage. Though the Sprouts were technically his wards, they seemed to have adopted Thorne as the nearest thing they had to a parental figure. They had flourished under Thorne's attention in Brighton, and he would not begrudge them that. Thorne was able to do many things that Roland could not.

"The noises in the castle," Wes began haltingly. "Lady Grace told us a story about how she had tricked her brother. Lord Felix was stealin' her ink pots, you see, an' getting her in trouble with the governess. Lord Felix said she was cracked, losing them herself. But she hid beneath her bed an' caught him doing it."

Roland nodded to show the boy he understood so far, and the boy wrung his hands a bit before continuing. "Willa wanted to see who was making the noises at night. She said it was prolly just the ol' duke, and she was going to go hide in your da's old room to see. The latch doesn't catch real good. It'll open if you push it right."

"And what happened then?" Roland asked Wes gently.

"I—I didn't go with her. I still thought it might be a monster... or maybe 'the Snatcher.'" Wes brought his fist to his mouth, biting his knuckle in a valiant effort to keep from crying in front of Roland. "If I wasn't such a scaredy-cat I would know. Maybe there was a snatcher, an' he took her cause I wasn't... I wasn't there."

Understanding, Roland directed his gaze at Thorne instead

to let the boy keep his dignity as Wes broke off. Thorne pulled Wes towards him, and the boy threw his arms around Thorne's waist, distraught.

"We've already checked the late Lord Percy's room, top tae bottom," Miss Fenton said when Roland looked inquiringly at her. "Where the lass has got tae, I dinnae ken."

"Easy, lad," Thorne said, resting his hands on the boy's shoulders. "Your sister might have gone wandering. Maybe she got turned around and she fell asleep in another part of the castle. Don't worry. We'll go looking for her."

"I'm—I'm sorry... Lord Percy," the boy sobbed against Thorne's chest. "You're mad at me and it—it's my fault."

"No, Wes, I am not mad at you, I do not think you are a coward, and it is most certainly not your fault Willa is lost," Roland told him, getting to his feet and gripping the boy's shoulder in sympathy. "We will find her and there will be no harm done. I promise."

Relieved, Wes turned in Thorne's grasp and hugged Roland so hard that he let out a surprised *oof*. Miss Fenton looked alarmed, and went to pull Wes away from Roland, but he stopped her. "It is all right," he said, stroking the boy's back.

The Sprouts had always been reserved around him, but Roland enjoyed being demonstrative with his brother and Grace. The boy's trust moved him, and for a moment, he caught a small glimpse of what it might be like someday to hug the child growing in Grace's belly.

It was into this tableau that Grace finally caught up with them. Seeing poor Wes' state, her face went through a sea-change of emotions from alarmed to affectionate sympathy.

"Willa was inspired by your story to catch the late-night wanderer," he explained to her over Wes' head, lifting one arm to let her approach.

Grace plucked Wes away from Roland, giving him a

squeeze and drying his face. "Well, then let us go find her. The others have started looking already. Shall you join them?"

Wes and Miss Fenton left, heading in the direction of the guest rooms, and Roland could hear people calling Willa's name. As Thorne, Grace and Roland made to join them, they were surprised when Mrs Yardley exited the duchess' suite, looking upset.

"My lord, Countess, I just discovered something that bears investigation," she said, gripping her keyring so tightly her fingers were white where the skin pulled taut. "The duchess' suite was unlocked. It is not the first time I have found it so, but before, I thought it had been a simple mistake, or perhaps a faulty mechanism."

Quickly, they hurried towards the door and the suite of rooms that adjoined the duke's. Throwing open the door, she pointed at a wall where one of the wall tapestries hung askew.

Thorne crossed the room in three steps, carefully pulling back the edge of the tapestry, revealing the edge of a dark hole behind it. "Mrs Yardley, did you know there was a passage in the wall back here?"

"I most certainly did not," the housekeeper said, affronted. "If I had, it would have been boarded up immediately!"

Roland moved to one side of the tapestry, reaching up to lift the hanging rod off its hook. Thorne lifted the other, and they carefully set the large wall hanging aside, revealing a wood-framed hatchway—one large enough to accommodate a man.

Turning to Grace, Roland asked her, "Would you please get Withers?" and then he lit one of the tapers in the room, bringing it over to have a better look. Thorne stepped back, allowing Roland to hold the candle inside.

It was cold, and the candle's flame flickered as a soft breeze disturbed the air in the passageway.

"Wherever this leads," Roland said grimly as two sets of

171

footfalls sounded behind him, "it finds its way to someplace outside."

"It leads past the outer wall." Withers sounded unhappy, and turning, Roland found the old butler standing there, jowls quivering with some emotion. "This was the secret tunnel built centuries ago to allow the Percy family to flee a siege. It has been boarded up for nearly fifty years—I ordered it done myself."

Roland touched the rough wood framing the hole, which indeed bore a few gouges and splinters from nails, hammered in and removed. And then he stuck his head back inside, seeing the remnants of the old wooden planks, set aside. "Well, clearly, it is boarded up no longer."

Thorne clenched his fists, turning to Roland. "If Willa lost her way inside the castle, it is only a matter of time before we find her. But if she went outside..."

She could freeze.

Almost as one, the men turned away from the dark hole in the wall. Thorne exited the room without a word. He didn't need to speak. Roland knew he would be bundling up, then heading to the stable. It was exactly what he planned to do himself.

"Grace," Roland told her gently. "Find someone to dress warmly and check the passage. Thorne and I will go out to check the place around the exit. I must assume that even if she had been underdressed, she could have returned before she got too cold in the passageway."

Covering her mouth with one hand, Grace nodded. "Yes, of course."

Thanks to Briggs' planning, Roland managed to beat Thorne to the stable, though not by much. The horses were already saddled and waiting, ears pricking as they picked up Roland's emotional state.

Anger would make Arion fractious. Letting himself feel the anger, however, was more productive than feeling the fear that lay just beneath it.

Thorne arrived before Roland could grow too impatient, and the men swung into their saddles, setting out at a fast trot into the biting cold. Withers had told them where the tunnel opened—near a yew tree and deliberately planted bracken that acted almost like a small labyrinth of living concealment. Behind it, the tunnel entrance had been turned upon itself. One would have to deliberately traverse a path around the nuisance plants and face the tunnel head-on to spot it.

But someone had. Roland could see, even as they approached, how the winter-withered bracken fronds lying on the ground had been crushed into the mud.

"Someone on horseback has been here, and recently," Thorne said with a grimace. He hopped down from Horse, examining the area. "Hoof prints coming and going. A man's boots." Thorne poked his head into the tunnel from this end.

"Any sign of Willa?"

"Not in the dirt. But all that might mean is that he was carrying her. The hoofprints came in from the direction of the Lion Bridge. But they're leaving to the east. If he was carrying a child, he would likely avoid the main crossing."

Arion flattened his ears, and Roland forced himself to relax, thinking. "I would be ready to wager that we have discovered our 'rat problem' and that somehow Willa and our intruder crossed paths. Perhaps he was forced to take unexpected action as a result of it. He could have killed her in that case, but he did not."

"Aye. We are missing a part of the equation. He has entered Alnwick Castle more than once, but stolen nothing that has been noticed? This person is no common thief, which begs the question... what has he been looking for? A child to ransom—or even snatch for another nefarious purpose—it does not tally well if he has been in and out of the castle more than once."

"I do not know, but we need to go back. Our intruder knew this tunnel existed," Roland said, gritting his teeth, "and I am entertaining a few unpleasant theories as to why Withers may have requested someone board up a tunnel nearly fifty years ago."

21

Fear made Grace's stomach roil. Sitting down and waiting for news was out of the question. Roland had told her to send someone through the doorway into the secret passage. Someone, but not her, was what he had implied. On this, she was in disagreement. If their child, for she thought of the Sprouts as their responsibility, was lost or hurt, she would not send a stranger to their rescue. She asked a footman to fetch Mrs Yardley.

"Are you afraid of tight spaces?" Grace asked, with no explanation, once the woman appeared.

"I am not," Mrs Yardley replied. "If you mean to enter the passageway, I will gladly accompany you. Francis," she added, turning to the footman, "Get a couple of torches and another footman. We will need plenty of light."

While they waited for the footman to do her bidding, Grace returned to the hallway in the family wing. There were no signs of a scuffle, and no drops of blood anywhere. There were plenty of hiding places for a child. Grace put herself in the young girl's shoes. Willa must have seen someone walking in the hallway and followed them. The girl was exceptionally good at moving without making a noise, a skill she had picked up while living as an orphan on the streets of London.

Perhaps that was what had happened. Someone had come in through the tunnel and left again, with no knowledge that they were being followed... except they must have noticed, for Willa had not returned to tell them what she had seen.

"A cloak, my lady," Mrs Yardley said, drawing Grace back to the present. The housekeeper wore a similar one.

Grace threw the thick woollen cloak over the simple dress she had donned in a rush. She still had her slippers on her feet. It was no matter. She was not going to go outside.

The strapping footman who had rushed off to do the housekeeper's bidding returned with an equally strong man and the requested torches. He took the lead, guiding Grace and Mrs Yardley back into the bedroom. He glanced back once, determination writ in the lines on his face, and then stepped through the hidden entrance. He disappeared from sight almost immediately, but soon called back that he had reached a staircase.

"Follow it down," Grace commanded in an unwavering voice, despite the fear freezing her bowels. "We are right behind you."

The passageway was as dark as a crypt and equally as eerie. There was no light save that which they had brought with them. The torches in the front and back fought against the shadows, their light surging forward in uneven charges, only to be repelled just as fast. The faint scent of old stone, a cold, mineral smell mingled with the dryness of dust, tickled her nose.

As promised, they reached the start of a narrow, winding staircase. Grace stretched out a hand to steady herself. The stone walls were covered with a thin layer of dust. She spotted a cobweb clinging to a corner and jerked her hand back in time to avoid it. To keep from shuddering, she focused on the small cracks in the walls that testified to the age of the passageway.

Down they went, past what must have been the ground and into the bowels of the earth. The dusty stairs turned damp in places where moisture had seeped through, leaving darker patches. It was enough to soak through her satin slippers, until her toes went numb from the cold.

The occasional drip of water from the ceiling created a faint, rhythmic sound. In some places, she heard the rustling of small creatures disturbed by her presence. Either mice or bats, she thought, though she was hard pressed to decide which was worse.

She prayed to find Willa around each bend, yet just as fervently hoped she would not. She could hardly bear the thought of the child sitting in the dark on her own. Injured... No, she refused to imagine the alternative. Willa had to be fine.

In the silence, her own breathing seemed louder, mingling with the slight hiss of air moving through the passageway. The lead footman trudged forward, as unnerved as the rest. Only sheer bravado and the women behind him prevented him from turning back.

"I see something," he called, his voice echoing off the stone walls of the passage. He held his torch high, illuminating a scrap of cloth on the ground.

Grace pushed past him, uncaring about the risk. Her mind said it was far too small to be the missing girl, but her heart drove her onward. She scooped the item up.

It was Anne Bonny—Willa's most favoured possession—tossed aside. Abandoned.

Grace clutched the doll to her chest, unable to stem the flow of tears falling down her cheeks. Keening cries filled the air. It was not until Mrs Yardley wrapped an arm around her that Grace realised she was the one making them.

"Come, my lady, it is far too cold and damp for us to continue. We will leave the footmen to carry on until they meet with Lord Percy and Sir Nathaniel." Mrs Yardley took a torch in one hand and used the other to turn Grace back in the direction in which they had come. She did not drop her arm until they reached the base of the narrow stairs. "Can you make it up on your own?"

Grace could not move. She did not know whether to give up and go back to the warmth of her chambers, or to throw off the housekeeper and charge back into the underground tunnel, her health be damned.

"You must protect the baby, my lady," Mrs Yardley murmured in a soft tone.

Her words jolted Grace out of her stupor. Protect her unborn child? The castle was meant to be a safe haven, yet someone had broken in. More than once, if the Sprouts were correct. They had complained of hearing noises on multiple occasions. Someone had been walking the halls for days. It was sheer luck that they had not been seen before. *Or, was it?*

Withers had claimed the entrance to the passage had been boarded up for nearly a half century. After all that time, what was the likelihood someone stumbled across it by chance?

No, Grace could not believe that. Whoever came in knew exactly what they were about. They had thwarted all security measures, not through luck, but through planning and care. Only Willa's midnight foray had led to their discovery.

The list of people both old and wise enough about the castle interiors had to be short. The duke had to have closed it off for a reason. Fifty years earlier, he would have been Roland's age, already carrying the title. His younger brother might have known.

Or... his sister Hannah. Hannah, who was presumed, but not proved, to be dead.

Grace took a fortifying breath and then passed Willa's doll to the housekeeper. She gathered the cloak and skirt in her hands, lifting them out of the way, and then hurried up the stairs as fast as her legs would carry her. Her thighs burned from the exertion, but she forced herself to move through the pain.

As soon as Grace and Mrs Yardley arrived back into the bedroom above, Grace turned to give a new set of instructions. "We need to know what our intruder was after. Can you have the servants check every room on this floor and the one below? They have entered more than once. Items may be missing."

"Nothing is gone, my lady," Mrs Yardley hurried to reassure her. "The staff are in and out of the same rooms, day after day. They would have alerted me of any changes."

"Search the rooms that are not in use, then. In a castle this large, there must be rooms that have not been entered in days. Pay close attention to any domains the duke claimed for himself."

Mrs Yardley bobbed her head in acknowledgement and hurried off to do Grace's bidding. Grace paused a moment longer to study her reflection in a mirror. She had a streak of dust across her cheek and a cobweb in her hair. She raised her hand to wipe them away but thought better of it. Let the Breaker see her as she was, dishevelled, frightened, and burning with anger.

Withers stood guard outside the door to the old duke's suite. Grace met his gaze head on, practically daring him to stop her. He must have seen something of her sentiments in her eyes for he shuffled out of the way.

Grace rapped twice, rapid fire, and then swung open the door. Once again, the duke sat by the fire in his sitting room. He glanced up, his face lighting up at the sight of her, but when she stalked closer, his pleasure faded, leaving behind only confusion. "Why have you come in unannounced? What is all this fuss I hear?"

Grace drew herself up straight and ignored his questions. "Who knew about the tunnel?"

The duke's brow creased. "What tunnel? There no tunnel. I made sure of it."

"The tunnel is in use again, by someone coming from the outside. Withers told us he ordered it closed nigh fifty years ago. How odd. That would be roughly the same time when Hannah snuck out to meet her lover. Did she use the secret passage in the duchess's suite to come and go with no one else the wiser?"

"That tunnel was a family secret! There for our safety, to give our family an escape route out in case of siege or attack. She could have put us all at risk, showing it to others!" The duke raised his shaking fist in anger, but he did not have the strength to keep up his rant. His hand dropped back into his lap and the fight drained out of him. He sighed heavily and turned away to face the fire. In a voice barely audible, he said, "She left me. She chose him. I will never know why."

A million and one reasons flashed into Grace's mind, but she stopped herself from voicing any of them. She was angry, but not cruel, and beating him further with his mistakes served no purpose at all.

"Someone has been coming into Alnwick Castle, night after night, using that same passageway to enter in secret. Was there anyone who knew of its existence outside of the family and Withers?"

The duke gave a slow shake of his head, still looking away.

Grace grasped the implications but she wondered if the duke did. "You claimed Hannah died that night, Your Grace. Clearly, she lived long enough to tell someone else about that tunnel. Her lover, perhaps her husband, after you cast her out? Mayhap she did it only to explain how she made her escape. I cannot imagine someone well into their seventies or eighties making that trek."

"My nephew—or niece, I suppose." He covered his face with his hand and his shoulders shook. "The child must hate me for what I did, just as their mother must have carried that same hate to her grave, if she is indeed gone."

"What if Hannah is still alive? Would you bar her return, even now, after all these many years?"

If the Breaker replied, Grace did not hear it. He wept silently.

Grace backed away on silent feet and let herself out the door. Roland stood waiting on the other side of it.

"I heard," he said. "You did not close the door all the way."

"Willa?" Grace asked, clasping her hands together, desperately hoping for good news.

"Whoever it was took her, though I do not think she was their intended target." Roland offered Grace his arm and escorted her to the stairs. "Our intruder spent a fair amount of time in my grandfather's study. Mrs Yardley found it in disarray. If it is Hannah's child, or some other relation, I cannot imagine what they wanted from there. Perhaps proof that would help their recognition—but instead they found someone to ransom for it."

22

Since they were already dressed for the cold, Roland left Grace with Mrs Yardley and took Thorne with him to head to St Michael's church. It was high time to solve the mystery of what had happened to the woman who would have been his great-aunt. The church records would be the first step in discovering what became of Hannah when she was no longer considered a Percy.

Christmas was still the better part of a week away, and given that it was the middle of the week, St. Michael's was eerily serene. The sunlight filtering through the windows was dappled by dust motes disturbed by the breeze of their entry, but they found the inside of the church otherwise empty.

A middle-aged man in a plain frock coat popped his head out of the vestry. "Lord Percy!" the man said. "Reverend Shepherd is not here at the moment. Is there something I might be able to assist you with?"

Roland didn't recognise the man. "You have the advantage of me, I am afraid, Mr..." Roland trailed off, waiting for the man to introduce himself.

"Oh, my apologies, my lord. I'm Edwin Crowther, the

parish clerk here at St. Michael's. I assist the reverend with church affairs and services."

The coincidence seemed almost too good to be true. "Church affairs, you say? Then you might be just the man we are looking for. Mr Crowther, this is Sir Nathaniel Thorne. He has been indispensable to me with several matters in Alnwick. Right now we have a bit of a minor mystery on our hands, and if you have access to the parish registers, you may be able to help solve it."

The man beamed. "It's so very good to meet you both. Yes, I maintain the registers, as you can, well... see." He lifted his hands, which were spotted with ink stains. "Where would you like to begin?"

"Perhaps the marriage records might be best to begin with," Thorne said, glancing at Roland. "Although we do not know if she got married. We're looking for any sign of a woman named Hannah marrying a man named John in 1765. And barring that, we would be looking for any sign of a child of hers, born the spring of 1766."

Hannah, the man mouthed to himself, scratching his chin. But he shook his head and gestured to the men to follow him into the vestry.

The vestry itself was cramped but tidy, and with the three men in the space, plus all the shelving, they barely fit. However Roland perched himself upon the rough wooden stool to one side of the room, and Thorne leaned against the wall behind the clerk's desk to stay out of the way. Crowther stood at the bookshelves, glancing within the covers at the first and last dates of entries. He discarded several tomes until he found the birth and marriage registers that would span the right period, and finally he took his seat with the tomes, opening them.

Wetting his fingertip idly, Crowther flipped through the pages of the marriage register, seeking the entries in 1765.

Marking the place with his left hand, he flipped forward a page, scanning the contents.

"I do not see any Hannah or John listed at all in either year, my lord. But this could simply mean she was married some place other than Alnwick," he offered. "We are not far from Scotland. Do you know if the lady eloped?"

"There is a possibility she could have," Roland agreed dourly. "Or have been married at one of the neighbouring villages. Or perhaps she was never even married at all. It was too much to hope for."

Crowther set aside the marriage register, and as he did so, the wooden front doors of the church banged shut. Lifting his head, Crowther paused. "I should check to see if someone needs assistance. Excuse me just one moment, gentlemen."

But footfalls were already coming towards the vestry even as Crowther navigated himself around the desk. Only a brief knock preceded the entry of Reverend Shepherd himself.

"Lord Percy, Sir Nathaniel!" the reverend said in surprise, squeezing into the space. To make more room, Crowther sat back down at his desk. "I was told you were seen heading into the church. Were you looking for me?"

"We were only seeking information, Reverend," Roland told the man. "Mr Crowther has been quite helpful already, so I apologise if you had other plans. I believe we will find what we are looking for, so there is no need for you to disrupt your day to assist us."

Reverend Shepherd let out a booming laugh. "Nonsense! I am happy to help if I can. Although I do have to admit I am curious—what might the, er..." he trailed off as he craned his neck to look at the page in front of Crowther, and then his eyebrows lifted in confusion. "Old baptismal records? Lord Percy, pardon me, I thought you and Sir Nathaniel were still investigating matters related to the missing children."

Crowther, who had continued perusing the ledger, ran his fingers down the list of births from both years. "I cannot find a date of baptism to a child born of a woman named Hannah in 1766. But... there is Mary, baseborn daughter of a woman named Anna—no family name is provided. She was baptised the first Sunday of May."

Thorne and Roland exchanged glances. If Hannah knew she was carrying in a child in the late summer or early fall, that child would have been born in April, or thereabouts. Hannah could have indeed shortened her name to Anna.

"Edwin, could you lend me the room?" the reverend said unexpectedly, interrupting Crowther's continuing perusal of the book. "I wish to discuss something privately with Lord Percy."

Both Roland and Thorne jerked, having forgotten Reverend Shepherd's presence while considering the information. The clerk blinked and then nodded, closing the old book as he got to his feet.

After they could hear the closing of the church front door, Shepherd turned a hard look at both men, though Roland couldn't help but notice that Thorne got the brunt of it. "Why are you looking into Hannah Percy?" the reverend asked mildly.

Roland was unimpressed by the reverend's disapproval. "It is a family matter. But I take it, then, that you are familiar with the scandal."

"Familiar with it, aye. One could say that. It all happened, of course, before I was born." The reverend looked to be only in his mid forties at best. "I do know, however, His Grace was quite adamant that the matter be kept silent and forgotten. So much so that my own predecessor made sure I was aware of His Grace's wishes before he passed on. You do not have the title yet, Lord Percy, and so neither do you have the authority to overturn the duke's wishes."

Steepling his fingers, Roland considered how to convince the reverend to cooperate. After all, he did not wish to reveal anything more about the tunnel, or Alnwick Castle's illicit visitor. "I do not wish to overturn his wishes. But it is imperative that I know what became of Hannah Percy after she left the duke."

"Is it?" The reverend looked at Roland sidelong. "She has been dead for many years. The dead do not recognise any mortal urgency, my lord."

"Dead to the line, or dead and in the ground?"

"Most assuredly, in the ground. She passed away some fifteen years ago, and I attended her funeral myself. Perhaps you should let her enjoy the peace she could not find in life, my lord."

That was a bitter revelation. No matter how much his grandfather might regret it, it was far too late for him to make amends with his sister. Still...

"I wish I could," Roland said, trying tact. "I am not at liberty to discuss all my reasons, but I assure you, reverend, I am not asking for this information for a trivial reason. Hannah Percy may be beyond time, but there is a young life at stake, not to mention that of her surviving family's."

Roland had anticipated the possibility that the reverend would be unmoved by his plea, but he still expected the man to pretend to consider it.

The reaction he got instead was wholly unexpected. "Hannah Percy conducted herself in a scandalously improper manner for a lady of her breeding, Lord Percy, and your fascination with the consequences of a lady's liaison with a man of the lower classes is nearly as outrageous as her disregard for her station. I will do naught to indulge your curiosity, and I must ask you to leave, my lord. Mr Crowther and I have other business to attend to this day, and I must lock up the office."

Surprised, Roland opened his mouth to argue.

"Lord Percy," Thorne interrupted him as he stepped around the desk, trailing his fingers on the wood. "The reverend is caught between your hammer and the anvil of the duke's wishes. There is no reason we cannot come back with the duke's permission this afternoon. But for now, Mr Harding is expecting us back."

The reverend swallowed heavily, and Roland, wondering what the devil his brother was about, slowly nodded his agreement. Shepherd opened the vestibule door for Roland, a clear invitation to leave, and Roland stepped out into the main church.

Thorne remained silent until they exited St Michael's, stepping quickly back down the street. The reverend did not follow.

"Well," Roland said slowly. "That was... odd. But I suppose you are right. It would be easier to forge a request from the duke than it would be to argue with the fool."

"We may not need to," Thorne replied, and he pulled a ledger from where it was tucked inside of the coat.

Roland let out a bark of laughter. "Sir Bastard, you surprise me. Stealing from a church? What would God think of that?"

"*Borrowed*. It isn't stealing if I do not intend to keep it, you barbarian," his brother replied peevishly. "And I suspect God will forgive me even so. There are many wrongs to set right in Alnwick, and the air is thick with deception."

Grunting his agreement, Roland held further comment as they returned to the castle and entered the foyer. Thorne continued towards his study, his brother barely pausing to shuck his coat and gloves. As they hurried past, Roland saw the drawing room's door was open, and Grace stood waiting just inside the open doorway.

"We learned a few things at least," Roland said, grabbing

Grace by the hand and taking long strides to catch up with Thorne again. Grace had to quicken her pace to a trot, but it was only for a few steps. "It seems Hannah stayed in the area, and survived to her forties at least. The question then is whether John the farmer did right by her."

Thorne threw open the study door in a hurry, nearly startling poor Mr Harding into knocking off the piles of paper forming on the table he had appropriated as his own.

"I believe he did," his brother said as he plunked the old book down on Roland's desk, flipping through pages quickly and tracing the dates. "As I was looking over Crowther's shoulder, I read a little further ahead. Here." His finger stabbed a line on the page opposite the entry about baseborn Mary, daughter of Anna.

Bertram Robson, son of John Robson (farmer), November 9, 1766

"Bertram Robson," Grace read aloud, having beaten Roland to Thorne's side. Across the room, Mr Harding paused his shuffling. "And the mother's name is not listed. You think this could be Hannah's son?"

"There are only a few reasons a clerk might leave off the mother's name, especially when he has faithfully recorded them even on the baseborn children like Mary. She might have died, or given up the child—" Roland began.

"Which she clearly did not intend to do."

"Or, she was deliberately absent for another reason. Such as obscuring a connection to the child," Thorne finished.

"Baptising a child months after his birth would also serve the same purpose." Roland dishevelled his hair again, thinking. Briggs would have a conniption next time he set foot in the hallway, so he crossed his arms over his chest instead. "Why does John Robson's name sound so familiar?"

"It is a rather common name in these parts, my lord,"

Harding volunteered from his table. He laid his hand on his ordered stack. "There are at least six in the church registry. I've got petitions from a couple of them somewhere in this."

"Was Robson not the name of the parish constable in Alnmouth? That seems like an odd sort of coincidence," Thorne added, closing the register and leaning on Roland's desk.

"If we believed it was a coincidence, we would be making cakes of ourselves," Roland muttered. "No, this fortuity was orchestrated by human hand. I will be making a trip to Robson's house at once, to see if I cannot find Bertram and learn if he knows anything about our missing girl."

Grace's eyes opened wide as she took in the light outdoors, already beginning to turn a more golden shade.

Thorne straightened. "We should ride in force. Mr Harding and Colonel Ellesmere can join us—"

"I will take Colonel Ellesmere. But you need to stay," Roland told his brother, gripping his forearm for emphasis. "Thorne, we might be grasping at straws. If we have guessed wrong, and Willa's kidnapper is still nearby..."

Roland would take leave of his senses if anything happened to Grace. Fortunately, Thorne understood him perfectly. "All right. I'll stay nearby and set a guard on Wes and Lady Grace."

"Thank you," Roland said in an undertone, ignoring Grace's apprehension. He turned to his lady wife, wishing he dared kiss her goodbye in front of Harding. Perhaps it was just as well he couldn't, because Grace looked like she might burst into tears if he did.

Had he really promised her that they would always take their risks together? A child's promise. She could not follow him now to Alnmouth and he... well, he would never know the dangers of the birthing bed.

But now was not the time to borrow trouble against the future. Roland had to settle for taking her hands, rubbing the backs of them with his thumbs. Before leaving, he gave one last order to Thorne. "Go back and keep watch on Reverend Shepherd. I am left wondering whether he was truly instructed to keep all information on Hannah from me or if it was a clever ruse to continue hiding some other bit of truth."

23

With the departure of Roland and Thorne, Grace was left behind with only the echoing silence and a sheaf of papers to keep her company. Francis, the burly footman who had led the search of the passageway had taken up guard in front of the door.

Thinking to go check on how Wes was bearing up under the strain of his sister's absence, Grace moved to set the papers aside. But before she relinquished her hold, a thought struck her.

What if Bertram Robson was not after ducal recognition, but something else?

Harding had recollected the surname. Grace shuffled through the papers, glancing at the names at the top of each. The first Robson complained of a broken fence. Harding had made a note that it had already been repaired.

The other request was near the bottom, one of the oldest in the pile. Bertram Robson's name was marked at the top of the page. Grace skimmed over the text. It took her a couple of passes to grasp all the details. The first part was a request for an amendment to his lease to allow him to convert it from strictly agricultural to mixed use. The second part outlined plans to divert a stream and convert an old barn into a mill.

A wool mill, Grace guessed, recalling Roland's mention of the constable being a sheep farmer and the carded and spun wool leaving Alnmouth.

Was this why he snuck into the castle? Had he lost his patience with the long wait and decided to seek the duke's approval directly? No, that did not make sense. If seeing the duke was his aim, he could have accomplished that in a night. Still, Grace could not let go of the thought that the request and his visits had to be connected. She got up and rang for Withers.

When he walked into the study, she asked him a question. "If someone wanted to petition His Grace, for permission or perhaps funding for some repair or project, what would be required? Previously, that is. Back when the duke handled such matters."

"They would submit a request to Mr Harding. Mr Harding does the assessment, and if he believes it is worth His Grace's review, he passes it along. If His Grace grants permission, or releases funding, he signs the petition and stamps it with the ducal seal on his signet ring." Withers pointed to an object lying atop Roland's desk. "It is there, my lady. Lord Percy claimed it after he learned of the duke's ill health."

Grace dismissed the butler and then went to pick up the ring. The object was worth a fortune, and not because of its solid gold make. With a drop of the duke's signature red wax and a single stamp, they could sign off on a sizable investment.

Or, on building permission.

What if this was what Bertram Robson had been after? It would certainly explain why he had spent so much time searching the duke's study the night Willa had caught him. He could not have known that Roland was handling business elsewhere, and had moved it. But again she returned to the question. Why now? Winter's cold breath froze the ground beneath their feet. No one would be doing any work now, not unless absolutely necessary. She checked the date on the petition more closely, noting he had submitted it in the early spring.

What if Robson got sick of waiting for permission? Might he have built the factory on his own? It seemed rather farfetched, but then again, Grace had no real clue what would go into such matters. She supposed a handyman might be capable of the woodwork, but once it was up and running, would he not need machines of some sort and workers to operate them?

The boom of Thorne's voice sounded in the hallway. Grace opened a drawer and dropped the ring inside, shutting it just as Thorne entered Roland's study.

Thorne's normally placid features had been replaced with a fiery anger that made even Grace flinch. It was entirely unlike the usually good-natured man.

He was not on his own. Thorne's good left hand had a firm hold on Reverend Shepherd's shoulder. He shoved the man into the room and kicked the door shut behind them.

With a fierce glare, Thorne ordered the man to sit and pushed him into a wooden chair.

Grace swallowed and struggled to keep her composure. Thorne was not angry with her, of course, though that hardly lessened the heated waves he was throwing about the room.

"I presume there is a reason you, err, escorted Alnwick's rector here, Sir Nathaniel. Would you care to enlighten me?"

Grace's cool tone went a ways toward banking Thorne's anger. "Certainly, my lady. Not long after Lord Percy set off for Alnmouth, the reverend dashed back to the parsonage and began packing a bag. I happened to overhear him telling his wife not to expect him back and that he would send word when he could. Before he made a break for the wilds, I thought we might want to have one last conversation with him."

"I was leaving for a short trip, sir. Am I not allowed to visit parishioners?"

"The bag of sterling hidden away in your things suggests a very different destination." Thorne reached into his coat pocket and pulled free a velvet bag. He poured the contents onto a side table. Shiny coins in gold, silver and copper gleamed under the candlelight. "This is more than a man of the church would earn in several years. Either you have been helping yourself to the village tithes or are involved in something lucrative, and likely illegal since you have hidden it from the world. Which is it?"

Reverend Shepherd turned to Grace, his hangdog expression pleading for her to intervene. Grace stood firm, crossing her hand over her chest and giving him a snooty glare of her own.

"Either way you are going to prison. Let me make the situation clear to you. Someone has broken into the castle and kidnapped a child. We have every reason to believe that our kidnapper is connected to Hannah Percy. Given the life of my ward is at risk, I might find it in my heart to suggest clemency should you aid our search. What do you, Mr Robson, and a wool mill have to do with our missing girl, Willa?"

Shepherd hunched in on himself, any thoughts of blustering gone out of him. "I had no idea Robson was planning to take anyone from the castle, Lady Percy. You must believe me on that!"

"But you admit it is him?"

Shepherd shrugged his shoulders but then gave a nod of agreement. "If your search has brought you to Hannah then his is the next logical doorstep. I can offer some hope, however. If he has put her with the other children, then she should be unharmed."

"*Other children?*" Thorne swung around to tower over Shepherd. "Do you mean to tell me that you have known the location of Northumberland's stolen children all this time?"

Shepherd blanched and sucked in his lips as though trying to retract his words.

Grace dropped her haughty pose and reached out to lay a hand on Thorne's arm. "Though I share your outrage, you shall give the man an apoplexy before we learn all we can. Let us all sit so Reverend Shepherd can tell us this story from the beginning."

Grace chose a chair a safe distance away from the rector. Though he seemed harmless enough now—terrified, if she was being honest—she had learned the hard way there were risks of being within arm's reach of a villain. Thorne stayed closer to the man's side, not wanting to risk he might make a second attempt at running. Grace was less concerned about that risk than she was that Reverend Shepherd might expire on the spot. She needed to bring the tension down, and soon.

"I am simply parched from all the worrying I have done today. Would either of you mind if I rang for tea?"

Thorne gave her an incredulous look, his eyebrows nearly up to his hairline. Reverend Shepherd, however, latched onto any hint of geniality just as she thought he would.

"Yes, please, though I may require something stronger before we reach the end."

Thorne poured a finger of his favourite whiskey for both himself and Shepherd while they waited for the tea tray to arrive. Shepherd accepted it with a fervent thanks and then stared into the glass bottom as though in search of a way out. Thorne left his sitting on the table, paused beside Grace's chair and whispered, "Roland has left for Alnmouth, not knowing that the children are hidden at his destination. Is now the best time to cling to manners?"

"Patience," Grace told him. "It is better to set out armed with knowledge. Besides, I do not think this will take too long. The man is a coward."

Shepherd tossed the whiskey back, hardly pulling a face at the raw alcohol. Despite expectations, he was an old hat at imbibing strong drink. "I have feared this day for so long, I can hardly believe it has come. For a while there, I almost believed I would get away with it all. More the fool me," he muttered.

"How did you come to be involved in this matter?" Grace asked. "I must say it is not obvious that someone of your vocation would find himself caught up in an illegal kidnapping ring."

"My confession to you must start much earlier than the current sins. Truly, the Percy family owns almost as much blame as I do." Shepherd held up a hand to ward Thorne off. "Lord Percy, that is the former lord, Thaddius Percy, suffered much in the isolation of the northern wilds. Far from his normal cohort, if he wanted to carry on with his craven lifestyle, he was in need of someone here to join him. He recruited me, first. Then others, Ellesmere for example, to play cards, dice, and other games of chance. Thaddius was a careless player, more interested in passing the time than winning each hand. I took advantage, landing pot after pot until I collected the tidy sum you see there."

"Robson was a part of this group?" Thorne asked.

Shepherd threw back his head and barked a laugh. "Sadly no, though he tried to find himself upon the fringes of it. When his mother died fifteen years ago, Bertram found the last piece of the jewellery Hannah had taken with her, tucked in a handkerchief embroidered with the Percy lion. John Robson was forced to explain the whole sordid past, and Bertram was, predictably, rather unhappy once he learned the truth. Better fortune could have so easily spilled upon his family."

Grace's heart sank as the rector confirmed her worst fears about Bertram's interest in the family. How deep did it go? Would he take out his anger and jealousy on poor Willa? Worse yet, Grace could somewhat understand his motivations. The Breaker's decision to cast his sister out into the cold had a ripple effect right into the present.

Reverend Shepherd was still talking. "After that, Bertram aspired to a better life than that of his father's. He believed it was his right. And he conceived of a way to stand upon his own through the profit of industry. He finally found a way to bend Thaddius' ear with a plan to prepare for the next spring's shearing. The earl, while in his cups, at any rate, seemed agreeable. So Robson applied for permission to build the mill... I assume you know that part."

"We do," Grace confirmed. "That permission did not come, however."

"And then the earl passed, and the duke's cruel silence was answer enough. Bertram's request was denied. So he came to me with an ultimatum. Either I helped him get the approvals, one way or another, or he would out me to the village as a wastrel and a gambler."

"Would anyone have believed him?" Thorne asked.

"Could I take that risk?" Shepherd replied. "My only saving grace was that Bertram was unaware of how much coin I had stashed away."

"But why did he begin stealing children?" Grace asked, unable to figure that part out.

"Greed? Why else? The profit would be better with borrowed children—"

"*Borrowed* children!" Thorne nearly roared, and then his face tightened as another thought crossed his mind. "You are the one responsible for appointing the parish constables. A striking convenience that this year Bertram Robson would be chosen to serve."

The reverend's eyes closed. "Yes, well, lest you think too poorly of me, I thought it was only to conceal his mill. I didn't piece together the rest until after the third child went missing. My head was well and truly in the noose by that point, but at least I did what I could to ensure the children were kept fed, clothed, and relatively comfortable, and I did *not* make it my business to inquire in such matters that might change things regarding the children's safety. Or mine."

"You could have done far more, reverend. If anything happens to a single one of those children, I will personally ensure you suffer the same injury," Thorne said, his tone icy.

Grace, too, found she had no appetite to continue the conversation. With the reverend's confession, they had solved not one, but two mysteries.

But... Only if they got word to Roland, however. If Roland only went as far as Bertram's home, he might never even know the children were there.

Grace leapt to her feet, startling both men, and hurried over to Harding's desk. She picked up the page she had been studying before and passed it over to Thorne. "Nathaniel, you must take Mr Harding and ride after Roland. If Roland does not know about the mill, he might not find Willa."

Thorne took the page, but did not move, looking deeply conflicted. Grace knew he was unwilling to leave her without some form of protection, particularly if they kept Shepherd in their midst.

Grace's patience shattered. She all but ran to the study door and threw it open wide. Francis, the footman, leapt out in front of her, his arm raised to enter the fray. She grabbed hold of his arm and pulled him inside.

"Take Reverend Shepherd into the wine cellar and lock him

inside. Station someone on watch to ensure he remains. And then come back here, and resume your duties as guard."

"Are you sure, Grace?" Thorne asked, dropping all pretence with her in a rare unguarded moment.

"Please. Roland needs you. Willa needs you, Nathaniel. Take Harding, the stableboys, whomever you need to bring the children home safe. I will take Wes and we will hide away in the castle. Francis can protect us should Robson be foolish enough to attempt a repeat visit through the hidden passage."

24

The sun was creeping steadily towards the west, falling behind some low clouds on the horizon as Roland approached the Robson farm with Colonel Ellesmere.

The farm was cold and quiet, the stone walls dusted with frost, and the pastures a dull, wintry brown. A hundred or so head of sheep huddled together in the shelter of the dry-stone walls and sparse hedgerows, and the small nearby stream that bordered the property on one side before it joined the Aln was still trickling beneath a thin glaze of ice, still feeding the troughs.

The Robson family had leased this parcel of nearly 100 acres for generations. Roland knew that Bertram had assumed the lease when his father, the love of Hannah's life, had himself passed a handful of years previously.

Did Bertram have Willa concealed in the walls of the farmhouse? When he had begun this journey, it had seemed a more certain thing. But now, he was riddled with doubt. The thick-walled stone cottage that sat near the front of the property seemed too quiet and small to hold Willa against her will.

Roland's lip curled as he thought back to when they found the Sprouts and he had managed to capture the girl. She had been dressed as a boy, then, and had done her best to bite Roland.

His amusement faded quickly, because if they were wrong, and Willa was not here, then he feared they would not be able to find her at all.

"Are you most certain of Mr Robson's involvement, Lord Percy?" the magistrate beside him asked, echoing his doubts.

"Yes," Roland said with more firmness than he felt. He could not be certain that Bertram Robson himself was guilty of kidnapping Willa. "He is the child of Hannah Percy. If he was not the one who used the tunnel to trespass in Alnwick Castle, he would have been the one to tell the person who had."

The magistrate nodded, accepting that logic as sound enough and, without further conversation, the two of them approached the farmhouse. Bertram answered to Ellesmere's knock, his eyes widening as he saw who stood at his threshold.

"Lord Percy, Colonel Ellesmere!" Quickly, the man backed out of the doorway, throwing it wide enough to allow them to come inside. Roland's hopes plummeted. If Willa truly was here, surely Bertram would not have been so quick to invite them unexpectedly into his home.

Colonel Ellesmere stepped across the threshold first, and Roland followed so that Bertram could shut his door. The inside of the rough cottage, he could not help but notice, showed no signs whatsoever of a woman's touch. No festive boughs of greenery on the mantle, or even a simple wreath.

"I am surprised to find you here. What may I do for you? Shall I make some tea?" he asked the men.

The signs of Hannah's influence upon the man's life had always been there for the viewing, Roland realised. Mr Robson's voice held the accent of the countryside, but it lacked the heavy burr of the rural farmers, his diction steady and clear. He had a body used to doing hard labour, but he held his back and shoulders straight, without slouching or leaning.

Roland shook his head, declining the offer of tea. "I wish to know, Mr Robson, whether you might have something to do with the kidnapping of the young girl who is my ward from Alnwick castle. I am prepared to offer a sum for her return and would be inclined to request clemency from the magistrate as long as she is hale and unharmed."

Bertram's mouth had parted in shock at Roland's first words, but the man's face quickly hardened into suspicion. "You must be jesting. Lord Percy, I can't even begin to imagine why you would show up at my door and accuse me of such a thing."

"Because your mother was a woman by the name of Hannah Percy, was she not?"

The man's face paled, but he grew grimmer. "She wasn't a Percy at all, my lord. My mother was Anna Robson, the wife of a sheep farmer."

Soul-deep cracks lay beneath those simple words. Flaws in the man's facade that stood brittle, threatening to shatter. Roland remembered how he had discovered the same cracks in Thorne only the week before, when he had told his brother he was still a man worthy.

Bertram straddled two worlds and found himself shut out from one. How close might Thorne's life have been to Robson's, had he never intervened between Thorne and Thaddius?

"She may not have been able to claim her name and heritage," Roland agreed. "But you knew who she was."

Unexpectedly, Bertram laughed, the sound bitter. "No, actually, I never truly did. My father and mother didn't breathe a word of it. Not once. Can you imagine, Lord Percy, what it was like to find out the truth only once she was dead? To discover your whole life was a lie only once you couldn't ask why she never told you?"

"I cannot. But I imagine it was even more shocking than me learning these last few days that my grandfather cast out his expecting sister."

Bertram's face creased. "You didn't know either? How amusing. I wouldn't have imagined we had so much in common, my lord."

"It does seem that the last two Percy generations kept far too many secrets," Roland agreed wryly. "Such as the hidden passage your mother used to meet with your father. I implore you, cousin. If you told anyone about it... if you know anything at all about Willa's disappearance—"

Bertram reared back as if slapped, and Roland knew that he had erred in extending that tentative, informal recognition. "How dare you mock the suffering my mother endured at the hands of the Percy family by calling me that. As if your small act of philanthropy with an orphan child forgives all of the sins of the Breaker."

"Mr Robson—" the magistrate rumbled, trying to stave off an argument.

Bertram thrust out his hand, palm upwards, inviting Roland and Ellesmere to search his home. "You wish to look for yourself? Be my guest. You will not find your ward here. Look your fill at my three small rooms, and then go home to your castle, *cousin.*"

Roland opened his mouth to argue, but then closed it. He had promised both a reward and a modicum of grace if Bertram could reveal Willa. Either the man truly did not have her... or ransoming her back to Roland was never in the cards.

Stomach cold, he nodded slowly and traversed the rooms of the cottage, checking every cranny and listening for someone hidden beneath the floorboards. Ellesmere, conducting the same search, shook his head when both returned to the main room.

Willa was not there.

Frowning, Roland paused, buying time as he struggled to think about what to do next. Ellesmere was drawn to the window while Roland pondered, and as he pulled back the curtain, the sound of approaching hooves outside grew louder.

"Lord Percy!" a voice shouted, and Roland started as he discerned Thorne's voice.

Roland did not even glance at the men to excuse himself. He found himself outside before he knew what he was about, nearly running to his brother and grabbing Horse's bridle. "Thorne? Why are you here? Has something happened to Grace?"

"Be easy. She is fine," Thorne told him, not throwing his leg over to dismount. "I am very glad, though, that we caught you before you and Ellesmere left, because your lady and I discovered more to the story."

Mr Harding and one of the sturdier stableboys gave their greetings to Lord Percy from atop their horses, and the stableboy took the reins of Mr Harding's mount, allowing the steward to get down.

"Is Mr Robson here?" Harding asked, a note of urgency in his voice.

"He is inside with the magistrate. Will one of you two tell me what the devil is going on?"

Thorne explained the barest bones of what he and Grace had learned from the reverend, and Harding withdrew the paper with Robson's request to alter the terms of the lease from the case in his possession. Roland was so stunned and incensed, he took Mr Harding's mount back from the boy, kicking the horse into a trot as he moved towards the distant outbuildings perched at the river's edge on the back end of the property.

Thorne's Horse quickly overtook Roland's borrowed beast, and his brother managed to dismount and throw open the old barn doors just as Roland trotted up.

"Willa!" Thorne shouted. "Are you back here?"

There was a little silence that lasted a hundred years, and then a high-pitched, tentative, "*Mr Thorne?*"

Roland's heart squeezed into his throat, and cursing, he and Thorne nearly tripped over one another to round a rather large bale of wool standing between them and Willa's voice. As they did, they found a scared-looking but defiant Willa, holding a heavy carding paddle in one hand like a mace, and a boy who might have been six years old under her other arm.

Willa let out a small cry of relief when she saw them, dropping her makeshift weapon and throwing herself at Thorne. Thorne swept her up, letting her cling to him like a monkey for a long moment. Roland coughed, smiled faintly, and turned to count the other small faces that were staring at him, uncertain if he posed a threat.

"Are you all right?" Thorne asked the girl, finally setting her back on her feet. "Did Mr Robson hurt you—any of you?"

Willa reordered her face into a mulish scowl, as if annoyed to be caught looking frightened at all. "Naw. He kept us, but he didn't hurt us. He fed us as long as we kept combing the wool, and didn't even need to lock us up," she said unhappily. "None of 'em knew where we were and they ain't dressed for the weather. I thought about trying to run off to find help, but I didn't want to leave the tykes alone."

She was the oldest of the seven children in Robson's makeshift mill, and clearly she had taken charge of the sprats.

"That was very brave of you, staying and taking care of them," Roland told her, and she pulled a face.

"It didn't feel brave," she admitted. "I bet Lady Grace would've found a way to get word to you."

She didn't see Thorne's face as he goggled in disbelief at her, and that was fortunate, because Roland barely kept a straight face as it was. "The countess," he reminded her gently, "is a woman grown, and you are not. Also, my lady has *clearly* neglected to mention the several times Sir Nathaniel and I have come to her rescue—without her help."

Her lips curled at that. "Like you did for me!"

"Just so," Thorne muttered behind her, but he ruffled her hair affectionately. "But what happened? Wes said you were trying to find whoever was making noise."

"Aye, and I found 'im. Mr Robson snuck into the duke's office, looking for something in the drawers."

"Grace thinks he was looking for your grandfather's ring," Thorne expanded.

"Guess he didn't find it an' that's why he was so mad," the girl remarked nonchalantly. "I saw him go back through the tunnel, and I followed, hoping I could get a better look at him. But I tripped on a rock and the geezer heard me." Willa grimaced. "He grabbed me then and took me with 'im so I wouldn't be able to tell on him."

Roland would have asked more, but he noticed one of the younger boys shivering. The barn door, thrown open with such haste, still stood open, letting the cold air in, and Roland was reminded about his anger towards Bertram. "Would you look after the gaggle for a few minutes more? Thorne and I have to settle matters with Mr Robson," he told her.

Willa nodded solemnly, and Thorne took off his scarf, wrapping it around the shivering lad. "Huddle together and stay warm. We'll be back shortly."

By the time they crossed back to the cottage to the unhappy cluster of men waiting outside, Roland was considering the merits of abandoning propriety so he could punch Bertram squarely in the nose. Fortunately, Thorne felt no such inhibitions, and he laid Bertram Robson out in the winter-dead grass with a single blow across his jaw.

"Sir Nathaniel!" barked Roland. "I *would* like to be able to put some questions to Mr Robson before you spindle him a little too much."

Colonel Ellesmere went to intervene between them, but Thorne was already stepping back, shaking out his right hand. Robson was a little dazed but not unconscious, and Roland could not be certain that would still have been the case if Thorne's arm hadn't been broken earlier that year.

"Yes, Mr Robson had the beginnings of a mill," he explained to Harding and Ellesmere. "We found seven children there, including Willa, and a great deal of washed and raw wool."

"*Why*?" Thorne asked the man. "Why would you take people's children? You could have hired hands."

Robson got to his feet a little unsteadily, and he gave Thorne the most venomous look Roland had ever seen turned upon his brother. "I know who you are, Sir Nathaniel. Bastard son of the late earl. Tell me, how does it feel to know that without this Lord Percy's outstretched hand, you would have nothing at all?"

Thorne looked stricken, and Roland knew that Robson had cut straight through to the scabs of Thorne's own half-healed wounds with those words. "You are wrong, Robson," Roland said regretfully. "I did intervene in Sir Nathaniel's life to spare him from my father's persecution, but he was always free to make his life afterwards. What he has, he earned with his sweat and blood."

"How fortunate for your brother," choked Bertram Robson, sounding unconvinced. "I, too, wanted to make my own life. A better one than my father's. I could have done so even without that outstretched hand."

"The reverend told us he wanted to become a man of industry," Thorne told Roland. "To stand on his own feet."

"Aye, Lord Percy. And to afford to do so, I sold the last things I had of my mother. I suppose you might argue I had a helping hand from the Percy family after all," Robson said, his voice grief-stricken. "All I needed was the duke's seal, and we would have been at quits. But then your father died, and with him, all agreement to sign the request to change the lease. To build the mill. Not that I didn't still try, but the requests went unanswered. My mother has been dead for fifteen years, and still the duke continues to punish me for her sins."

Sudden understanding rippled up Roland's spine. "So your next thought was to forge the approval yourself. The duke did not deny your request, Robson. The duke—" he stopped, before he could confess in front of everyone that his grandfather was mentally unsound.

"There was a regrettable lapse in paperwork, Mr Robson," Mr Harding volunteered. "After the former Lord Percy passed, your request never found its way to the duke."

A soft moan of comprehension tore itself from Robson's throat, and he dropped his face into his hands. "Small comfort, that it wasn't a personal slight. It ruined me nonetheless. All I had—every penny—trapped in the promises of wool and a mill that I couldn't build. So to answer your question, Sir Nathaniel, I couldn't afford to hire hands. I've merely been trying to recoup my funds before the wool rotted. As you doubtless might guess from the bales of wool remaining, I have not been turning a great deal of profit."

"He was late on his last quarterly rent," Mr Harding whispered in an undertone to Roland.

"We have a confession of guilt, it seems," the magistrate said when the silence dragged on, wiping off the ice crystals forming on his moustache. "It's regrettable that so much ill has come from what sounds like a misunderstanding and an unfortunate series of events. Housebreaking. Kidnapping. Attempted forgery and not to mention breaking your lease agreement. Usually, the punishment for such actions is severe, Robson. Lord Percy, since one of these children was your ward, what punishment do you think Robson merits?" Ellesmere asked him, giving Roland a say.

Robson wasn't looking at the magistrate. He was holding Roland's gaze.

The man's face held all the same terrifying resignation that Roland had seen in his mentor, Sir David, when he was caught for his crimes. But unlike Sir David, Robson was not holding a knife to an innocent person's throat. No. This time, Roland felt like he was the one holding it.

And Robson, silent, waited for a third generation of the Percy family to change his life for the worse.

"I forgive any slight against the dukedom, but I cannot countenance the kidnapping of children." Roland tore his gaze away, looking towards the sun setting on the horizon. "We are not discussing punishment. We need to consider the matter of justice. How do we serve justice here? For the moment, I shall freely admit it. I have no earthly idea."

25

The matter of Bertram Robson's punishment proved to be more complicated than anyone imagined. By law, the magistrate could sentence him to death by hanging. Transport to the penal colonies was another option. Some in town felt he deserved the worst the law could throw at him.

Roland, however, was less sure. After listening to his logic, Grace found herself in agreement with his position.

Robson had done wrong in kidnapping the children. Of that, there was no doubt. But he had not ended up mired in the mud of misdeeds without a little help from the Percy family.

Grace had counselled her husband to speak with Ellesmere about the matter. And so he had gone off and come home a scant hour later, with a hangdog expression marring his handsome face.

"Ellesmere says it is out of his hands. If he lets Robson get away with such a high crime, the people in Northumberland would rise up in arms. Nevermind that the children returned home in good condition. Their families went through hell and back during their absence."

Ellesmere's reply gave Grace the start of an idea. She sat behind Roland's desk, helped herself to a fresh piece of foolscap and a sharpened quill, and penned a note to the magistrate with a suggestion. Roland raised his eyebrows, but he had nothing to lose.

Ellesmere agreed.

On the afternoon before the longest night, the castle gates opened wide, allowing a half-dozen local families inside. Withers showed them to the drawing room, where a toasty fire and Lord and Lady Percy awaited their guests.

Garlands of fir and holly hung around the doorways and across the mantles, while beeswax candles made up for the weak light of the winter day. The castle smelled of a warm and inviting blend of fresh evergreens, wood smoke, and spices, all mingling with the subtle sweetness of candles and dried fruits. Grace adored the rich, layered scent that brought to mind the cosy festive seasons of her childhood.

In preparation for the event, the drawing room furniture had been rearranged into a concert salon of the style Grace remembered from her days among the London ton. Settees and chairs sat in short lines in one half of the grand room, while tables of food and drink beckoned from the other. Grace and Roland plied their guests with tea, hot chocolate, and fresh baked goods, doing their best to bring everyone into good humour.

As for the guests, they were the parents of the six children Robson had kidnapped in the dead of the night. Grace took time to speak with each one of them, inquiring about how their children fared, and commiserating about how difficult it had been to live with the fear of their absence. On any other day and at any other occasion, those farmers and labourers would have never dared to speak so openly to the Lord and Lady of the castle. But somehow, the shared experience of the missing children had bridged the gap between their stations.

After a while, the magistrate invited everyone to take a seat, so that they might discuss the fate of Bertram Robson.

The parents, dressed in what passed for their Sunday best, took the places in the front three rows. Roland and Grace did the opposite of what was expected, waiting until last to sit down at the back.

Colonel Ellesmere gave a polite cough into his fist to call the attention of the room. "Good afternoon, lord, ladies, and gentlemen. As magistrate, it is my duty to ensure peace is kept, and to uphold the law against those who dare to break it. You are all here on the matter of Bertram Robson's crimes."

A few people grumbled under their breath, but none so loud as to interrupt him.

"Had he hurt, or killed, any of the children, I would have already seen him swing for his crime. Because he did not, I have some latitude in my verdict. Lord and Lady Percy have suggested that you, the wronged, have a voice in his punishment. Though this is certainly unusual, I am of the mind to abide by their suggestion. Before I ask your opinions, Lord Percy begs a moment of your time. Lord Percy?"

Colonel Ellesmere waved Roland to the front of the room. Grace watched, along with their guests, as her husband crossed the floor. She had to give Briggs credit for choosing Roland's clothing well. His suit was made of the finest brushed wool and in the latest cut, but his cravat was tied simply and his hair mussed from running his fingers through it too often. The dark colour of the fabric and lack of other adornment allowed Roland to almost blend in with the others.

At the front of the room, Roland grabbed a wooden chair from against the wall and placed it so he could face their guests. He sat down and surveyed the room.

"Before you decide Robson's punishment, I want to give you all my apology."

"You?" a woman said, her voice heavy with confusion. "You did your best, my lord, and brought 'em all home, you did."

"True though that may be, your children might never have been taken in the first instance had the Percy family—my family —not done the first wrong. Some of you may know the story. Others will not. Bertram Robson's mother was Hannah Percy, the sister of the duke. When she was barely seventeen, and not long after her father passed, she fell in love with a man below her station. My grandfather cast her out. He struck her name from the family records and considered her dead, despite knowing she was heavy with child." Roland stopped to clear his throat. "Both the duke and my father made many decisions with which I do not agree. My grandfather believed strength and power came from eradicating flaws. In doing so, they failed in their duty to all of you."

Finally, a burly man with a thick black beard raised his voice from the back row. "So it's true, eh? I heard tales but I didn't put no ken to it. What do you want from us now? To save his neck?"

"The colonel has asked for your opinions, and I will not stand against you, should hanging be what you demand. But I want you all to know the full truth. Robson did not set out with the intent to kidnap children. He invested in the materials for the millwork, expecting approval from my father during his tenure as steward. After my father's ill-timed death, Robson had no choice but to press on with his request. His petition landed in a growing mountain of items needing approval from my grandfather. Like many other projects in Alnwick, that approval did not come.

"The rest of the locals waited patiently for my grandfather to do his duty and arrange for repairs and approvals. Bertram misunderstood the silence. He believed the duke was punishing him, just as the old man had punished his mother all those years ago. In utter desperation, facing ruin, Robson made a horrible, foolish, wicked decision. But his was not the first error. That honour belongs to my grandfather."

Grace laced her hands together and squeezed to keep from rushing to Roland's side. Silence stretched tauter than her nerves.

"Colonel Ellesmere asked me what punishment did I believe Mr Robson merited for his crimes. I told this dark chapter of my family's history, because I believe we cannot pass judgement on Mr Robson without considering the whole story. To pass judgement without it—that would show no compassion. It would not be an execution of justice. Only retribution.

"For this reason," Roland said in a soft tone, "I wish to propose another path for your consideration. That is, if you all will give me the opportunity to do so."

Grace watched as the couples leaned their heads together, first with their spouses and then with their neighbours. She caught a couple of the women glancing her way, but she took care not to influence them one way or another.

The bearded man kept shaking his head. He had his mind made up, and was not interested in hearing any of Roland's pleas, no matter what the reason. Most of the rest of the parents seemed unsure, until a tall man with a lean frame spoke from the other side of the drawing room.

"Lord and Lady Percy suffered the same as the rest of us, even if for a shorter time. None of our children would be home if it weren't for their efforts, which started, I remind you, before their ward went missing. I can't see any harm in letting the lord speak. Anyone who disagrees is a fool."

Grace braced herself for a battle, but the bearded man held his tongue.

Colonel Ellesmere, choking back a laugh, stood again. "I

will give you the first two options—death by hanging, or transport to a penal colony for a term of no less than seven years. Now, Lord Percy, what do you have to add?"

Again, Roland remained seated. On this, he had taken counsel from Thorne. Appearances went a long way. If Roland rose, some might see it as him lording his station over the rest of them. By staying in his chair, he positioned himself as, perhaps not their equal, but at least as someone who had shared in their experiences.

"Robson's original intention was to build a mill and hire local hands. None will work for him now, no matter what I say. So I propose we allow him to serve his sentence in a different manner. First, there is the matter of the mill where your children laboured. Regardless of what sentence you choose for him, the mill will become yours. What income it brings will go toward providing a future for those children."

"Even if he swings?" the bearded man asked.

Roland swallowed but gave a nod of confirmation. "The land belongs to the Percy family. I give you my word that this will be so. Let us move on to Robson's punishment. The Old Testament speaks of an eye for an eye, but the New Testament cautions us to forgive and allow he who did wrong to make amends. If we load Robson onto a boat bound for the penal colonies, we achieve eye for an eye. But what if we sent him to America instead?"

"To America? How is that fair?" This time it was the level-headed man who spoke up.

"Robson has a head for business, and my father clearly agreed. Things might have been very different if he had not died with this business unresolved. For everyone. That mill would have brought jobs and income to families like you.

"It is our error that kept it from happening, and our error that nearly ruined Robson financially as a result. I do not

215

absolve him for his choices. But I would argue that hanging him might also be unfair, when in the context of the entire story. The Percy family needs to make amends. We would send him there to oversee an investment. He would have enough money to cover room and board, but nothing else. Like our children, he would be torn away from all he knows and all those he holds dear. And in the meantime, the yield from our investment would come back to the people of Northumberland. It would pay for a proper lawman, to make sure something like this cannot happen again. This, I think, might be justice done.

"Before I let you decide, there is a last matter to be discussed. During our searches, I promised a reward to whoever found the children. All of you and many others set aside urgent tasks to lend a hand. In recognition of your efforts, I will make good on my promise. A portion of next year's sheep shearing will be donated to the village school. Let there never be a moment's doubt as to whether Castle Alnwick treasures the children of Northumberland."

Having said his piece, Roland stood and walked back to where Grace sat. She laid her hand in his, and together, they exited the drawing room, leaving the magistrate to oversee the final discussions and announce his verdict.

"Do you think they will hang him?" Roland asked, holding Grace tight against him in the quiet of his study.

Grace did not have time to reply. A footman knocked on the door, calling them to return almost immediately.

Colonel Ellesmere's expression gave no hint as to Robson's fate. Grace clung tight to Roland's arm, her legs shaking with fear for the man she both despised and understood. Wrong upon wrong upon wrong would never make things right. But would these parents, those most hurt, find their way to forgive?

"Robson will go to America, my lord," Ellesmere announced in a gravelled tone. "The good people here ask that you put all your commitments in writing, so there can be no question about them in the future. If you do all you have said, they will give Robson a second chance."

Roland squeezed Grace's arm against his side, but took great care to keep a solemn expression on his face. "I had the documents drawn up on the chance you would accept my proposal. With your permission, I will bring them here, so that you may all witness their signing and sealing."

With that, for the first time in weeks, Grace felt at peace.

26

After the events of the week, the night before Christmas was a quiet one. Grace seemed to have more energy during the day, but she was often half-asleep at the dinner table in the evening, and went to bed long before Roland was ready to turn in.

He had taken to spending the long evenings with his brother, often in silent company in his study, as they worked on their own pursuits. Tonight, they lingered at the table and enjoyed drinks and conversation.

"I'm glad you don't insist on port after dinner," Thorne said, playing with the rim of his glass of whisky.

Roland snorted. "Not here, not with you. And I will admit, I am not particularly fond of it either. But you should learn to cultivate a palate for something better suited than that swill, at least. You are a proper gentleman now, after all! Port is for camaraderie and manly conversation."

One side of Thorne's face curled in a sardonic smile. "It might be swill to those high in the instep, but I believe even they would hesitate to describe whisky as 'unmanly.' Certainly not in front of any Scotsman, at least."

Roland stretched out one leg, grinning at the image of what would likely result. No doubt, it would end the way Bertram Robson had, stretched out upon the lawn. Although as satisfying as that moment had been, it felt hollow now. Now, he only felt bad for what the man had endured.

How alone he was in the world. How much more so he would be, once sent to his virtual exile across the Atlantic.

"You seem easier now than you did when you arrived. I trust things are better now between you and Grace?"

"Can you actually believe she was afraid to tell me we would have to delay our plans to leave Alnwick? Am I really so fearsome?"

"You aren't," Thorne smirked. "But given the tender relationship between you and the Breaker, I cannot blame her for fearing the knowledge you would be extended guests might make your head pop right off."

Roland rolled his eyes expressively, tossing back his brandy, and Thorne considered his brother a moment. "You talk about you and Grace, but you haven't really said much else on the subject of her having your child. Just how do you feel about the idea of being a father?"

A small twist of nerves fluttered in his stomach, and he scoffed a laugh. "Curiously elated... and a little bit terrified, both at the same time. You know, it is not as if I never experienced fear in my lifetime. But this year, it feels as if we have made a rather different acquaintance. How can I be so suddenly afraid of a hundred different things I never even conceived of eight months ago? How can any person be worthy of the trust of rearing another life?"

Thorne's gamine smile made Roland hear his own words, and Roland scowled at his brother before he could hoist him with his own petard.

"Yes, clearly many fools have somehow muddled through it,

and you think I am being ridiculous. But now, you—you are a natural as a father. I see how the Sprouts are with you, and I wish..." he frowned, losing the sense of what he was trying to say. "I do not know what I wish. All I know is that I envy you a little bit. When I think about being a father to my child the way you are with them, I feel... inadequate."

Thorne spun his glass some more. "You are worrying for naught. The Sprouts restrain themselves because they feel safe and happy in your household. Their greatest fear is that they will lose you and Grace if they test your patience too far. In time, they'll know better. And you *will* make a good father. When you trust someone with your heart, you do so unreservedly, and I believe the moment you find that bairn in your arms for the first time, you will fall in love. And when you do, you will see. Everything will be all right."

There was something melancholy about his brother, and Roland wondered if perhaps Thorne was lonely. He had hoped the man would start to find his way to the edges of the social scene. To find friends there. Perhaps even a lover. It seemed that might take a little time.

"I would wish that for you, you know. Love, I mean," Roland blurted out before he could think better of it. This was a mistake. He was too intoxicated for such a serious conversation. Or perhaps not deep in his cups enough. He tried to salvage the conversation with humour. "After all, you managed to win *mine*, and you said that was no easy task. A lady's love—that should be easy as a winking for you."

Thorne's raised eyebrow gave Roland enough time to gird for a return salvo, and he pretended to wince, ducking. But the words died upon Thorne's lips, and as Roland looked up, he saw his brother was looking over his shoulder, rising to his feet.

The tapping of a cane became so loud behind him, Roland wondered how he had missed it, and he belatedly stood as well.

"Grandfather," he said in surprise, before correcting himself. "Your Grace. We did not expect your company."

"I should retire—" Thorne began, but the Breaker's expression kept him rooted in place.

"You do not have to leave, Sir Nathaniel," the duke said, a trifle archly. "In fact, I would be pleased if you would stay. Sit, both of you."

They sat, and with the aid of the footman, the duke took the head of the table with only the barest wobble. "Would you like some port, sir?" the footman asked him quietly.

"That vile stuff? *Hmph.* No, I believe I shall try some of what my guest is drinking."

Thorne's eyebrows lifted. "Er, it's highland whisky, Your Grace—"

"And?" the Breaker rumbled irritably, but then he gave Thorne a sly grin that was so unexpected, so shocking, even Roland sat straight in his chair. "I have lived here in the north all of my seventy-five years. Surely you do not think it would be my first time attempting it, *pup.*"

Blinking rapidly, Thorne inclined his head. "Well then... I hope you like Glenlivet's efforts."

The Breaker seemed thoroughly entertained by Thorne's confusion, and he lifted his glass to his lips slowly, being careful to avoid spilling it. "Good on you for knowing where to find the better stuff."

Thorne's eyes slid to Roland's, and helplessly, Roland shrugged one shoulder. He did not know what the duke was about any more than Thorne did. There was a silence filled only by the duke's approving rumble and the footman stepped forward to fill his glass again.

"Your rather rude remarks the other night gave me much to ponder, Roland," the Breaker finally said, cupping both hands around his drink. "To my greatest irritation, I fear you might be right. Withers has told me what you discovered about... Hannah, and her son. Perhaps what I did, in the end, was the inevitable outcome. But what I must admit, seeing your solution with Bertram Robson, is that I never offered Hannah another real choice she could have accepted instead."

The duke exhaled, a long, heavy sigh. "I took too long. I failed to even attempt to make amends with my sister, and you are right. It was my pride that prevented it. I would ask you for a boon, Roland."

"Of course, grandfather," he replied unhesitatingly, wondering what on earth the old duke was about to ask.

"When you send Bertram away... send him with all of Hannah's remaining effects you can find. Including her jewellery, if it can be reclaimed. I... do not want him to be forced to leave England without anything of his mother's."

Bertram Robson was living quietly, just until Roland could finish plans for investments, and passage could be arranged to America. Roland had some time to make that happen.

"That is generous of you. I also was thinking of the same thing. At least I thought we should give him the letters from his parents that Grace found, and the chest, if he can find room in his luggage for it."

The duke grunted, and then grew a little distant, his eyes turning in Thorne's direction, but seeing through him as if he was having another spell. "Where did all the time go?"

"*Sorrow never comes too late, and happiness too swiftly flies*," Thorne said softly, quoting Thomas Grey.

"Well spoken, Sir Nathaniel," the Breaker agreed after a moment, drinking off his whisky as he focused sharply on Roland's brother, as if he had not truly ever looked at the man before. "I say, you are rather well cultured for a bastard," he continued, but there was an amused lilt to his words.

"The opportunity to become so was entirely your grandson's

doing, Your Grace. I hope you don't mind my saying so, but in the time I have been fortunate enough to know him, I have found him to be a rather remarkable man."

The duke turned back to Roland at that, and humiliatingly, Roland felt his cheeks colour slightly.

"Yes," the duke said simply in his gravelly voice. "I agree. But I hope you do not plan to give your half-brother all the credit for becoming a person of excellent character." The duke struggled to his feet before either one of them could respond to that shocking comment. "Besides, he will get a swollen head."

Fortunately, his shuffling gait gave them the moment they needed to collect their wits.

"Grandfather—Your Grace," Roland hastily amended, and the man turned slightly. "I know you are uncomfortable interacting with many others, but I want you to know we would welcome your presence in whatever capacity you feel you wish to give it."

There was more than a small chance it would be the duke's last Christmas, Roland thought. Despite whatever awkwardness he might present, it seemed a cruelty not to make it clear he would be welcome to participate. And yet, as he said the words, he felt a strange shifting in the room. A sense of power changing hands.

The duke inclined his head, and Roland knew he felt it as well. "We will see what the morning brings."

27

Christmas morning dawned with a heavy fog blanketing the land. Instead of casting a pall, it made the residents of Alnwick even more grateful for the warmth of their cosy homes. By the time the bells of St Michaels rang to call the town to worship, the sun had cleared the low clouds from view.

Nearly everyone in town turned out for the morning service. The news of Reverend Shepherd's involvement in the kidnappings, and subsequent dismissal from the ministry, had spread like wildfire through the streets. All were curious to see who would take his place, particularly on such short notice. Roland had seen to the matter, sending a message to the kind minister he recalled meeting in Alnmouth.

Curate Treadwell had been delighted to step into the gap. He stood out front, dressed in a long black cassock with a bright white surplice and matching stole, offering a smile and word of welcome to all upon arrival. During the service, he provided a rousing message from the pulpit, marking the day as one of celebration.

Grace, dressed in a new gown of emerald velvet with matching jewels winking in her ears, nestled close to Roland's side as the pastor spoke of the birth of Christ and the return of the missing children. For the first time in her life, she understood something of how Mary must have felt—terror, joy, and hope all mixed into one. Roland reached over, taking her hand in his, and gave it a reassuring squeeze. Whatever trials lay ahead in their future, as with everything else, they would face them together.

Before they departed for the castle, Grace made sure to introduce the Sprouts to Miss Whitby. Come January, they would join the other local children for daily lessons. Never ones to shy away, the twins peppered her with questions about which books they would read and whether they would have to do sums and such. The schoolmistress held strong against the barrage until Roland stepped in to suggest they join the other children in a game of French and English.

After the children dashed off, Miss Whitby bade Roland and Grace to wait another moment. "I would like to extend my personal thanks to the both of you. Eight families have contacted me about enrolling their children in the last week alone. The additional funds coming our way will allow me to accept them and anyone else in the area."

Roland and Grace brushed her thanks aside, saying they had only done what was right, given the circumstances. The law saw the children returned safely home. Justice demanded reparations, both to them, and to everyone who had been left unaided by the Percy family in the past year.

They excused themselves from Miss Whitby, left Thorne to speak with the other local residents, and then went off in search of the Sprouts. Gleeful shouts echoed from the nearby village green. As they walked, Grace caught sight of a familiar white cap and black wool coat.

"Is that Elsie?" she asked Roland, as he was taller and had a better view.

"I believe it must be, because I am positive that it is Briggs in stride beside her. I cannot imagine my valet is taking anyone else out for a walk."

The pair seemed to be going in the same direction, their steps meandering along at a comfortable pace. Briggs was busy chatting, while Elsie, Grace noted, appeared to be searching the area for something. When the pair turned onto the green and wandered toward the old oak tree, Grace figured out Elsie's intentions.

"Stop here," she said to Roland, pulling him off to the side. She nudged his arm and nodded toward the tree. Sure enough, Elsie coaxed Briggs onward until they stood directly under the kissing bough. Only then did she interrupt him to point upwards.

For a moment, Grace feared for her maid, for Briggs froze like a fox at the baying of the hounds. Elsie fluttered her lashes at the man and that irascible servant actually seemed to be bashful. Still, it seemed that he succumbed to Elsie's charms. Before all, he tilted his head down and kissed her right on the lips.

A cheer went up from the nearby children, led, unsurprisingly, by Willa and Wes.

At her side, Roland gave a sigh. "I suppose I cannot dismiss him now."

Grace elbowed him. "If that is the price we must pay to have the help stay happy in our service, I do not think either of us should complain."

"I will tolerate his presence, for a price," Roland said thoughtfully, but he could not hold a stern expression on his face. "Perhaps if you would drop a comment to your maid that you no longer find my burgundy coat so fetching?"

Grace pretended to consider this. "Only if you let me consult with the tailor for a new one."

"If you must. But if I end up looking like a peacock, the gardener will find not just one but two coats buried in the garden come spring." He waved for the children to join them and then offered Grace his arm. "Come along, we do not want to be late for Christmas dinner."

What a dinner it was, indeed. The long dining table was filled end to end with steaming bowls and trays. In addition to Grace, Roland, and Thorne were the Sprouts, Mr Harding and his wife. Belowstairs, the servants enjoyed a similar feast. It took some insistence to convince the twins to taste the oyster soup starter. Roasted goose, stuffed and served with gravy, potatoes, and root vegetables proved popular all around. By the time the footmen presented the trifle for dessert, Grace wondered where she would find the space. But the thick cream and soft sponge cake proved too enticing to resist.

No sooner was the last bite scraped clean from her plate than Willa voiced a question. "Lady Grace, when can we open presents?"

"Who said anything about gifts?" Roland replied. "Has this wondrous meal not been sufficient enough celebration to mark the day?"

Wes and Willa exchanged glances, their faces wearing matching expressions of concern.

Grace decided to put them out of their agony. "The meal was divine, Lord Percy, but that was a gift to all of us from the kitchen staff, and not a heartfelt expression of love from one to another. I suggest we take our coffees and teas to the drawing room where, if I am not mistaken, a few wrapped packages await us."

Wes leapt to his feet so quickly that his chair rocked back. Only the quick action of a passing footman saved it from hitting the floor. The footman pulled Willa's clear, and she went dashing off after her brother.

Roland motioned for Thorne to lead the way, with Mr and Mrs Harding following behind. Roland helped Grace from her chair and wrapped his arm around her.

"Roland, the footmen—"

"Have all headed belowstairs to partake of their own dinner. Now, allow me to gift my lovely wife a kiss before someone else interrupts us."

One kiss led to two, and would have continued on had they not heard the halting gait marking the arrival of the Breaker.

"This truly is a Christmas miracle," Grace murmured as she pulled away. She and Roland hurried to the doorway. Sure enough, the old duke's bent frame was making slow progress down the stairs. He glowered at Roland's offer of a hand.

"I can still make my own way in this world," he muttered darkly. But he stopped himself from speaking further, instead giving a single nod to show his appreciation for the offer.

It was not much, but for the Breaker, it was more than Grace would have ever expected.

Cheered by the fragrant holiday decorations and warmed by the roaring fire, the others were chattering brightly in the front drawing room. Their conversations tailed off when they caught sight of the Breaker following behind Roland and Grace.

"I will take my normal seat," the Breaker announced.

Before the old man could make his way to the wingback chair he preferred on the far side of the room, Roland hurried ahead of him. "Thorne, give me a hand." Together, the brothers lifted the chair with ease and carried it across the room, placing it near where the others sat.

Grace braced herself for an argument, or at minimum a complaint, but the duke took their intervention for what it was.

An invitation to be part of the family, if only for this one day of the year.

Withers served hot drinks and left wool-wrapped teapots and a plate of sweets behind, before taking his leave as well.

Together, Roland and Grace took gifts from the stack and handed them around to their intended recipient. There was something for everyone, from the silver snuff boxes Grace had purchased in the village, to a hand knitted scarf for the children from Mrs Harding. The children soon overcame their reticence of speaking around the duke, their excitement for their gifts too much to contain. Wes received wooden soldiers, a chess set, and a new adventure book. Both children delighted over the battledore and shuttlecock set and dissected map of England. Even the duke had a present or two to enjoy.

The last present in the pile was an oddly shaped box with Willa's name printed on the front. The little girl untied the cord and lifted the top free. A squeal of pure joy escaped her lips.

"A doll," she sighed in awe.

"With hair and eyes just like your own," Grace said. "Look what else is inside."

Willa dove back into the box, finding several changes of clothing in just the right size for her new toy. "There's a ballgown, and a riding habit—"

"And a shirt and pair of trousers for when she needs to accompany you on some of your wilder adventures. Adventures for which you have permission," Grace hastened to add. "If you can behave, you might find a dollhouse coming in time for your birthday."

"Lady Gra, err, Percy," Wes said, casting a quick glance at the duke. "Lord Percy didn't get you a gift."

"I have not yet presented my gift," Roland corrected him. "If Sir Nathaniel will agree to showing you how to arrange the chess pieces on the board, Lady Percy and I will excuse ourselves for a moment. My gift is awaiting her in my study next door."

Thorne leapt into action, with Mr Harding offering to help while Mrs Harding asked Willa to show her the doll up close.

Grace let Roland help her to her feet again and followed behind him, mystified for what awaited her. What kind of gift needed to be given in private, but could be done in the confines of his study?

Roland's eyes sparkled with humour, though she could sense him growing more tense with every step. He was nervous. That baffled her thoughts even more.

The study chairs had been shifted around to make space for a large, cloth-covered object in the middle of the room. The contours made it immediately clear what the object was, but that knowledge was not much help.

"A trunk?' Grace asked. "We are not going anywhere, are we?"

"It is a trunk," Roland confirmed. "If you will allow me to properly give it to you, you will understand. Now please, sit here." He motioned to the chair nearest the covered object.

Grace sat on the edge of her seat, unable to take her eyes off the strange gift. Slowly, Roland lifted the edges of the cloth and pulled it aside, revealing inch by inch the treasure.

It was a satin birchwood trunk, its polished surface gleaming in the candlelight. Iron studs, arranged in elegant swirling patterns, caught the light like tiny stars, creating a delicate, sparkling design that wound gracefully across the top.

He opened his coat and pulled a key from his inside pocket. "Open it."

Grace took the key, now fully engrossed in seeing what else Roland had in store. The key turned smoothly in the oiled lock. She lifted the lid to find a velvet-lined tray, and underneath, a deep chamber lined in the same deep blue velvet.

"This is a memory chest, where you can safely store trinkets and mementos, both past and future. I have a few items to help you get started." Roland went behind his desk and came back with a box. One by one, he handed her the items he had saved. "The first is this pack of letters. Inside, you will find the invitation to the Fitzroy ball where we first met, Prinny's invite to the ball where we waltzed, and... the messages we exchanged during all of our adventures this summer."

"You saved all these?" Grace could hardly believe it.

"Most of them. I will admit I had some help from Thorne and Elsie." He handed her more mementos from their days of courtship and travels in Brighton. "This last item, however, is one for which I will take full credit."

Grace unfolded a bundle to find a square baby quilt made in shades of the pale green of spring grass and yellow buttercups.

"It was mine, years ago, and my father's before that. With your approval, I would like our child to continue the Percy tradition. Our son, or daughter, whichever one we are blessed to receive next year."

Grace's eyes filled with tears and for once, she did not try to hide them as they rolled down her rosy cheeks. She threw her arms around her husband and sniffled against his chest. "Oh Roland, this is the most lovely, thoughtful, perfect gift I have ever received. My poor little snuff box pales in comparison."

Roland forced her to pull away and tipped her chin up until their eyes met. "Grace, you are carrying my child, the most precious, unexpected, and wholly welcome gift a man could ever receive. Between that, and having you in my life—I need no other present for Christmas, my darling."

Epilogue

Christmas swiftly progressed into the New Year, but the next few months were bitter. The severe weather experienced in the early months of 1814 would become known later as The Great Frost. Outside of London, there were fewer hardships dealing with the scarcity of fuel. But the terrible cold still claimed its fair share of the elderly and infirm.

The Breaker would be one of them.

Roland kept vigil at the old man's bedside as lung fever ravaged him. The Breaker's periods of lucidity grew fewer and far between as he coughed and burned with it.

"Roland," the Breaker murmured on the third day.

Startled from his doze, Roland leaned forward, taking his grandfather's outstretched hand as he reached over to light another candle with the other. The duke seemed tired, but he sounded better. Perhaps he would rally? But no. As he brought the second candle closer, he beheld the way the old man seemed to almost be lit from within, and he knew that death was coming.

"What is it, grandfather?" Roland asked him.

"You will be a good duke."

The Breaker had not exactly cleaved to the family since that unexpected Christmas eve. But he most certainly had thawed. And the right side of Roland's mouth kicked up in a half smile. "Do you think so?"

"Yes. You have the spirit and the sensibility. You have surrounded yourself with good people." The duke stopped, tired and out of breath from his long statement.

"It is all right. You do not need to talk," Roland told him.

"Glad you're here," the man mumbled, already slipping into stupor as his breath began to bubble. "I should go make up... with Hannah now."

Roland somehow did not think he meant Grace, despite regularly confusing her for his sister the last month. "All right, grandfather."

Within a few minutes, the Breaker sighed and stilled. And Roland set the old man's hand down gently, his feelings chaotic. Tamping them down to sort through later, he opened the door. "The duke has passed," he told the footmen stationed next to the room. "I trust Withers can begin seeing to arrangements. Until you need me, I shall be with my wife."

After the death of the old duke, Grace and Roland officially took on the full mantle of responsibility for the duchy. Roland spent long hours in his study, with Mr Harding at his side, coming to grips with all that was involved in managing such a complex mix of estates.

Given the weather, Grace was left to find ways to pass more time indoors. Together with Elsie, she sorted through the old nursery items stored by previous generations of the Percy family. Custom furniture such as the cradle and dressing table were deemed suitable, but provisions for clothing, toiletries, and napkins were woefully low.

By March, the ground had thawed enough to allow travel to recommence. Though on schedule with the change in season, for Grace it felt far too long. Roland had taken one look at his wife's worried face and promised to dispatch riders to London and Edinburgh to order whatever she needed. Within a few weeks, wagons laden with goods began to arrive at the castle portico.

Though there were more than enough servants on hand to sort the arrivals and store them away, Grace insisted she wanted to oversee the matter. London's finest drapers and linen merchants sent fabrics in the finest cotton and muslin, decorated with delicate lace and embroidered with the Percy crest. From Scotland, she procured caps and gowns in the softest wool, trusting only them with the delicate skin of her expected child.

So many deliveries came and went that the arrival of a wagon or carriage was hardly cause for remark. Yet, on a day in early April, the clip clop of horses' hooves on the paved drive was followed by a sharp rap on the door of Grace's sitting room.

Francis, elevated from footman to under butler, entered at Grace's bidding. "You have a visitor, my lady. The Duchess Atholl," he added.

It took Grace a moment to grasp the meaning of his words. "Charity? Charity is here? Show her in. No, wait, I should go to the drawing room."

"You will do no such thing," Charity's voice rang out from behind the under butler. The man stepped aside to allow the exquisitely dressed blonde woman to enter the room. "Your letters have made it abundantly clear that this is one of the few rooms where you can sit comfortably. I will not have my dearest friend in the world be discomfited on my behalf."

As if to prove Charity's point, Grace could not hold back a small groan as she struggled to her feet to properly greet her unexpected guest. She sent Francis off to fetch a tea tray and then held out her hands to Charity. "For the first time, I have no fear of standing in your shadows, beautiful as ever though you are. Given my expanding girth, one would have to be blind to miss me."

Charity's delicate laugh tinkled freely. "You are the picture of health and radiate joy besides, Grace. It is I who am envious, and not the other way around."

Over steaming cups of tea, Charity explained that she was on her way to London, to rejoin the ton for another season. "Not the marriage mart," she made a point of noting. "Our good queen has invited me to be a lady-in-waiting."

Anyone else would have offered their congratulations, but Grace had spent enough time with Charity and Queen Charlotte to know such an honour did not come without strings.

"And what does Her Royal Highness expect from you? You are barely out of mourning."

Charity brushed a blonde curl from her shoulder and squared her shoulders. "I have mourned enough for this lifetime and the next. The Queen and I agree it is time I reclaim *my place* in society."

Grace sensed a world of meaning lying under those words, but Charity refused to be drawn out on what they were. Though part of her longed to beg Charity to take her along on what was no doubt the start of some new intrigue, the child kicking in her womb reminded Grace of her place.

When it came time for Charity to leave the next morning, Grace demanded a promise. "You will write to me, do you understand? And if you have need of anyone, or anything at all, you will not hesitate to ask."

"I will send letters as often as I can," Charity replied. "And you must do the same. I take great heart in hearing of your life now. Somehow, we have ended up on opposite paths from what we planned. You have everything you never wanted, and yet could not be happier. I hope that one day—soon, even—I will be able to say the same."

~

Briggs, if one could believe that, was actually the one who chased Thorne down when Grace went into labour.

At the end of her pregnancy, the new duchess' discomfort was so great that Roland had not left the castle for nearly a fortnight. Feelings ran high and tempers were short, so Thorne determined to make himself both useful and scarce, spending his time exercising both Arion and Horse and assisting Mr Harding by checking on the repairs progressing around Alnwick.

Briggs stood in the stables, arms crossed in pure displeasure. "I shall thank you for having enough sense to time your return well. I would never forgive you if I had to get on top of one of these stinking beasts to find you."

Thorne handed Arion's reins to the stableboy, looking down at the shorter valet. "Now I am disappointed to have missed that. I suppose the next thing you are going to tell me is why you were looking for me at all?"

"The duchess is labouring," Briggs said shortly, and Thorne's sour mood shifted immediately. "If you do not get in there and help me distract the duke, he will end up as bald as a turnip. The duchess rather *likes* her husband's full head of hair."

"Ah," said Thorne comprehensively, smirking at the man as he read between the lines. "Did the duchess's labour begin at a most inconvenient time for you?"

Briggs' eyebrow lifted archly. "Quite. Now, would you go, or would you like me to go find some rope to truss the duke up instead? He is also wearing a place on the rug in his study."

"I'll go," laughed Thorne, and he hurried into his room to shuck his riding clothes quickly. He knew Roland would not care, but Thorne did. After the extended morning riding, he positively reeked of sweat and horse. It took him only a few minutes to make himself decent with a quick rinse using the pitcher, and he gratefully threw on the clothes Briggs had set out in anticipation of the need.

Briggs was a thorn in everyone's backside, but one had to admit, he was also a very good valet.

The study's door was closed, and Thorne paused outside for a moment, surprised that it was so quiet. He knocked on the door with one knuckle, and very quickly, Roland pulled open the door.

Roland looked awful, his eyes reddened as if he had gotten no sleep the night before, and his hair... No wonder Briggs had been concerned for it.

"How on earth did you manage to do that to your hair?" Thorne stepped close to his brother, lifting his hands to bring a semblance of order to the man, but Roland threw his arms around him in a hug instead.

Thorne glanced around, used to being mindful of Roland's propriety, but there was no one else in the study. He had been waiting alone. A small wonder he was taking leave of his senses. So he patted Roland awkwardly with one arm, his other caught above his head.

"God, I am so glad to see you," Roland grumbled. "How long is this going to take? It has been hours!"

"And it could be hours yet," Thorne told him reluctantly. "These things can take some time." Gently extricating himself, he found Roland's brandy, pouring him a glass. "Here. This will help. Have you eaten?"

Roland blinked at him, and so Thorne decided that was most likely a no. As Roland nursed his drink, Thorne asked the footman to bring whatever they had at hand. Small cakes for tea, or even bread, although the footman looked affronted at the idea that they could not find something less crude to serve the duke.

"Are you hoping for a boy or a girl?" Thorne asked, jollying his brother along.

Roland uttered a short laugh. "I know I am supposed to say a boy, of course. But at this moment of time, all I find I can care about is Grace's wellbeing. So, I really do not care, not as long as she is safe."

Thorne smiled, understanding completely, and he sent a short prayer in his thoughts that it would be so. He could not imagine Roland having to deal with any other outcome. It would devastate him.

"I wanted to ask... although I was afraid to tempt fate," Roland murmured as he perched on the edge of the wing chair by the fire. "No matter whether it is a boy or a girl... Would you be willing to serve as godfather?"

Eyes wide, Thorne found himself speechless. "You want... me? But—"

"I meant what I said. I cannot imagine someone who would be a better father. Should the worst happen to either one of us. Not that I expect that to ever happen... but still. I would want our child to know that sort of happiness that I know you would be able to give them."

"Roland," Thorne said, his voice growing suspiciously hoarse. "That is an incredible honour. Are you—no, I can see you're sure." Roland's brows had drawn together, as if offended Thorne questioned his judgement. "Nothing will happen to you and Grace. But... yes, of course I would be happy to stand in."

"Good." Roland stood, dusting his hands on his knees as if that was all there was to the matter. "Now there is nothing to do but descend slowly into madness until the child shows up."

"I am surprised you were here alone," Thorne commented. "Where are Mr Harding and Curate Treadwell? I thought for certain they would keep you company."

"I sent them away," Roland admitted. "I did not think I could maintain the appropriate face of... bored indifference to the whole matter and play cards—"

Roland's voice cut off as he cocked his head, hearing something. Thorne listened too, hearing the creak of floorboards and hurried footsteps. He got to his feet before Roland could, opening the door just as a happy Mrs Yardley showed up.

"Oh, Sir Nathaniel! Your Grace! Are you there? Come see."

"She is all right then?" Roland asked urgently, pushing past Thorne to grip the housekeeper's hands.

"Yes, the duchess is well. Better than well. You will want to see her now."

Roland was out of the room like a shot, and Thorne shared an amused glance with Mrs Yardley before walking slowly back towards the family wing. He did not think Roland and Grace would make him wait until the christening to meet his new godchild, but surely the new father and mother would need a few days.

And so, he headed towards his room, only to have Roland throw the door open a few moments later, completely unlike himself. "Thorne! Brother! You must come see this. Mrs Yardley was... Well, you might decide you no longer want to accept the honour."

Dumbly, Thorne let himself be dragged towards the duchess' sitting room, the hallway door still standing open. Fortunately, the lady's bedroom door was firmly closed, and there was a sound of great industry coming from behind it.

Roland went back into Grace's room, and Thorne lingered near the hallway, not wishing to intrude even though his curiosity had been fired. It was less than a minute again before the door cracked open, and Roland returned, a tiny bundle cradled tenderly in his arms.

"They said I could show you while Grace is resting." Roland stood beside his brother, and Thorne could see right away that the newborn lad had the Percy dark locks, passed down three generations now from the Breaker. "I have a son," Roland said, almost looking as if he didn't quite believe it.

"*And* a daughter," Elsie said, although she was smiling at Roland's addled state. Thorne whipped up his head to see Grace's maid, standing outside the door with a second baby in her arms.

Almost immediately, Grace lost track of her days and nights. She refused to do the done thing and hire a nursemaid to care for her babies. Motherhood was her new adventure, one which she was determined to share with Roland and no one else. Between feeding and changes, she had little time to wonder how the new season's debutantes were getting on. Once in a while, a passing traveller would bring along news from London, but little of it caught Grace's attention.

However, when a footman delivered a letter sealed with a familiar emblem, Grace found herself eager to read the contents. After a quick skim, she asked the footman to send Roland to her side.

"Is something amiss?" her husband asked, almost as soon as he walked into her sitting room. "The children?"

"Are sleeping," Grace assured him. "The nursery maid is under strict orders to let me know when they wake. That is not why I called for you. I received a letter from Charity. It seems trouble is once again afoot in London. Here, have a read for yourself."

She could not hide the fraught edge in her tone, so it was little wonder that Roland required no further urging to take the letter from her hand.

My dearest friend,

I cannot begin to put into words everything that has transpired in London since I last saw you. But I expect you'll hear this sooner rather than later—there is scandal afoot again. When is there not, you are likely asking? This time, it involves the Prince of Orange and his betrothal to the princess. Or his lack of one, rather.

I wish I dared speak my next words more plainly, but tell your husband to be on guard. I believe there is a possibility that our dear departed enemy, Lady F, has again set her sights on England. To what end her ambition lies, I am not yet certain, but if she decides to take aim against the throne, it would be easy for her to place us in the crosshairs as well.

Do not worry for me; I am taking precautions. But I would not want you and your family to be caught unprepared if she decides to retaliate against you.

Your husband may be particularly interested in the news of Lady F's son, Peregrine. He is back from the front, and he has already found himself in trouble with the crown once again. Some would think me a fool, but I have my doubts as to his guilt. Fear not, I

will keep you apprised of anything I uncover. Please do
the same, should any news pass your way.
All my love,
Charity

NOTE FROM THE AUTHORS:

With Roland and Grace living happily ever after in Northumberland, we did not want you to miss out on what happens in London during the season of 1814. As you can see from her letter, Lady Charity has a front row seat to all the activities, secret and known.

The regency mysteries set in the world of the Crown Jewels will continue - with a brand new series. Follow along with Lady Charity and Lord Fitzroy in the Diamond of the Ton Regency Mysteries.

The first book, **Brilliance and Betrayal**, will be out in 2025.

With the royal engagement on the line, can these mortal enemies turn allies long enough to solve the crime?

London, 1814: As Britain is set to celebrate the end of war and the possibility of a royal wedding, a poisoned foreign prince becomes the first victim in a deadly game of power and intrigue that threatens to reshape the continent.

A man determined to clear his name

Lord Peregrine Fitzroy knows the effects of this poison all too well—after all, it is one of his traitorous mother's favourites. Either the dowager Lady Fitzroy is playing a new, deadly gambit, or someone wants to implicate him in the crime. If there is one person in London with the motive to set him up to take the fall, it is Lady Charity.

A woman set on regaining her place in society

Lady Charity's debut season was fraught with scandal. Now back in London, all she wants is to reclaim her status as Diamond of the Ton... and get even with the family who nearly ruined her. When Lord Peregrine shows up in the dead of night, accusing her of framing him, she finds herself cornered.

A crime only they can solve

With the crown demanding justice and their own futures at stake, Lord Peregrine and Lady Charity forge an uneasy alliance. Their hunt for the true culprit will unravel dangerous secrets. Can they trust each other, or will betrayal destroy them both?

Immerse yourself in the Diamond of the Ton Regency Mysteries—perfect for fans of court intrigue, twisty crimes, redemption, revenge, and a slow-burn romance.

Order your copy now on Amazon.

Brilliance and Betrayal
A Diamond of the Ton Regency Mystery

With the royal engagement on the line, can these mortal enemies turn allies long enough to solve the crime?

London, 1814: As Britain is set to celebrate the end of war and the possibility of a royal wedding, a poisoned foreign prince becomes the first victim in a deadly game of power and intrigue that threatens to reshape the continent.

A man determined to clear his name

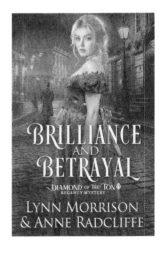

Lord Peregrine Fitzroy knows the effects of this poison all too well—after all, it is one of his traitorous mother's favourites. Either the dowager Lady Fitzroy is playing a new, deadly gambit, or someone wants to implicate him in the crime. If there is one person in London with the motive to set him up to take the fall, it is Lady Charity.

A woman set on regaining her place in society

Lady Charity's debut season was fraught with scandal. Now back in London, all she wants is to reclaim her status as Diamond of the Ton... and get even with the family who nearly ruined her. When Lord Peregrine shows up in the dead of night, accusing her of framing him, she finds herself cornered.

A crime only they can solve

With the crown demanding justice and their own futures at stake, Lord Peregrine and Lady Charity forge an uneasy alliance. Their hunt for the true culprit will unravel dangerous secrets. Can they trust each other, or will betrayal destroy them both?

Immerse yourself in the Diamond of the Ton Regency Mysteries—perfect for fans of court intrigue, twisty crimes, redemption, revenge, and a slow-burn romance.

Order your copy now on Amazon.

Historical Notes

Gentle reader,

When we first began tailoring the universe in which Roland and Grace began their books, we departed from true historical accuracy a wee bit in a couple places. The Percy family and the Duchy of Northumberland was one of the larger liberties we took early on, although some of the dates might have been easily overlooked by readers up until this book.

Northumberland was and is a real dukedom, and the locations we have mentioned are equally real. In fact, Northumberland had been a dukedom twice before, but the title was stripped from John Neville by Edward IV only a few years after being granted, and John Dudley was executed only two years after being granted the title by Edward VI.

The current title, still in existence, was created in October of 1766 for Hugh Percy. When we began writing book one, *The Missing Diamond*, we wanted Gideon Percy to be the second duke of Northumberland for our tale. You can see he is well old enough in 1813 to be the first if we established his title in the original year. We elected to consider the dukedom a little older than that well before *The Emerald Threads* was even a glimmer in our thoughts.

Incidentally, it might be amusing to know we had originally only planned to write a trilogy for Roland and Grace. Then we decided to add a Christmas short story. Then that became a novella. And then by the time we finished this book, we realised it was even longer than the originally-planned final book for Roland and Grace, *The Sapphire Intrigue*. So I suppose we are writing quartets now for future familiar faces.

At any rate, when we conceived of the terrible, complex man who became the Breaker, it worked better if he was not the first to hold that title. If he was just old enough for his father to have died relatively young, leaving a Gideon Percy in his late 20s to inherit both title and sense of duty from his father—keenly aware of the past history of the dukedom, afraid it was endangered following the death of both of his sons.

And in the end, that choice was just as well, because if we hadn't, the story of John and Hannah would have had to look very different.

History records the months of December of 1813 to February of 1814 as a spectacularly (and notably) cold winter. To give you an idea of just how cold it was, the Thames froze over solidly enough to support the weight of thousands of people and a giant ice fair in February. It was the winter that would later become known as "The Great Frost."

By 1813, Europe was still in—but beginning to come out of —the grasp of a period of global cooling known as "The Little Ice Age." During that period, which lasted from the early 14th century to the mid 19th century, yearly average temperatures are estimated to have decreased by as much as 2 degrees Celsius (3.6 F).

There is unlikely to be just one cause of that period of cold. In fact, scientists have identified as many as seven contributing factors. But during The Little Ice Age, the reduced solar activity and general increased global volcanic activity are suspected to be among the top culprits for creating the conditions that would lead to The Great Frost. In 1812, the La Soufrière volcano in the Caribbean erupted. It was a significant one, and this might be the very volcano that set the stage for The Great Frost.

People who survived this winter would have had a chance to see volcanic-induced weather changes once more, during "The Year Without a Summer" in 1816, after Mount Tambora erupted in Indonesia in April 1815. While we won't see it, it might be interesting to know that Mount Tambora's eruption was one of the most powerful in recorded history, releasing such an enormous amount of ash and sulphur dioxide into the stratosphere that the volcanic particles created a veil that reflected sunlight away from Earth. In 1816, countries in the northern hemisphere would see snow falling in June and frosts in August, bringing crop failure and famine to Europe at a time where it was still struggling to recover from Napoleon's wars.

Bertram Robson's plan to build a wool mill would have been a good one... in theory. With wool being used to make soldier's uniforms, the price of wool and wool cloth cloth was quite high during the Napoleonic wars.

However, it is just as well for him that he got sent to handle another investment in America, because once the wars ended, demand dropped sharply. By 1816, not only was England suffering The Year Without a Summer, the wool market was flooded with more supply than demand, and the price of wool crashed, adding to the hardship for a lot of British sheep farmers and rural communities.

∿

If you recall the part where Roland and Thorne talked about "The Vampire of Alnwick," 12th century chronicler William of Newburgh did record a tale that would become something of an urban legend, since many people supposedly held it as true. In this record, one of the deceased masters of Alnwick Castle rose from his own grave during the night to prowl the village.

The citizens of Alnwick hunted the creature down and burned it, according to William's recounting in the *Historia Rerum Anglicarum*, which you can find in some digital archives in its original Latin and a few English translations.

They armed themselves, therefore, with sharp spades, and betaking themselves to the cemetery, they began to dig. And whilst they yet thought they would have to dig much deeper, they came upon the body covered with but a thin layer of earth. It was gorged swollen with a frightful corpulence...

William's tale is one of the earliest documented vampire legends in England, and indeed, in the 12th century, it predated the word vampire itself, which wouldn't become popularised for roughly another six centuries. He referred to the monster as a revenant. It wouldn't be until 1819 that the modern vampire we're more familiar with evolved from the publication of "The Vampyre" by John Polidori, and then the later 1897 novel *Dracula* by Bram Stoker.

We hope you enjoy these bits of history as much as we did.

Acknowledgments

Thanks to Melody Simmons for creating another fantastic cover for us.

Thanks to Ken Morrison for reading along as we write, letting us know we are on track and cheering for us to keep going. We super appreciate Brenda Chapman, Anne Kavcic, Ewa Bartnik, and Lois King for pitching in again as beta readers. They drop everything to read our book as soon as we put it in their hands, and get back to us with feedback, typos, etc straight away.

Thanks to Mary Fields for being a fantastic support for our writing team (and for sharing cat pics with us).

As always, we send a heartfelt thanks to you, our lovely readers, for loving our stories as much as we do.

About Anne Radcliffe

As an American Expat living in Ontario with a husband and teen son, Anne Radcliffe spends a lot of time editing or writing in order to avoid having to become a Maple Leafs fan. Anne loves a great story no matter the genre or medium - books, graphic novels, TV, movies or video games. You can find out more about Anne on her website at AnneRadcliffe.com.

BB bookbub.com/authors/anne-radcliffe

g goodreads.com/anneradcliffe

a amazon.com/stores/author/B0D1VMVDZ1

About Lynn Morrison

Lynn Morrison lives in Oxford, England along with her husband, two daughters and two cats. Born and raised in Mississippi, her wanderlust attitude has led her to live in California, Italy, France, the UK, and the Netherlands. Despite having rubbed shoulders with presidential candidates and members of parliament, night-clubbed in Geneva and Prague, explored Japanese temples and scrambled through Roman ruins, Lynn's real life adventures can't compete with the stories in her mind.

She is as passionate about reading as she is writing, and can almost always be found with a book in hand. You can find out more about her on her website LynnMorrisonWriter.com.

You can chat with her directly in her Facebook group - Lynn Morrison's Not a Book Club - where she talks about books, life and anything else that crosses her mind.

facebook.com/nomadmomdiary

instagram.com/nomadmomdiary

bookbub.com/authors/lynn-morrison

goodreads.com/nomadmomdiary

amazon.com/Lynn-Morrison/e/B00IKC1LVW

Also by Lynn Morrison

Stakes & Spells Mysteries

Stakes & Spells

Spells & Fangs

Fangs & Cauldrons

Midlife in Raven PWF

Raven's Curse

Raven's Joy

Raven's Matriarch

Raven's Storm

Wandering Witch Urban Fantasy

A Queen Only Lives Twice

Made in the USA
Las Vegas, NV
02 December 2024

13153093R00152